The Universe Crack'd

I0566323

CHRIS JOHNSON

Johnson, Chris, www.facebook.com/ChrisJohnsonAuthor

The Universe Crack'd

ISBN: 978-0-9945233-6-5

Cover design by Chris Johnson

Internal design by Chris Johnson

Typeset by Chris Johnson

Keep up with Chris Johnson behind the
scenes HERE and receive a free gift!

DEDICATED TO

My wife
My daughter
My readers
The members of my Facebook Page
And especially my email newsletter buddies
who cheered me on.

Chapter 1

Large eyes, silent as glass, gazed at the shapes sneaking through the dusk. Lightning flashed close by and briefly swallowed their silhouettes: three young humans. Angry thunder thumped and shook the ground, then rolled away into the night, before darkness returned enveloped the surroundings. A mere finger of dim yellow light danced across the nearby gravestones, illuminating the marks that scored their surfaces as the trio progressed.

Another lightning bolt, much closer, flashed, yet the watcher didn't flinch, its focus riveted upon the teenagers under the tree in which it sat.

Hunger boiled its grumbling stomach. Loud and annoying, the creatures below posed no threat to it, but they had frightened its prey into hiding. Starving, it launched itself on its pinions towards the teenagers. It swooped three feet above their heads, causing one to flinch — much to his companions' amusement — before it landed upon another tree's branch and sat as though listening.

"It's an owl, you dork."

The boy puffed himself up to disguise his embarrassment. "No! It was a bat. I saw its fangs." He flashed his torch after it. "See?"

"It has tail feathers... See?" The second girl rolled her eyes and shook her head with a disappointed sound. "You can be such a pansy, you know?"

James ignored the verbal dig and pointed to where his torch's beam now shone. "That patch there looks good."

He hadn't wanted to come out tonight, anyway, but his crush on Tamsin had spurred him to follow. To his knowledge, she didn't yet know James' feelings. Or maybe she did because she enjoyed teasing him about things. But their friend, his best mate Amy, knew. She had invited him along to spend the night at Hilltop Cemetery.

Both girls were both into séances and spooky stuff. James didn't go for that sort of thing, but he enjoyed the thrill. Besides, he had an Ouija board that had belonged to his father's wife, which he figured was the perfect currency to impress his crush. And he loved the prospect of Tamsin grabbing him if something scared her, either, if the story of the woman in white held truth.

The rumours were that a phantom red-headed lady dressed in a long, flowing dress haunted the cemetery. Sometimes people glimpsed her at sunset as she walked along the path between the thick trees. She would walk towards a prominent large tree, then disappear into its wide trunk as if it had a door in it. But no one had ever learned where the spectral resident vanished. Nor did they know her name.

Whose idea was it to venture out through the storm? He hated wet weather, which he considered good for lazing in bed with a book, but not for traipsing in soggy clothes and risking a chill.

James followed Amy's finger as she pointed at something. "That's the best place," she said, "Over there. We'll be right next to the tree and can watch when she appears." She led the way and dropped her backpack on the grass near a large tombstone.

Tamsin reacted to the noise. "Careful! Don't wake the sleeper."

Amy snorted with a laugh as James guided his torch beam across the words incised in the stone. The lad's lips moved as he read the dates, his gaze thoughtful. "I remember this guy. He died last year. My dad was friends with him."

Tamsin passed a cursory glance at it. "So what?"

"Today is the first anniversary of his death."

Amy's white teeth appeared to glow in the dark when she grinned. "You're such a romantic with anniversaries. Isn't he, Tamsin?"

James froze at the joke. Was she putting him on the spot on purpose? His crush shrugged and removed a blanket from her backpack to spread on the ground by the tombstone. He cleared his throat, glad the shadows hid his furious blush, as he wondered about the meaning behind her shrug. It was too soon to admit his feelings yet, and he didn't want them to tease him about it, either. Not tonight.

Amy's voice sound like she enjoyed the opportunity though. "What do you reckon, Tamsin?"

"About what?"

"Does it turn you on when a guy remembers birthdays and anniversaries?"

Tamsin flicked the raven-coloured hair from her face and pondered. Did her eyes flick towards him? He couldn't tell in the gloom. "I'd like a boy with balls and the guts to mean what he says."

Quick! Say something now. The thought raced through James' mind, blurring by so fast he wondered if he should answer. By then, Tamsin had spread the thin blanket across the ground and was looking at him with an air of impatience. "Well?" she said, her demanding tone making him jump.

"What?"

"Come on, doofus." Tamsin's eyes rolled. "The board!"

James dipped into the bag, a painful flush of disappointment crossing his face. He sure was stuffing up a bit with Tamsin. Damn his awkwardness. Impressing her seemed an uphill battle. "Give it to me." Amy snatched the board from him, which twisted a dagger of embarrassment through his heart.

Amy's teeth flashed with a sly grin that only James had glimpsed. The bitch! She was enjoying this, making him squirm in front of Tamsin. Wasn't she supposed to be on his side? He mouthed a "What?" to her, but she gave her head a slow shake. "Wake up," she said with equal volume.

Amy put the board on the blanket and lit the candles, and the darkness retreated into the surrounding trees. Lightning flashed again. The tiny flames flickered in the breeze and went out. The shadows lunged forward, held at bay only by the lights of their torches. And the thunder rolled and rocked the ground under their feet.

"Couldn't we have done this at your place, Amy?"

A grin of sadistic pleasure spread across her features like a spooky clown's makeup. But she didn't answer him.

With great deliberation, she put the wooden planchette onto the board that must have been older than Methuselah. "Let's get on with it."

James opened his mouth to protest, but Amy's head shook and quietened his unspoken words.

The trio sat around the blanket on the grass. Shadows danced from the light of the re-lit candles.

"The planchette!" His jaw dropped.

Amy shot him an impatient expression. "What's wrong?"

Tamsin's voice trembled too when she replied. "It moved. I saw it too." She pointed with a shaking finger.

"Look!"

"But we haven't started yet."

Amy rolled her eyes to scoff at them when something caught her attention. A scraping sound. She spotted it and gasped as the planchette danced and skipped across the board by its own volition, its mahogany feet tapping and scratching the surface.

All three scrambled back in surprise. James knew Amy loved practical jokes, but her blanched features revealed all. This was no gag.

Then it jumped—a whole inch off the Ouija board—then landed with a clatter on its wooden castors. Its scraping sound reached their ears, scratching like fingernails on a blackboard. Like a dragonfly over a still pond, it strayed back and forth and pointed at the first letter.

"H."

No sooner had Amy said it aloud than the pointer drifted towards the next one.

"E."

"We haven't even started." Tamsin's voice shook with horrified wonder.

The unseen force must have been waiting to be sure the teenagers understood. Upon their realisation of the starting word, it pushed the planchette faster.

"C. O. M. E. S."

The wooden pointer stopped.

This was James' first time in a séance, and the looks on the girls' faces said it was theirs too. The board belonged to his father. He thought he would look cool if he brought it. Somehow, his gut told him this wasn't the fun he expected.

Tamsin wondered aloud. "Who comes?"

The explosion came from nowhere. The lightning strike's shock threw the trio from the board and the graveside. A terrible pain flared in James' shoulder, paralysing it, when it collided with something hidden in the dark. A squealing noise pierced his ear drums, and his vision blurred. The strike had flung the girls away, too, tossing Amy onto a grassy patch. Tamsin lay sprawled elsewhere.

James wobbled on his legs, stumbling before trying to stand again. The ringing in his ears had dulled but remained like a persistent mosquito. Steadying himself on a tombstone, he stumbled towards Tamsin, one wobbly step at a time. Something told him to deal with her first, while another said he should get the hell out of there.

James tried to speak, but his voice was like an echo inside his skull.

Tamsin stirred at her name's mention. She lifted her head as he flopped beside her. One smooth hand reached for him when he put his hands on her shoulders. The other stretched out and slapped him aside as she pulled herself to her feet and staggered away. He was aware of Amy running past, too, but missed her shouted words.

Then James saw it, another movement in the corner of his eye.

A hand stretched above the tombstone of the guy who had died a year earlier. It searched, scraped across the top, and reached forward again to grip the stone's edge. Spiky brown hair jutted upward from behind it.

He comes?

Then the creature groaned, loud and mournful, like in the movies, but worse because this was real. The spiked head dropped out of view. Something slipped and thumped on the soft earth. Then strong fingers, crusted with mud and grassroots, gripped the stone's top side, tensed and held the weight of the ragged thing that pulled itself up on shaky legs.

A sudden knot twisted in James' stomach. His mouth gaped like Luna Park's entrance as moisture and something warm and mushy filled his pants. Instinct drove his feet into carrying him from the dark shadow that rose from the grave.

Chapter 2

Thunder and lightning cracked the darkness again, but further away, and the creature pressed its palms against the side of its head. Ears ringing from the loud noises, it raised itself from the ground on unsteady limbs. One hand slipped across the headstone's smooth rain-slicked surface as it stumbled to regain balance.

Ripples of pain radiated through its head as another lance of lightning flashed. Its fingers, encrusted with mud and slop, rested on the tombstone's face. Then a spark of recognition ignited in its tortured mind.

What was that?

Patting his hands across the stone, he gripped the grave marker's edges and leaned his head over it. Painful shards slipped through the man's skull as he concentrated upon the images flooding his mind. Visions of a minister delivering a long-winded sermon filled his brain. Snippets of other things: the crunch of a spade in the earth, a gravedigger's cuss, silent teardrops that fell and hit the ground, names, faces — some familiar, a few not. Then came the teenagers stealing through the night. Their hushed voices and giggles met his ears. Lightning flashed in his vision, and he spotted the tombstone's inscription. A name — familiar, yet alive in a faint memory - flickered into his consciousness. His name! Craig Ramsey!

An anguished cry ripped past his parched lips. Startled, nearby birds chattered from the darkness, their chirps echoing through his mind as he stumbled and fled from the resting place.

It couldn't be. No. Wouldn't he remember that?

A protruding grave curb caught his foot. He tumbled to the ground in a heap. Yet he crawled forward still and lurched through the night until he reached a path that led him through an archway of trees that loomed overhead. He'd been to Hilltop Cemetery in recent memory, a lot. Yes. He had fought here. And won. Or did he?

Ahead, voices echoed through the night. Was it the cemetery's residents? Maybe. But why weren't more around?

One torturous step after the next, he pushed forward, fighting the dizziness that steered him like a drunken monkey from one side to the other. The voices — a male and a female - were his beacon, drawing him closer to their hushed conversation until he spotted them outside the graveyard's wrought-iron fence.

Silhouetted by a pale yellow streetlamp, the couple didn't notice him until he burst from the foliage and reached through the railings.

"Help me," he tried to say, but only a dry, rasping stammer floated from his parched lips and throat.

Startled by his growl, one of them gaped open-mouthed at him. Although the light behind the woman's face hid her features in shadows, enough illumination allowed him to see the horror that contorted her mouth. The man lashed out and swatted his outstretched fingers, then paused as he took in the creature's appearance, and gasped. "No! But you're dead!"

The woman screamed, a piercing squeal that hurt his ears, and tripped past her escort as they fled into the night.

He had died? Yes. That's what they said. That confirmed his greatest fear. Yet why was he above ground and

9

walking, hungry and thirsty and tired?

And the couple had recognised him!

One hand over the other, he scuttled along the fence, peering through the rails at the couple's retreating figures, until he reached the gateway, then loped down the gloomy street.

Visions flashed through his mind as he lengthened his running stride and picked up speed. Memories. Fighting on the metal stairwell of the city's main bridge with a man whose name he couldn't recall. Flash of a gun's muzzle followed by its thundering roar. Pain in his mouth, his teeth threatened to crack as they trapped a bullet between them. The red curtains covering his vision as he fell unconscious. Voices. A gorgeous woman's features filling his sight when he opened his eyes, his head cradled in her lap as she ran soft fingers down his cheek. Beautiful tears shimmering on her face. Who was she? Her name teased the tip of his tongue. The other woman with the thick Scottish accent knew her, too, and addressed her with in a thick Scottish accent. She was familiar to him, too, but their names eluded him.

A bus whizzed past him on the street, its brightly lit interior signalling the warmth he craved. Anything would be better than the rain that suddenly bucketed from the sky upon his bedraggled figure.

Instinct drove him forward, pushing him down the streets until, at last, he entered the city. Here was a sea of faces and people that bustled their way along the footpaths and mall strips. Bright lights, colourful and gay, bounced everywhere with spiritual warmth. Familiar lyrics from a beautiful song rang through the air. Their notes resonated in his heart.

The first Noel, the Angels did say, was to certain poor shepherds in fields as they lay

It brought back more memories. Childhood. His sister — no, his cousin — taking him through the suburban streets to gawk at the Christmas lights.

Christmas?

It couldn't be! It was Christmas when he —

How much time had passed since he died?

Strangers brushed past him. Random images popped to mind. Memories. But not his.

Why was that? Whenever he touched things or people, he heard and saw what they thought, what they had experienced. He didn't know how, but he could do that.

Was he always able to do that?

The lyrics of "I'll Be Home For Christmas" drifted to his ears and stirred emotions deep inside him. Yes! He needed to get home.

He changed course towards the river that snaked through the city. Something told him he if he kept following it past the tall Ferris wheel, lit up in blue like a beacon, he would reach his home. Wherever or whatever that was.

He shambled by the stores, lurching to avoid the people to save experiencing the torture of their souls' voices in his mind: forgotten birthdays, angry spouses, first kisses, wishes, dreams, events. They all intruded in his brain, sometimes their sounds echoed in his thoughts; other times bright enough to blind.

At last, he reached a street that meant something to him. Yes! He didn't know the name, but he knew the houses. But a few looked different somehow. Was it the trees? Maybe the guttering on that one had changed colour. Not that he could tell much without the same streetlights.

And there it was!

His bones aching, he dragged himself along the street, catching himself as he tripped on the footpath's gutter. For there was his home. It looked different, but the house was the same.

He patted his pocket, reached into it, and retrieved his keys, and smiled. Soon he would be inside, warm and dry and safe from the downpour that he spat from his mouth.

The key stopped at the handle. Puzzled, the vagrant stared at the unfamiliar brass door knob. It was the same kind, with a ring of metal above it, which he always used to pull it shut, but where was the keyhole?

He arched an eyebrow and bowed his head to look closer, squinting at the pale grey light that glowed from the edges of a glass panel next to the door. He stood erect, one eye narrowed as he scratched his scalp. Since when did he have a palm-print reader installed? There was only one way to find out. He pressed his hand on the edges. It felt warm. Then, yes, more images flickered through his tired and scrambled thoughts. A familiar face appeared in the vision, but known only from photographs, or an associate. He struggled to remember how he knew or who it was.

Perhaps he had died. It just had not occurred to him that someone else would have moved into his home now, however much time had passed since that day. Why wouldn't they? He was a member of the nearly departed, right?

The palm-print panel buzzed, its warning indicator glaring at him with a threatening red hue that blinked three times. Security lights thumped to life and bathed him in blinding whiteness. Pain speared his blinded eyes. He lifted an arm to shield them, staggered backward, and tripped into the nearby cacti. Their spikes impaled his leg and provoked a curse a moment before the door opened.

A boy of about fourteen or fifteen poked his head out, then looked down at him. Recognition flickered on the surprised boy's face, then turned to horror. The lad was familiar to him, but from recent memory. A few hours ago. He'd seen him fleeing with two girls.

A wave of vertigo swept over the stranger, overwhelmed him as he hit his head on the concrete pathway. The boy's voice echoed. "Dad!"

He mumbled in surprise. "Dad?"

Then the darkness took him.

Chapter 3

The first hints of Saturday morning presented themselves to Brianna as she slept. The grass, short from her father's having trimmed it too low, provided no protection from the hard ground. Although cooler than the boiling bitumen road, the footpath's close-cut lawn was hot enough to make her jog on the spot as she waited for the Mr Whippy van, which made its tortoise-like crawl along the street twice as unbearable.

She licked her lips in anticipation and imagined the velvet-smooth ice cream and how it would help beat the summer holiday heat when she sat under the mango tree in the backyard. Of course, her alsatian, Tango, would make her share it with him.

Then the dream world dissolved around her. The sun disappeared, and the room's darkness surrounded her where she lay on the bed.

Brianna groaned, rolled over and patted the space beside her.

Empty.

The strains of Greensleeves floated past the lace curtain that danced with the warm breeze. Why do ice-cream vans always play the same tune? The imagined icy treat's sweet chocolatey taste remained on her lips, which she licked, then disappeared. She stretched on the bed. The music grew louder as it approached her house, enticing her like a siren's song to buy some, confusing her between the present and the dream that still lingered.

Downstairs, the screen door squeaked open, then

slammed shut. The sounds of four-year-old feet running towards the van, which idled outside her home, followed. Brianna opened her mouth to call out for a chocolate cone, then stopped in hesitation.

Why was an ice-cream truck operating at this time of night? The first light of dawn was still young. No normal person had even thought of breakfast yet, let alone a sugary treat.

"Hayley!" Brianna had bolted downstairs and outside before she realised what she was doing.

An end of the little girl's nightie, its hem just above her tiny bare feet, disappeared inside the back of the grey vehicle a moment before its door slammed shut. Its wheels protested with a light squeal as they carried its passengers down the street.

Brianna bellowed and sprinted after the van as it sped away and turned the corner without slowing at the intersection. Her feet splashed on the wet bitumen, her arms pumping as she puffed faster downhill and along the pathway in pursuit. Her eyes narrowed as she took in its details and noted the truck's colouring was blander than other ice-cream trucks she had known. It didn't even have a cone on top!

The van's brake light flickered for a second as it approached the next intersection. Instinct told Brianna the van was turning left again. She changed course and cut the corner through a grassy park, easily hurdling a bench that otherwise blocked her path.

The manoeuvre brought her close enough to read and memorise its registration plate before it disappeared. But she couldn't let go.

Red, raw, her naked feet stung. Still, she ran on impulse,

dogged determination pushing her. She wouldn't give up. Not on her niece.

A car beeped its horn behind her, then sped past. She waved her arms for it to stop, but the driver gave her the finger. Then she heard the roar of another engine. A motorbike!

Its rider slowed a bit as he approached her. She opened her mouth to speak, but her voice stuck in her throat. Luckily, her hand suffered no problems as she grabbed a handlebar, then pushed the biker off with the other. A moment before the startled man crunched to the bitumen, Brianna had already popped the bike's clutch and toed up a gear to pursue her quarry.

Ignoring the speed limit, she ripped the Indian Scout past the sleepy-eyed 4am commuters. Horns blared as she ran the red lights, her vision locked on the van ahead.

The quiet suburbia transitioned into an industrial area. The traffic changed, too.

Her quarry zipped by a construction site. Without warning, an oncoming truck veered into Brianna's path to turn wide into the property. Brianna swore, braked hard, and skidded in time to avoid a collision. Obscenities spewed from the driver, leaning out his window. "Watch what you're doing, ya crazy bitch."

She revved the engine and took off onto the gravel beside the road and roared after the van. Astonishment registered in the truck driver's eyes for a second. Brianna toed through the gears fast. Her surroundings blurred. Then she realised she was wearing her pyjamas — a crop top that barely covered her assets and a bikini bottom. Little wonder the driver had gawked.

Meanwhile, the van had passed a roundabout. She was

close now, but shift-workers in their souped-up sedans and oversized 4WDs approached from both sides. Her teeth clenched, jaw set, she skidded and weaved between them. Cars and utilities crunched together behind as the right-hand traffic braked. But the utility driver ahead to her left wasn't watching. Oblivious and ignoring the oncoming motorbike, he nosed his car into the intersection.

Brianna's eyes felt heavy, but her thumping heart kept them open. Fingers clenching the handle grips, she braked again, flicking her high-beams to alert the driver.

Bad move.

His head turned. He screamed, stomped the brakes, and gawked at Brianna's charging motorbike.

A split-second decision saved her.

Brianna swerved. A moment sooner, and she would have collided with another oncoming car from the other direction. The Indian bore her along the right-hand side of the street against the traffic. Brakes squealed. Horns blared as she weaved between the cars with ease.

Her eyes flicked upward towards the brake lights ahead. The van! Was that it? No! Where had it gone?

While she searched, quick calculations zipped into mind. Had it turned at the next roundabout to head into a different industrial area? Or had it circled at the first exit to enter the motorway?

She opted for the highway. A moment later, she spotted it. The van had gained a significant lead after her near misses before. It would get away unless she changed tactics. She steered the Indian across the road towards a lump of dirt at the side. The kind that formed a jump, like what she used to ride on her BMX as a nine-year-old. But Brianna was an adult now. She wasn't jumping over another kid on the ground.

The Indian flew. Brianna's stomach heaved as she fought not to shut her eyes. Some twenty feet below stood the outbound motorway, headlights passing each direction in the early grey of dawn. The wind blew her face and hair. For a moment, things slowed down as the motorbike reached the peak of its upward arc. Her adrenaline-filled mind took in the sights as they flashed by her vision. The car lights, the light pole she had barely avoided, the fuse near its bulb, the clouds scudding across the horizon, and the truck below. Then the ground lurched upwards toward her like a hungry shark.

Somehow, she separated herself from the motorcycle. It dropped faster, its frame heading straight for the road just ahead of the van. She landed on the vehicle's roof, jarring her shoulder with a paralysing blow. Brakes squealed. Her fingers clawed at the smooth metal. Then her legs swung over the speeding van's front windshield.

The van jumped. No, it shook as it ran over the motorbike. She grabbed the edge and clung on tight.

Veering off the path, it headed towards a ditch beside the motorway and crunched to a complete stop. Brianna didn't. Her body zipped off the slick roof to crash in a deep pool of water, the impact winding her.

The sounds of traffic slowing filled Brianna's senses for a few seconds before she painfully dragged herself to her feet and limped to the van. Its driver sat motionless in the seat behind tinted glass. Anger fuelled the adrenaline that carried her in stumbling steps towards the driver's side before she wrenched open the door.

Brianna had expected a fight. But not with the four-legged fury that erupted as a growling mass from the cab.

She yelped, side-stepped in time to avoid the alsatian, its fur grazing her bare arm. A deep snarl escaped its bared teeth, its head lowered for a second before it lunged for her throat. She dodged again, conscious of its raking claw that scratched through her shoulder.

Painfully aware of her nakedness, therefore her lack of protection, she faced the canine as it turned towards her. All sounds around her dulled except for the dog's warning growl as it rounded its shoulders and lowered its head, stalking her careful step after the other.

Avoid eye contact, her combat instructor had taught her. It can excite a savage dog, which provokes and challenges it. Give it time to calm.

Fat chance.

Forty kilos of solid muscle and fur lunged. By instinct, Brianna pivoted and punched. She yelled as her fist crunched on a strong skull. The dog yelped and thudded on the rough ground. An instant later, she had sprung on the creature's back and pinned it under her.

It was powerful, and her muscles screamed for rest. Survival spurred her. It was the canine or her.

The mutt fought hard to escape her clutches, but Brianna's arms persisted. Her fingers inched around its chest, hugging it tight to her. The dog tried to twist, barked, and snarled at her. If not for her first blow to its head, events could have been worse.

The alsatian squirmed in her grip and snapped at her, missing her face by an inch. Brianna clung on until she captured the furious growling mass of fangs, muscle, and fur in a full Nelson and pressed hard. Teeth gritted, she twisted. The resounding crack of the dog's breaking neck was like a gunshot. A nearby stranger, who had rushed to help, stopped shocked in his tracks, uncertain what to do.

Her hands trembling from fatigue and shock, Brianna rolled from the warm, shaggy corpse. The dog or her. This time, it was her. She wanted to follow a primal urge to shout and beat her chest like a savage hunter, but she couldn't. Brianna's legs were heavy as lead and trembled as she staggered to the vehicle's open driver's door.

No, it was empty!

The nearby stranger approached with hesitation, his head cocked at an angle as his eyes scanned her, careful to avoid her exposed flesh. "Lady, are you okay?"

"Call the police." Brianna waved away his helping hand and limped to the back of the van. With one shaky hand, she yanked its door open.

There, strapped in a seat, was her niece. "Hayley!" She crawled inside and checked the young girl's inert body. Although unconscious, the child's heart beat strong. "Thank God."

Another sound. To the left. Brianna turned and saw two more girls crying, their contorted faces streaked with tears. She unbuckled Hayley and lifted her from the seat, cradling her sleeping form, and moved next to the closest girl.

Brianna's voice croaked. She coughed, cleared her dry throat. "It's okay, honey. I'm a policewoman." She collapsed on the van's floor, panting. "I'll call your mummies, yeah?"

* * *

Three hours later, Brianna was on her second cup of coffee.

The first one, delivered in its burnt and bitter flavour from the hospital's vending machine, hadn't held the same comfort for her. The doctors had examined Hayley and the other girls, given them the all-clear.

Earlier, another detective had seen Brianna in the hospital gown that provided little dignity and fetched spare clothes from her work locker.

Now they were back at the station. A social worker had arrived and sat in while an officer interviewed the girls, who were old enough to answer questions. Brianna had opted out of the questioning. While glad for the other children's safety, she felt more responsible for her niece. Her brother would never forgive her if something had happened to his little girl, who represented all he had left since his wife had died a year after giving birth. She wouldn't have forgiven herself, either.

Her desk phone rang, shocking her from her thoughts. She grabbed it, guessing the caller's identity without needing to look at the incoming display. "Detective-Inspector Cogan."

"Brianna?" the man's voice asked. She allowed a smile, knowing that she had guessed right. "Are you both okay?"

"Yes, Mick." She turned her gaze towards the corner of the office where her niece was sleeping fitfully in a chair and covered by a light blanket. "Hayley's fine."

A sigh of relief on the other end. "Good. Do you know if-"

"There were two other girls in the van too," she answered with a yawn. "The driver escaped."

"Schick. At least you're all safe." A pause. "Brianna," Mick's deep voice continued. "I have to talk to you, anyway. When are you bringing Hayley home?"

She looked at the clock and thought for a second. "Give me half an hour. I'll need a lift. Really, everything is fine."

"Not that, Bri," Mick responded. "Something else has happened. Just as big."

"What?"

"Not on the phone. Talk soon. See ya."

Chapter 4

Craig Ramsey awoke with a start. Sweat had drenched his clothes, and disturbing images packed his head. He blinked against the sunlight that streamed through the open curtains, then upon recognising his bedroom, he lay there and took a breath. A butcher bird's song floated in from the branches near his window and coaxed him to rise, but he rested a hand on his head until the swimming sensation in his mind ceased.

What had he done on the previous night to feel so terrible?

His knuckles were smooth, yet ached as though he'd hit bone. If he didn't know better, he would have sworn he had fought someone last night. But that was only a dream. And that taste in his mouth. What was it? He reached for the glass on the bedside table and grunted in surprise to find only a lamp there. Odd. He always kept water there, in case he woke up thirsty. He glanced at the other side of his king-sized bed — empty; that's odd — and stood.

The snippets of dreams slipped through his thoughts: a graveyard, running children, a long walk home, and someone else living in his home.

The dream had been so vivid, his muscles ached as though he had trudged for many miles. Dreams can appear so real; to Craig, an expert astral traveller and lucid dreamer, it also carried differences his trained mind perceived most times. For instance, the carpet; its design matched one he had replaced ten years ago when he first moved into the house. Brianna had changed them from the mosaics to cream-coloured not long after she moved in. She hadn't put them back again, had she? The carpet was the same, the walls too. Even the paint's texture on the dense brick and plaster walls matched. This was definitely his home.

Ah, home! With a satisfied smile on his face, Craig Ramsey rose from the bed and stood and stretched again. Relief flooded him as the gentle aroma of bacon and eggs drifted past his nostrils. Ah! Emily, his familiar ghost guardian since childhood, or perhaps Brianna, his wife, was cooking breakfast. Its pleasant sizzle reached his ears, triggering eager saliva in his mouth as he trudged barefooted down the hallway to the kitchen.

Then he stopped.

For there before him stood Brianna and a man he had met a few times but wasn't familiar enough to be cooking breakfast in his home! The black-haired stranger turned towards him before studying him for a moment with an eyebrow lifted.

A smile melted into view upon the stranger's face as he dished sausages, bacon, and eggs. "Craig Ramsey, I presume?"

Craig shot a questioning look toward Brianna. He leaned forward to kiss her, only to stop when she flung her hands upward to block him, her palms facing him.

He paused — Odd. Why would she do that? — and turned back to the stranger in his kitchen, his forehead puckered. "Yes, that is me." Then a thought occurred to him as he swung towards Brianna again. She remained quiet and showed a smile, too brief for his liking, and a creepy sensation shivered through Craig's spine.

"I'm Michael." The stranger offered him his hand. "Do

you remember me?"

Craig hesitated a moment before grasping Michael's firm hand in a shake. "You look familiar, but beyond that, I don't know." He turned his mind inward, processing the images that played across his tortured psychic consciousness from the touch. In the vision, he was friends with this man named Michael. They had fought together, saved each other's lives, yet he couldn't recall him! No memories sparked.

Shocked, Craig released Michael's hand and walked around the living room, aware of the other two exchanging glances.

"I don't understand," he muttered while running his fingers across the books. He recognised them as volumes he'd collected, writings about various phenomena that unconventional sources avoided. And as he touched the surfaces, more facts zipped through his mind, but they weren't what he expected. Some were familiar, but others differed. "I know these books. I purchased them myself, yet the memories I see are not mine. We've never met, Michael, but I appear to have given this house to you somehow. How?"

A terrible idea crossed Craig's mind. His hand dropped to his side, shaking. "Am I dead?"

Brianna stood from beside the kitchen counter and beckoned towards a waiting lounge chair. Craig waited for her to sit first before complying. All the time, she watched him with keen searching eyes, the same gaze he remembered as her "thinking face". He had often joked with her about that, but now he couldn't bring himself to mention it.

"So," Craig said, "tell me. What's happened?" He reached

to take her hands in his. Again, she moved away. "What is it?"

Michael cleared his throat. "You're being too forward. Perhaps you should keep your mitts off her."

"Forward?" Craig reacted to Michael's protective tone. "What the hell? She's my wife." He shot a meaningful look at Brianna, hoping that she would come to her senses.

"What?" Brianna's reflexive stiffening surprised him further. "What planet are you from?"

Craig glanced at Michael, who observed him with a heightened interest, then back to Brianna. Too surreal, he thought, and considered that perhaps this was a dream. He withdrew towards a lounge-suite that looked like the one he had once owned but since replaced after a sword stroke had disembowelled and spilled its stuffing three years ago. His fingers brushed it. Images filled his mind, but none included the memories he recalled. He moved his lips to speak, but no sound came.

The man named Michael stepped toward Craig, lifted a defensive hand, and waited as though assessing his mood. Craig nodded and plonked himself on the lounge-suite.

"There seems to be some confusion around a few things," Michael said. "Let's start with the obvious." His smile was friendly, open, calm. "Then we will hear your story. Yeah?" He waited for Craig's nod.

"I believe I should ask questions," Craig responded. "You know who I am, and I see you have obviously acquainted with my home enough to cook in my kitchen. How, I don't understand, Michael, because, although you're familiar to me, I never invited you here." Then he turned to face Brianna. "And somehow, my wife of two years, the mother of my daughter, doesn't recognise me.

Yet you and she are close to each other. What the hell is going on?"

The puzzled looks on Michael's and Brianna's faces confused him further.

"Well?" Blood warmed Craig's face as his heart quickened.

Brianna cleared her throat. Craig opened his mouth to speak, but she silenced him with a wagging finger. "You say your name is Craig Ramsey, and you share his resemblance." She glanced inside his leather wallet, which she held, and bobbed her head to the side. "Your ID says you are too." She shot him a hard stare as she snapped it shut. "But you aren't. You can't be."

Craig scoffed, shaking his head in disbelief. "You hold all the evidence you need. How can you say that?"

Brianna took a breath and replied in a softer, calmer voice. "Because you — that is, the real Ramsey — is dead." Her expression softened despite her pensive eyes.

"You've got to be bloody kidding me. I'm alive. Look at me!"

Michael stepped forward beside Brianna. "We attended your funeral, and you even left this house and property for me."

"Garbage!" Blood surged to Craig's face, heating his mood as he stood up to point a finger straight at Michael. "I don't know you. That's impossible."

"Last year," Brianna replied. "You... That is… He died, murdered in the street, a hit-and-run. We identified you ourselves."

"Killed?" A recollection of the previous night's dream struck Craig. Struggling through the muddy graveyard dirt. He gazed at his hands, conflicting emotions and thoughts

27

tangling in his brain. "Last year?"

Brianna's tone relaxed, just a little. "Yes." She leaned toward Michael and whispered something, to which he nodded.

"You sound convincing; I'll admit that, but there's no way you're Craig Ramsey."

His face planted in his hands, Craig's mind grasped for words. Then he raised his eyes and set his gaze on her. He took a breath, and asked in the calmest voice possible, "Where's Emily? She can tell you." Brianna and the stranger glanced at each other and shrugged. "Come on! You must know her. Remember? Scottish, red hair, cheeky, a bit possessive." He delivered the last part, which was a joke he and his wife shared. Surely she'd recognise that.

But the woman shook her head and wrote in a notebook he hadn't noticed earlier. "Who is she?"

"Never mind," Craig said, his voice trailing as a train of thought steamed behind his eyes. Emily Fraser had been his spirit companion since childhood and known only to him and a select few, including Brianna. While Craig was famous for being able to divine information from holding objects, few people knew he could see and communicate with the dead. Was this woman an imposter? He studied her features and still found it hard to believe. Maybe this was someone impersonating the woman he had married. That could explain why she shied from his touch, but he needed to find something she had held. It was best to change the subject for now until the time was right. "What about Tyrone?" She had to know his adopted nephew; they had a close bond.

Again, Brianna shook her head, the same blank

expression on her face as she wrote Tyrone's name in her notepad. "Afraid not."

"This is ridiculous!" Craig stormed as she leaned back away from him in her chair. "I can't be dreaming this."

Michael stepped between them — a protective posture - and faced him. He spoke in a calm and reassuring tone, without the slightest tremor. "Simmer down, please."

They were interrupted by a fresh voice that appeared to be all around them at once. "The DNA test checked positive."

"Who-?" Craig said, searching for the disembodied voice, thinking it was an unseen spirit, but Michael interrupted.

"Are you sure, Sparks?" His eyes stared into the air above them. "How?"

"The DNA sample you took from this gentleman's hair matches Craig Ramsey." The voice said, "Michael, this is Craig Ramsey."

Chapter 5

"DNA?" Craig blurted. "You took my DNA?"

Michael's eyes flicked toward Brianna and back again. He nodded.

"Why?" Craig strode toward a wall, his eyes searching for anything, fingers grazing the surfaces.

His brown-haired host paused a moment. "Sparks, are you sure?"

"Is the Pope a Catholic?" This time, the disembodied voice responded from the opposite side of the livingroom near the kitchen. Craig spun in confusion towards its source. "Skids, he's the real deal. Fingerprints check. So do the saliva and tissue samples."

Heat surged into Craig's face, his heartbeat picking up pace. "What the hell is this?" He studied the walls, fingers drifting across the surface. "Speakers built into the wall? Where are the cameras?"

Michael shrugged again and replied to the voice he called Sparks. "He recognises the house and Brianna. Why doesn't he recognise me?"

"I recognise you," Craig Ramsey replied, stepping into his kitchen to examine it closer, and opened the top drawer. "You just don't belong here in my home. Knives, forks and spoons. All how I left them." Then he cast a glance towards the books in the living room, his library. "Everything as I remember!"

"Except for me." Michael's strong voice held curiosity, but remained calm.

"And this is my wife!" Craig nodded towards Brianna,

whose jaw dropped in surprise. "We married and have a daughter. Where is my little girl?"

"Hold up there, sunshine." Brianna stepped back from Craig. "You're wrong there. That never happened."

Craig stopped and drew a breath. "What the hell is happening here?"

"Look," Brianna said, her hands raised, palms facing Craig in a calming posture until she was close enough to him. "You obviously have a lot to process, Craig." Brianna spoke in a soothing tone as she placed a hand on his shoulder to lead him to the living room. "Let's relax a moment. Have a seat."

A sigh escaped Craig's lips as he sank into the armchair's familiar depths. He often sat there to relax, but now the serenity refused to come. Across the room, Michael dropped into the armchair's twin. The same in which Khan, another friend of Craig's, had sat just the other week. At least, that was in his recollection. Brianna left him and hunted for a mug in the kitchen while Michael regarded Craig for a moment.

Meanwhile, the cuckoo emerged from the German-crafted clock nine times to mark the hour.

Michael's right eyebrow raised. "You're pretty spry for a dead man, you know?" The corner of his mouth rose in a lopsided grin. "I just about scooped my underpants when I saw you at the front door."

Craig nodded his thanks to Brianna, who had returned with a steaming cup of hot tea. Its aroma teased his nostrils, evoking memories of Brianna as his wife. Was it even real?

"Dead, you say?" Craig took a quick sip. Ah, peppermint tea. She remembered that about him, at least. "For how long? A year?"

Michael nodded. "What's the last thing you remember?"

"I was…" Craig searched his memories. Good question. With his mind rattled from the recent discoveries, he wasn't sure what was real. What was the last thing he recalled? "Christmas shopping. I was after something for my daughter."

"Do you mean Julia?" Brianna asked from the side, a hot drink cradled in her hands as she sat on the long sofa between them.

Craig faced Brianna. "Julia's dead. You know that." How could she bring up that name? A fatiguing wave of confusion drifted through his head as Brianna gave an apologetic look. "Sorry. She-"

"It's okay," Michael's calming voice interrupted, his face unreadable. "Focus. Where were you?"

"The Myer Centre," Craig paused, the comforting texture of the leather armchair's familiarity calming him. "Yes! Then I stopped by Hilltop on the way home."

"The cemetery?" Michael exchanged a concerned glance with Brianna. "Why did you visit the cemetery?"

"To visit my…" Craig paused, remembering how he had visited Hilltop Cemetery the previous day. It was Christmas season, the time when his first daughter, Julia, had her birthday. That little girl had died in a car crash with his first wife, Celina. Murdered, he later discovered, by a demon. Yes, he had bought a Christmas present for his youngest daughter by Brianna. He had also purchased a teddy bear for Julia, a yearly ritual he performed at her grave. Brianna knew that. She had talked to Julia's ghost before, too, as he did every year on her birthday. Craig turned to Brianna, noting her reactions, which remained as blank as Michael's expressions. Disappointed, he shook his head and regrouped his thoughts. "Hang on a minute. You're in my house. You should answer my questions. Why are you so curious?"

Michael returned Craig's stare for a moment before gazing upwards at the point from which the disembodied entity's voice came. "Sparks, can you confirm again this is Craig Ramsey?"

Sparks' sigh reminded Craig of a teenager impatient with the questioning adult. "Fingerprints match. Voiceprint matches. So does his DNA. Blah, blah, blah."

Michael's expression remained thoughtful. "Is he a clone?"

Craig huffed. "What? You're doubting me—"

"He's definitely Craig Ramsey, Michael," Sparks replied in a somewhat amused tone.

"Sparks?" Craig asked, his eyes searching the room again. "Who the bloody hell are you? Are you even here?"

Sparks' voice chuckled through the air and sounded young. "I'm here, but not the way you think. I'm just wrapped in computer chips, not skin." Craig's confusion prompted an explanation. "Human intelligence, not artificial."

"But I have installed nothing in my house." He looked toward Michael and Brianna, who both swapped knowing looks at each other. A grin, the kind one gives with a party trick. "What? What's so funny?"

Michael smiled, leaning forward. "Sparks, is he a clone?"

"No."

"Are you sure?"

"DNA signatures match completely. There is no evidence of genetic alteration or degradation."

"Can you confirm that again?"

Sparks replied with an indignant air. "Are you joshing me, Skids? This is THE Craig Ramsey, except for a few notable differences." Craig uttered a protest, which Sparks interrupted. "His memories differ from what we know about him, but he's telling the truth. His truth. The polygraphic analysis shows a normal heartbeat, although stressed from the conversation, alongside other physiological signs."

This time both Craig and Michael glanced at each other, their visages a mirror image of the other. "What?" they said.

"He is the real McCoy, Skids," Sparks confirmed, emphasising his words. "He's just experienced things differently to what we know."

"How?" Michael asked, his brow crinkling.

"Check his left hand. A wedding ring. He's married, and his wife is indeed Brianna Cogan."

"What?" Brianna gawked at the corner of the ceiling. "Hang on a minute. How?"

"The family photo in his wallet, Brianna. You're in it. You, Craig and a little girl." Sparks' voice registered further amusement. "She looks like you, Brianna. A bit like Craig, too. And it's not Photoshopped." Sparks chuckled at Brianna's overt discomfort, and prompted an uneasy laugh from Craig, too. "What have you been up to, Bri?"

Brianna reached for the leather wallet that she had earlier left on the counter. She opened the wallet and examined the photo inside. Her eyes glowed with surprise, a hand lifting to her face to trace its contour as she inspected the picture before she snapped the wallet shut. "Doesn't prove a thing," she muttered and tossed the wallet to Michael, who viewed its contents with equal interest. At last, he closed the wallet and returned it to Craig's waiting hand with a nod.

"Craig," Michael said, leaning back in his chair. "We have a problem, quite a few, actually." Craig snorted but allowed his host to continue. "To us, you died and returned. In fact," Michael's voice turned sombre, "you died in my arms."

Craig's eyes widened, one of his fingers brushing back and forth across the surface of his wallet's leather finish. Dead? How? Memory flooded back to him as he remembered staggering from Hilltop Cemetery in the darkness. "In your arms, you say?"

Michael took a deep breath and released it with a nod. "I owe you my life for saving me from the base that night. And you had left me your estate in your will, which is how I came to live here, like I said."

Craig nodded, sliding his wallet back in the hip pocket of his jeans. "I know. I don't remember it. But I believe you." He caught Michael's raised, quizzical eyebrow, and winked. "I read your vibrations on my wallet just then. A moment before handing me the wallet, you were thinking about my death."

"Psychometry!" A grin melted into view on Michael's face. "Holy Schick! It is you!"

"I need to know more," Craig responded. "Such as, how did my killer survive what my nephew did to him."

"Your nephew?"

Craig nodded. "Tyrone killed Colonel Blaze three years ago. I was there when it happened."

"But it's Blaze who killed you!"

Confusion hit Craig with the subtlety of a brick in a

cotton glove as he processed the shocking information. Stubbornness laced with cockiness pressed his reply. "Well, now I'm back, I guess."

Chapter 6

Meanwhile, in a concrete-walled room, deep under an old car wrecker's yard, two young children huddled in the darkness. They had met as strangers hours ago when they woke in the cell from the same shared dream — ice cream on a hot summer day. The oldest, an eight-year-old named Jackson, hugged the other closer. The little girl under his left arm snuggled against him, her tiny body hitching with each heartbreaking sob.

"Mummy." Her bottom lip trembled like a leaf.

Jackson shushed her with a gentle voice, just the way his own mother used to comfort him. The urge to cry too grew strong in his chest, but he fought it back. His father always told him to stay brave, even when you're scared. That's how he kept calm in the dark. The darkness might hide the Boogeyman, but it also hides you if you stay quiet. His father taught him that. But the men who took Jackson weren't Boogeymen. They wore uniforms, the heavy kind coloured with different shades of green and white. Camouflage, his father used to call it.

"I want Mummy."

"Someone will find us, Beaulah." Jackson sniffed back a tear. Don't cry. Be brave, he told himself. "Don't worry."

But that's just it. People already knew Jackson and Beaulah were here. The wrong people. And the right ones did not know the kids waited here.

And not just them.

Other kids were here too. Jackson could hear their voices in his head. The same way the old man's voice spoke inside his head that day at the playground. The old man knew. He could hear Jackson's inside voices just as Jackson heard the old man's. In that instant, when their eyes met, the old man winked. *G'day, Jackson, it's good to meet you. Be good for your mother.*

The other kids had similar gifts. Their voices spoke in his mind, and he heard them thinking about their mothers and fathers. And he caught other words: tests, subjects, double-blind experiment, sensory deprivation. Those words came from grownup thoughts.

Heavy footsteps reached his ears. Faint at first, their steady rhythm reminded Jackson of his father's steps on the wooden floorboards at home in the hallway. The way he walked with purpose. Steady, confident, and strong. But these footsteps weren't his father's. They belonged to another, a man with a cold and angry heart. The feet stopped before them. Both children held their breaths, waiting. A quick sliding sound punctuated by a hard thump made them jump, and a square of light appeared before them.

Cold eyes glinted, squinting into the darkness at first, then focused on them. Jackson clutched the little girl closer. Something in the eyes warned him. They belonged to a wicked man.

The hatch slid shut. "Bring the girl," said the man.

Beaulah's scream in his ear deafened Jackson. It rocked his chest, made him gasp hard for breath. Brilliant light splashed over them from outside. A large man, round as a gorilla, strode through the open door into the room and took Beaulah by one of her tiny hands. She screamed again, called for her mother. The gargantuan brute smiled with teeth full of shiny metal that gleamed in the light.

Jackson tried his best to fight the man away, shouted for him to leave Beaulah alone. A meaty hand slapped Jackson in the face, stinging him as stars danced in his vision. Pain in the back of Jackson's head crunched his thoughts, weakened his grip. The gorilla man carried the screaming Beaulah out the door as Jackson watched in helplessness from the floor.

Then the door slammed shut, plunging the room into sudden darkness, except for the tiny square of light, which disappeared soon with a sliding click.

Jackson screamed into the darkness. "Bring her back!"

But the footsteps mocked his cries as they retreated down the hall with the screaming Beaulah.

* * *

The uniformed officer watched the ham-fisted soldier strap the young girl to the chair through the one-way glass. The corner of his mouth flickered when the little girl kicked at Tabua. *Such a spirit, she has*, he thought. Perhaps she holds promise.

That would depend on the test.

The little girl's wide eyes studied the room. They lit upon the straps that held her tight to the chair. She scowled before regarding the flat screen television in front of her, then the helmet-shaped device beside her. They flicked toward the mirror, behind which the officer stood in darkness. Her eyes didn't just look in the mirror as other children's eyes had. No, this little girl looked through the glass and directly into his eyes. Her chest heaved with heavy breaths as she panicked. A scream echoed in fright and pain as a needle pierced her skin. The girl's eyelids sagged, her breathing calmed, and her head flopped to the side.

Another door opened, through which a grey-haired scientist with owlish glasses entered. With a cursory glance at the giant standing nearby, he turned his attention to the little girl slumped in the chair. With gentle hands, he lifted her head so that it sat straight in the chair.

He turned towards the giant soldier. "Why is she sleeping?"

The giant shrugged and looked away.

With a disgusted shake of his head, the scientist placed his fingers on the little girl's wrist and counted her pulse against his watch before grumbling. "How the hell am I supposed to test her if she's sleeping, Tweedledum?"

The officer pressed a button on the desk and leaned towards his microphone. "Is there a problem, Professor Lee?"

The doctor raised his hands in exasperation. "Yes! How do you expect me to test her if she's unconscious?"

"Then bring in another subject, Professor." The officer flicked something from the front of his jacket. "Must I do all of your thinking?"

Professor Lee rolled his eyes, turned to the giant, and hollered. "Well, go on! Do as the colonel says!" The giant remained still, moving only his head to face the scientist with a snarl. "Get another subject and try not to scare them, will you?"

With mute precision, the giant unstrapped the little girl from the chair and lifted her into his arms as the professor watched. He stared into her face, his expression unreadable for a second, before carrying her out the door.

In the other room behind the one-way glass, a knock on the door caught the colonel's attention. He looked up in time to watch the door open and leaned back as a major entered.

"Major Oates," the officer said, the hint of venom in his voice. "You look like someone stole your lunch money. What is it?"

The major, a touch older than him, saluted the superior officer. "Strange news, sir. You must see this."

"What is it?"

Major Oates lifted a remote from the desk, switched on a monitor and tapped a channel number into the controls. An image came to life on the screen. "Our tracers on the local surveillance cameras picked this up."

The superior officer gazed at the video stream as a silhouetted, lanky figure loped along a dimly lit street, lurching side-to-side. As the video's subject leaned against a brick wall, the watcher squinted his eyes for a minute. "What's this? A drunk?"

Major Oates shook his head. "Does the man look familiar to you, sir?"

The commanding officer shrugged. "I don't fraternise with lushes, Oates." Then his eyes opened wider, a glimmer of recognition. Could it be? He waved his hand. "Is this the best image you have?"

Major Oates pressed another button. "The boffins enhanced the video for us." He zoomed the video a few frames until the subject's features appeared brighter in a nearby streetlight.

Onscreen, the lean figure lifted its face towards the camera without noticing it or caring. His spiky hair looked a touch darker, but that could be the dim lighting. The stranger's facial shape rang bells.

The superior's heart skipped a beat, and his surprised eyebrows raised as he leaned forward to scrutinise the image through squinted eyes. "Is this a joke?"

Major Oates shook his head. "It's real, sir. I confirmed it myself." His voice lowered. "That's Craig Ramsey... or a damn good facsimile."

Oates' superior crossed his arms. "No way. Impossible." He checked his watch. "How old is this video?"

"Twelve hours."

Twelve hours? Could it be? That was when the Neurolyser had malfunctioned on its third test.

"Twelve hours!" His hand slammed the desk, shaking its contents, and drawing the attention of the scientist in the adjoining room. Red-faced, he hissed. "And you just brought this to me now?"

Major Oates shrugged. "I only saw it half an hour ago, sir. I had to check it first before wasting your time."

"A year." On the screen, the thin man staggered into the shadows off-camera. Slack-jawed and eyebrow raised with curiosity, the superior watched. "Where has he been all these months?"

The footage flipped to another camera's angle to show his nemesis staggering along a footpath towards a group of five men. They looked less than charitable as they approached the raggedy man.

He watched the gang surround Ramsey. "Where did he live?" Engrossed in the video, he nodded at the major's reply. "Amazing. Could he have been heading straight home? He wouldn't be that stupid... Could he?"

"We don't know where he went, Colonel," the major replied. "Surveillance cameras lost him soon after this footage. Camera troubles in the area."

Oates' superior nodded. "This happened less than an hour after the Neurolyser malfunctioned."

"A coincidence."

"Not likely. He upset the cameras." But how?

Onscreen, the group's leader attacked. Ramsey dodged aside as though by a breeze and dispatched the assailant with a rapid triple punch to the head before flooring a second thug. Soon, he had either crippled or maimed the remaining gang members, except for the fifth attacker, who had fled down the street in a panic.

Colonel Blaze zoomed in on the subject's face as he surveyed his downed assailants. "There you are, Craig Ramsey." He shaped his fingers like a pistol, aimed at the screen, and mocked a gunshot. "Got you, you son-of-a-bitch."

Chapter 7

Brianna glanced at her watch. "I should get out of here, boys." She yawned. "Some of us have to catch up on sleep."

Craig glimpsed Brianna as she stretched, caught the hint of curves through the material of her top. His eye lifted towards her face before she spotted his gaze. "Going home?"

Brianna blinked and took her cup to the kitchen sink. "After this…" She stopped, changed her mind about what she almost said. "I could use some shuteye before tonight's shift."

What was Brianna about to say? Her eyes had flicked towards Michael. Had Michael shaken his head, told her to say nothing?

Craig left his chair and picked up Brianna's backpack to hand it to her. Brianna hesitated a moment, her eyes raised to meet Craig's. He smiled. "Your bag?"

Brianna took it, almost snatching, with a nod. "Yes, thank you." She turned to leave, then stopped to face him again. "I don't know who you really are. But if you're Craig Ramsey, I wish you the best."

Craig opened his mouth to answer. Of course, I'm Craig, your husband, he wanted to say. Yet he could only nod. "Thank you."

A smile flickered on Brianna's face for an instant before she turned and headed for the door. Craig watched, noting the walk of the woman who resembled his wife in so many ways. But his fresh discovery proved otherwise.

The Brianna Cogan he saw had some similar experiences to the Brianna he knew. But they weren't the same.

Michael cleared his throat. "Mate," he said, "are you okay?"

Craig said nothing. He could only nod.

As if he guessed Craig's thoughts, Michael put a supportive hand on Craig's shoulder. "I'll see Brianna off. We'll talk more soon."

"I guess I'll make myself at home," Craig replied, looking at the house which was his but wasn't.

"You've got the idea." Michael winked and followed Brianna, who was already heading out the door.

The couple shut the front door behind them, but their muffled voices still permeated it. Although their words remained unclear, Craig guessed the subject: him. Michael and Brianna still had questions about him. The impressions Craig had gleaned from touching Brianna's backpack — a sneaky move on his part — and from shaking Michael's hand had provided as many questions as answers.

Michael's handshake confirmed his words. He believed Craig Ramsey had died a year earlier. So did Brianna. Michael had told the truth too about how he'd died. Craig had seen it himself in the vision, bleeding on the street, his head resting on Michael's lap, unfocused eyes staring upward at nothing while his lips stuttered incoherent words. That wasn't the most comfortable revelation so soon after waking. At least, he didn't feel the same death rattle or final breath.

Craig listened to the outside voices. Still unsure of their words, he decided the conversation had deepened, which gave him some time. The backpack didn't tell him much about Brianna's view of Craig, nor had his wallet, which she had held, but he'd seen enough of what looked like a frantic motorcycle chase. The little girl in the vision, about three-or-four years of age, he determined, was still upstairs sleeping. He wasn't sure yet of the kidnapping attempt, but he'd worry about that later. What would the cup tell him? He strode towards the kitchen sink and grabbed Brianna's cup by its handle.

Ah! Here we go.

Craig paused at hearing Brianna's words in his mind. Her thoughts. Their tone spoke volumes. Yes, she knew Craig Ramsey on some level. But not the way he knew Brianna. He probed further, held onto the impressions, and delved deeper, until the discovery that had nearly shocked him enough to drop the mug. This Brianna hadn't married him at all. She'd never even considered it. At least, until that moment when...

The cup slipped from his fingers and into the sink. He jumped at the loud thump it made, then feeling guilty, he checked he hadn't broken it.

So, that's why Brianna didn't want him to touch her! It explained the hesitation when she realised he had touched her backpack. Never mind. Her secret's safe. And he would keep it in mind.

"Is everything okay, Mr Ramsey?"

Craig jumped at Sparks' voice in the speakers. He had forgotten the house could see him. He gazed at the ceiling. "You bloody startled me. How long have you been watching?"

The computer chuckled. "Does it matter? Is everything okay?"

Craig managed a smile. "Yes." He paused. "No, it's not

okay. You must realise that some things aren't right for me."

"Disorientation?" Sparks asked, his voice emanating from a microwave in the kitchen's recess. "I kind of understand what you mean. More than you know."

Craig reacted to the tone. Something spoke volumes about it, not the empathy he expected from a computer. "Sparks," he said, "I get the feeling you're more than artificial intelligence."

A chuckle laced with sarcasm. "No shit." A moment later, it replied in an apologetic tone. "Despite the hardware, I forget, Craig. You don't know me as well as Michael, who has known me for years… before this."

"Years?" Craig asked. "Didn't I only die a year ago?"

Seconds ticked by before Sparks replied. "Amazing. You surprise me, Mr Ramsey. Don't you remember me at all?"

Craig shook his head. "The last I recall, my house never talked to me."

How was he going to bypass the computer here? He needed to move fast to solve the conundrum he faced.

"That's true. Michael installed the hardware necessary for me a fortnight after your… untimely demise. May I add we're both thankful to you for letting us have the house?"

"Don't mention it." Craig waved a dismissive hand, noting another oddity. No time to worry about that, though. "Do you mind if I have some privacy? I have to process things."

"No worries," Sparks replied. "I'll go back to playing Warhammer. Shout if you need something."

"Of course."

Craig paused for a second to listen. Michael's voice filtered through the closed door. Whatever he and Brianna discussed, Michael must have been holding up Brianna from sleep. She'd be getting cranky soon if Michael didn't let her go.

Once certain he had some peace, Craig wandered through his library of books that remained in the living room. This was his "small" library. The really good stuff — books of ancient history, mythology, and esoterica — were in an upstairs spare bedroom he'd converted into a library. But in the wake of his demise, who knows what Michael had done to his library.

Interesting. One of those books' titles looked wrong. Craig's fingers slid over the leather spine and retrieved the volume to check it closer. The Revisited History of the Mabinogion. Craig raised an eyebrow as he flipped through the pages. The text inside was close to what he had read — only a week ago in his memory — but the title was different. The psychometric vibrations were different, too. He focused on the vision.

@ @ @

Craig Ramsey held the book up to the hallway mirror, his eyes peering at his reflection above the tome. He raised an eyebrow, and still gripping it, he lowered the volume below his image.

"Hullo!" He flashed himself a grin. "You're me. Or I'm you. I can't tell for sure, but I know you will find this book in the bookcase. It looks different to you, right?"

Vision-Craig nodded. "Yeah, pretty different. You probably think it's The Revised Arthur of the Mabinogion." He glanced at the cover as he walked towards the living room. "Here's the thing. I don't think I'm going to be around much longer. For me, it's October 2019. You will see it at around -", he checked his watch, "just after you have breakfast on 29th November 2020-ish."

@ @ @

Craig blinked at the vision. What the hell? A message for him from himself? No way!

He concentrated again.

@ @ @

"Yes way, Craig," the Vision-Craig said. "Like I said. I'm you, you're me. At least, that's what you told me the other day." The Craig in the vision took a breath, a thoughtful expression on his face that made him appear as though considering his words. "I don't know the how or the why. But I don't have time to explain. You have only a few minutes. Go to the safe in the master bedroom. Open it. You know how."

@ @ @

The vision faded.

A shiver of anticipation etched its way along his spine as he replaced the thick book on the bookshelf and headed upstairs towards what was once his bedroom. Once there, he paused and took in the decorating. The king-sized bed he once shared with Brianna had changed. Someone — Michael — had replaced it with a large oval bed. A thought flashed through his mind. Could it be?

He stretched his fingers towards its spread, pressed it, and the surface wobbled.

A waterbed! What could he discern from it?

@ @ @

Vision-Craig appeared on the bed like a translucent projection and stared back at him, waggling a thin finger at him as he tutted. "How'd I know you would look here?"

With a grin, he sat up and stood almost face-to-face with

Craig. "You won't find anything about Brianna here. She's not your wife. Got it?" Then after a pause, he added, "Come to think of it, she's not mine either." Was that a sigh? "Forget Brianna. Go to the safe, I said."

@ @ @

Vision-Craig vanished.

Craig turned towards the wall, attached to which sat the flat-screen television. Could it be true? He pressed the wall panelling, which popped open to reveal a safe in the recess. Yes, it was exactly as he'd installed. Not even Brianna knew of this. But although the safe looked like the one he knew, it looked different. What was it? He peered at its brand. Yalle? No, this had to be a different safe. His brand was a Yale. Not Yalle.

The moment he touched its dial, Vision-Craig appeared beside him. "What are you waiting for? Yes, it's my safe, or your safe, whatever. Open it." No sooner had his doppelgänger spoken than he disappeared.

"Who the hell are you?" Craig whispered as he sucked in a breath. So far, his vision-double knew enough about him to guide him and even knew what he would do. He smiled to himself, thinking how clever this double was in leaving messages, and turned the safe dial clockwise, then anti-clockwise, and back the other way again. 38-24-36.

The safe clicked open.

Ye gods! It was the same combination, after all.

Craig paused a moment to process this before he reefed open the safe to discover its contents. A Japanese wooden puzzle box, about the width and length of an A4 sheet of paper, but three inches deep.

Such beautiful workmanship! Comprising many slats and levers and sheets, each coloured according to the unique wood types used, it responded to his touch. In thirty-two quick moves, he solved the puzzle. Child's play to someone with psychometric ability who could tap into the object's memory and determine how previous people opened it. But he recognised this box. Although this didn't carry her vibration, Brianna had gifted him a similar one on the Christmas before their daughter's birth.

Christmas. He realised it was close to Christmas now. A tear welled in his eye as he wondered what happened to his Brianna and their daughter. Would he see them again?

The box clicked open.

And within, he found a greater puzzle than before.

"What?"

Chapter 8

Once outside, Michael shut the front door and hissed to Brianna. "What do you think?"

Brianna shrugged. "I'm unsure. He sounds the same as Craig but… no, I can't believe it."

Michael chuckled. "You don't reckon it's him back from the dead, yet you believe in psychics."

Brianna rolled her eyes. "Don't be a dick. It's one thing to see you in action, and another to have seen Craig work on those cases with me…"

"But?"

"You're talking about someone who died in your arms, Michael." Brianna shook her head and looked across the yard towards the street. "Dr Kroot did the post-mortem, the undertaker prepared him, and we buried him. The Craig we knew was a good escape artist, but he can't have got out from a coffin covered by a ton of dirt then wandered back home a year later."

"Yeah, he would've escaped quicker. Maybe the box wasn't that comfortable?" Michael grinned. Brianna snapped a stony gaze at him, but he looked right back at her with a straight face until she snorted a laugh. "Seriously, yes, I think it's possible. Don't forget what you know about me."

Brianna's brow furrowed. "That's different. He's not —"

"He's not what?" Michael interrupted. "Psychic? Alive?" Another grin, slyer than a rat's, crossed his face. "I noticed you didn't shake hands with him. What was that about?"

Surprised at Michael's words, Brianna turned away, a

slight redness tinging her features. "I don't trust him."

"Bull. Schick." Michael squinted hard as he watched her. "Something else is going on there."

A memory flashed across Brianna's mind, one that she had pushed back for over a year. She stayed silent. "You're full of it, Michael. You might have psychic abilities, but you can't read minds. And stop doing the Craig Ramsey thing too." Michael continued his gaze, and she felt it boring into her as he stared. "Anyway, we haven't talked about this morning with Hayley yet."

Surprised guilt broke through Michael's visage, distracting his stare, and he nodded. "Yeah, true." He took a breath and exhaled in a sigh. "Tell me what happened."

"An ice-cream van drove through my street, playing its music. Remember the tune the vans used to play when we were kids?" Michael nodded, and she continued. "The same one. This was at four o'clock in the morning, mind you." Michael's eyebrow rose at the news as Brianna spoke. "It woke me. And Hayley must have heard it and wanted ice-cream, so she went out. By the time I had caught up with her, she was in the van, and it took off."

"Why did Hayley step outside at night?" Michael asked, shaking his head. He couldn't believe it. "She knows better than that."

"Hayley isn't yet five," Brianna said. "She doesn't think that way."

Deep in thought, Michael idly slid his finger along the spike of a cactus plant. "You mentioned hearing the Mr Whippy tune."

"Yeah, it woke me."

"And no one else came out to see what the noise was about, right?" Michael replied. "For something so loud at four in the morning, it's a wonder not one person rang the police, or the council, to complain. You didn't even have the old biddy from next door investigate?"

"I was already there," Brianna replied, half-jesting, and stopped when she caught Michael's glare. Hayley was his only child, not that it made it less important, but the little girl was the spitting image of his partner who had died three years ago. Losing Hayley would have killed him. "Listen, Michael, there's more to it. The van was large, kind of reminded me of the units I've seen used in Libya and Afghanistan."

"What?" That grabbed Michael's attention, and he glanced at Brianna's wounds from the escapade. "So you caught up. What else did you notice?"

"The driver's tattoos," she replied. "I got a glimpse before his guard dog attacked me. A kangaroo flicking an Ace of Spades at the Grim Reaper."

"What about it?" Michael asked.

"I've seen it on the guys from my unit who returned from Afghanistan. It means they escaped without dying," Brianna answered, "but I didn't recognise this guy."

"Commandos? Christ! I should have known. He's still poking around for me."

"Why you?" Brianna asked. "It wasn't just Hayley they took. There were two other little girls there too."

"Attracted to the music?"

"More than that. Other kids have been going missing, too, Michael." Brianna brushed her tired eyes. "I didn't tell you before because I hadn't connected the dots. We are receiving reports from all over Statton of children disappearing from their homes. Not just here either, but in different places around the state. You must have seen it on the news."

Michael shrugged. "Kidnapped by Mr Whippy? I've never heard that."

Brianna shook her head. "No one else has mentioned an ice-cream van before, or the music. I'm the first to learn that."

Confusion mixed with worry on Michael's face. "How many kids are missing?"

"Eight, so far. Hayley and the girls would have made eleven."

Michael turned towards the front door and hesitated a moment. Then he faced Brianna. "There's a connection between that man inside and what has happened to the kids," he said. "I'd bet my life on it."

"You've got to be kidding. How?"

Michael opened his mouth to reply, but the throaty roar of a car engine filled the air. A sound familiar to Michael that blanched his face. He spun towards the noise to catch sight of a gleaming silver Jaguar leave the garage and enter the street and zoom down the road. It happened so fast that neither Brianna nor Michael could stop it in time. But they knew the driver.

Craig Ramsey.

He'd found his old Jaguar and jumped protective custody.

Chapter 9

It's amazing the difference a year away can make, Craig thought to himself, although that didn't seem right to him. For he'd been here the whole time, yet the world believed otherwise.

The houses he passed in the suburbs were the same. Well, almost. While some matched his memory, some sported major differences, but most were subtle. For example, one particular house he knew thoroughly from a past gig as a psychic entertainer had changed. He was sure it had three mature pine trees shielding it from the street, but today four stood there. How could it have grown in such a short time? And something else seemed odd, too. People didn't have their faces glued to social media on their mobile phones, either. How could the public have cured themselves of such introverted behaviour so fast?

Perhaps Colonel Ryan would know, he decided, as he travelled towards North Cemetery. An old friend of Craig's for as long as he recalled, the deceased veteran officer would doubtless tell him what had happened to Emily, his longtime ghost companion, and explain his revival.

The blank paper from the Japanese puzzle box had instructed: "Visit the Cemetery."

Craig drove the Jaguar through the cemetery's front gateway and along its muddy trail to a familiar duck pond, beside which he parked the car and stepped out into the sunlight. Everything looked the same. Graveyards rarely change.

But something struck him as wrong about it.

It was quiet.

As a graveyard.

Craig approached the modest marker that bore his phantom friend's name. There it stood, a lonely testament to an Australian war hero who died in a plane crash on the way home from Vietnam, blanketed in purple blossoms from the overhanging jacaranda tree.

An uneasy feeling crept over Craig as he knocked on the headstone three times. "Colonel," he called aloud. "It's me. Ramsey."

He smelt the air, hoping to catch a whiff of the colonel's trademark cigar.

Nothing.

"Ryan?"

Still no reply.

Craig scanned the surroundings for any signs of spirits. Other times, he'd have spotted them. The dead centre, pun not intended, of Spirit Force in Statton, North Cemetery always teemed with them as they trained. Not even civilian ghosts wandered the silent grounds today.

What was going on?

Craig returned to his car and sped along the gravel path to the main road. His guts told him there was more to this situation than his resurrection. Ghosts don't just disappear. At least, not until they complete their business. Not usually, anyway.

Then he remembered the trees out the front of his client's place. The psychic visions of his double. And Brianna's odd behaviour. Those and every other oddity he'd witnessed didn't add up.

If only this were a dream.

North Cemetery was merely one spot, though. What

about Hilltop?

He stamped the accelerator to pass a stale green light and headed to the hills overlooking Statton. Perhaps new answers awaited him there.

His eyes snapped to the rearview mirror and narrowed upon spotting a dark-clothed man on a motorcycle. The motorcyclist had remained back at first, a random amongst the other vehicles, but now he was almost beside Craig's Jag.

Craig turned his vision to his side window as the black-clad rider came level with him. A gloved hand pointed to the roadside. Was this a police officer who had spotted him dashing to meet the light? But he hadn't been over the limit — much.

He pantomimed the question while pointing to the side. "Do you want me to pull over?"

Yes, came the reply, and Craig recognised Michael Mach's eyes behind the visor and smirked to himself. Well, he couldn't get in trouble by not stopping, could he?

He pressed the Jag faster through the traffic to distance himself from his follower and steered without indicating. Anything it would take not to telegraph his intentions. Three knocks on the driver's window startled him, almost causing him to veer. He corrected his direction, then looked to find Michael's narrowed eyes glowering at him through the helmet's visor. The pursuer's finger jabbed the air, telling him to pull over.

Yeah, right. Craig burst out with laughter. The more he sped, the closer his pursuer came. And he loved it.

He cupped his ear and delivered a mocking grin. "What?"

Was that an amused expression in Michael's eyes? Never mind, Craig thought. Let him follow me.

And the Jag's wheels squealed as he floored the pedal. This was the most fun he'd had in a year. His Jag powered him through the side streets like a juggernaut to Hilltop Cemetery. Near the top, he slowed only to cross the cattle grid at the gateway. He saw no need to ruin his car's suspension for the sake of his amusement. Michael had chosen instead to follow at a safe distance until Craig stopped under willow trees.

Craig stepped out, amazed upon noticing how silent Michael's motorcycle was as it braked beside him. Ignoring Michael, he strode between the graves with his host hot on his heels.

"Oi!" Michael shouted. "Where the hell do you think you're going?"

"This way. Keep up, will you?"

Déjà vu struck. Craig stopped, his eyes darting back and forth at the stones until they rested upon one marker.

Michael stepped in front of him, his hair dishevelled from the helmet, and stared him in the eye. "What are you doing?"

But Craig ignored him. The tombstone ahead held him entranced as he went down to it, disbelief marching arm-in-arm with horror in his mind at the sight. "Oh, shit."

"What?" Michael said, then stopped.

Craig pointed a shaky finger at the stone. "What is that?"

Michael lay a comforting hand on Craig's shoulder. "I'm sorry, mate." He paused a moment. "I don't know what to say."

Words trickled from the psychic detective's mouth in brief spurts. "That's... my name... on the grave." He glanced at his companion. "Is this real?"

"Yeah, it is." Michael nodded matter-of-factly. "It's

where we buried you."

Craig shot him an incredulous look. "This is where I woke after the lightning struck." With wobbling knees, he stumbled towards the grave, a shaking hand reaching forward, and collapsed beside it. "I died?"

Michael nodded in sympathy for a moment. "Craig, we can't hang around here, mate." He scanned about the area as he spoke, his agitation growing. "I get it. It's a shock. But let's go home. Leaving like that was a bad idea. Blaze has eyes everywhere. There's no telling what—"

A footfall to the left interrupted him. Then a twig cracked behind them. Michael whirled as a dozen men in camouflage approached them from different directions, their fists flexing.

"Oh, schick."

Chapter 10

Craig's mind ticked as the first heavy-set opponent lumbered towards him from behind the trees. In the few precious moments before he ducked the brute's ham-sized fist, he wondered how many visits to the Reaper he had accrued. Two seconds later, he danced backwards after uppercutting the granite jaw. He'd punched hard, hard enough to feel pain lance his arm. The other guy blinked once and advanced.

Craig heard Michael trading quick blows with one or two other men. He couldn't go to his aid though, for soon blurs registered in his peripheral vision as more soldiers closed in on him. With no time to think, he swung his hips, kicked, and smashed his first opponent's knee, which cracked a second before his jumbo-sized enemy crashed like a boulder to the ground. He ducked on instinct. Something as heavy as a python wrapped around his neck and forced him to the ground. The smell of sweat made him want to chuck. Without thinking, he buried his face in his adversary's body an instant before a fist hit his skull. Shaken, he snaked one hand to his assailant's foot, hooked it while grabbing the man's hair with the other, twisted both arms. His second opponent released his headlock and landed on the other soldier with a yelp. Craig caved his nose and cheeks with a triple punch but missed spotting the new fighter attacking from the other side.

Craig's nose exploded. The blood filled his sinuses, flowed to his mouth. Hands raised, he fended off more blows, danced to the left, and attacked without seeing. His palm met a chin, smashing teeth, and rendering its owner unconscious. It grunted and struck the earth in a heap.

With a shake, his vision cleared enough to see his third opponent. He heard Michael's voice, high-pitched battle cries in rhythm with speedy thumps like drumsticks. Craig wasted no time. Years of training drove his blocks and counterattacks. Fists pounded flesh and bone. Another thump. Silence fell.

Craig staggered, still dizzy, and slow clapping reached his ears. He glanced in Michael's direction to see him sitting on a pile of seven men, all dead.

Michael raised an eyebrow. "I thought I'd have to help you then, mate. I had no idea you knew Wing Chun and whatever style you used then."

"He busted my nose." Craig held one hand up, requesting time from Michael, and squeezed his nose while his unique metabolism healed the injury. It still hurt like hell, though. His teary eyes fell upon the corpses, but not for long. The faint scraping sound accompanied by muffled screams of tortured souls reached his ears. And a smile crossed his face.

"What is it?" Michael asked.

Craig shushed him. "Wait."

There it was. The first sign of normalcy he'd seen since he woke. His heart leapt like an eager puppy. Ghosts! From each of Michael's victims came the spectral visages, translucent copies of their physical bodies. They moved to attack Michael, who remained oblivious to their presence. When their phantasmic limbs passed through his body, their angry expressions changed to confusion. They stood and gaped at each other, opening their mouths to utter inaudible words thanks to their inexperience as spirits.

Meanwhile, Michael approached Craig's unconscious opponents. He kicked one of them hard, eliciting a groan, and shook his head. "Sloppy, Craig. We can't let them live." Before Craig realised it, Michael had broken their necks with three rapid strikes of his hand.

"Why did you do that?" Craig demanded, watching their spirits appear beside their predecessors.

"They're not really alive, anyway," Michael replied. He gripped two men's heads by the hair and lifted them for Craig to see. "They're all the same person. Clones. Blaze sends clones to do his dirty work."

"But they —" Craig stopped himself. He was about to say they had spirits, but he didn't want to reveal that ability to Michael yet.

"They what?"

Something else caught Craig's attention. From the ground behind his grave rose a dark-cloaked figure, one that Craig recognised as a Death Reaper. Once fully present, it turned, face hidden in its dark hood's depths, and assessed the situation. After surveying the dead, it stopped, its gaze set in Craig's direction.

Then, with a nod and its black cloak flowing behind it in an ethereal breeze, it strode towards Craig.

Chapter 11

Craig's heart thumped hard in his chest as the preternatural creature approached. Memory of meeting a Reaper, the Head Reaper, otherwise known as The Grim Reaper or Death itself, sprang to Craig's mind, and he took an involuntary step backward, almost tripping.

"Wait," he said, an idea forming. "Is this a late visit?" The Reaper stopped and cocked its head in question. Then a skeletal hand rose to remove the hood to reveal Craig's next surprise by recognition. "Debbie?"

The name conjured a smile on the familiar face belonging to his adopted daughter. "Hello, Uncle Craig. Fancy meeting you here."

A smile blossomed on Craig's face upon recognition of the same young girl he'd known before her untimely murder four years earlier by a crazed man's astral projection. "Is that you, Deb?"

Brilliant white teeth flashed from the Samoan girl's face as she hugged him. "You should know. You raised me after Mum and Dad died, you old duffer." She gave him a welcome hug that made his day. At last, she stood back and offered a questioning look. "But you shouldn't be here."

Craig relaxed his smile long enough to ponder her words. "Here? What do you mean?"

Debbie laughed. "You don't know, do you?" When Craig shrugged, a thoughtful expression crossed her face for a moment before it brightened and the curiosity faded. "You're in a parallel world."

Craig gasped. "A parallel world?" The cloud lifted from his cocky brain as the penny dropped and clinked in the glass. "Another dimension! Of course." He turned toward Michael and paused upon observing his companion, frozen like one of Medusa's victims. "What's happened to him?"

Deb dismissed Michael's stillness with a cursory wave. "He's fine. We're on my time, in a side dimension, so we can talk. Just for a few minutes though because I have work to do." Deb noted Craig's puzzled expression. "Don't worry. When we're done, Michael won't even notice you've been talking to me."

"At least you didn't come for me," Craig grinned, wiping mock sweat from his brow. "Tell me about this place. I just woke up here, if you know what I mean."

"Actually, it's a parallel universe, Unc," Deb explained. "Imagine another universe like the one you know. The same, but different in some ways." She paused a moment to tap on the wandering soul of a nearby clone. It shrank, turned to vapour, and disappeared into her finger like dust in a vacuum cleaner. "Don't mind me if I work while talking, but, Unc, you're not supposed to be here. How did you get here?"

Craig explained how he'd visited Julia's grave. The last thing he recalled was putting the toy on her headstone a moment before thunderheads appeared in the sky. A second later, everything had turned white and thunder rumbled. "The rest is blurry. I remember staggering through the night all the way home because I couldn't find my car. Then I passed out and woke this morning in this nuthouse of a world."

Deb picked off the remaining souls, collecting them in

their vaporous forms, and nodded. "I've heard of mortals moving between worlds. We Reapers do it all the time because dying is universal, after all. But there has to be a purpose to your appearance here. Somehow, someone or something has summoned you here."

"By whom?" Craig asked.

Deb shrugged. "No idea. But, Unc, you have to know this. You might remember Tyrone killed Colonel Blaze on your world." Craig nodded, and she continued. "I picked that prick myself, but —" A puzzled look on her face, she said, "I've got eleven. Weren't there twelve to collect?"

Craig gave a nonchalant nod. "Yeah, there were. But you were about to say Colonel Blaze is her on this world, too, right?"

Deb cast an eye about the area and stopped. "Ah, there you are!" Her eyes narrowed, and a kris appeared in her hand, which she threw just past Craig. Its wavy blade whistled past his ear, and he turned in time to see it thud point-first into the last clone's spirit. "Slippery little sucker," she muttered as the weapon flew back to her hand and the clone's vaporised soul retracted into her grasp. "Last one." Deb's lips moved as she confirmed her count. "Where was I? Oh, yeah, Blaze is here too. Not the same guy you remember, but he's deadlier. Watch out for him. And your other self is supposed to be dead here too. I say 'supposed to' because I never met him; I was grabbing souls from a natural disaster in Bali."

Craig nodded. "I guessed as much. These clones remind me of some heavies he used to send after me."

"Well," Deb said, pulling a pocket watch by its chain from her robe to check the time. "I've got to fly. There's going to be an epidemic starting in China soon on another world." She smiled at Craig before they melted into a deep and long hug. "I miss these hugs, Unc. You did good by Tyrone and me. Thanks. And say hi to Emily." She stopped. "Oh, that's right. Emily. You know there are no ghosts or spirits here now, right?"

"What?"

"Not many, anyway." Deb frowned. "They disappeared just over a year ago. Not sure of the full story, but check with Blaze about that." She turned and headed back towards the nearby grave. "Say hi to my little brother for me."

"Wait, Deb!" Craig called. "I have a question. You and Tyrone used to find a way past my psychometric powers. How did you do it?"

The young Reaper stopped in her tracks and looked over her shoulder at him. With a wink, she faded to nothing.

A second later, Michael spoke. "Are you going to finish what you were saying?" Confusion appeared in his face, and he spun about before he looked at Craig. "Hey. Weren't you standing just here a moment ago?"

Craig realised he had been walking along with Deb in her side dimension before she left. To Michael, it must have seemed as if Craig had teleported five feet away from him. "It doesn't matter," he replied, and stopped. He bent down and picked up the object that caught his eye near his namesake's grave.

A spirit board pointer.

The moment his fingertips touched the planchette's polished wooden surface, the vision hit.

@ @ @

Three teenagers were sitting around the Ouija board, their fingers light on the planchette. One of them, a boy, appeared familiar, and Craig watched him through the eyes of one girl: Tamsin. James was the lad's name, and he had a crush on the other girl who didn't even like him. Then the perspective changed so that Craig saw events from James' viewpoint. He glimpsed Amy's face, so pretty in the schoolboy's thoughts. Why didn't she notice him, and why was she so standoffish? Interesting. Craig realised he recognised the teenager as the one who had sneaked the device out of his father's possessions.

He cast a furtive glance at one of the two girls with him. Tamsin, a pretty girl, placed the planchette on the board. It moved, spelled out letters, a message: HE COMES.

Lightning and thunder.

The girls fled, leaving the boy — his name is James — to fend for himself.

The shock nearly forced Craig from the vision as he witnessed the dishevelled man stand from behind his namesake's grave. He paused the vision's events, then stepped towards the shadowy newcomer and gasped with recognition.

This was his arrival in this world!

@ @ @

The vision segued.

Vision-Craig appeared before him in the present, one hand on the gravestone, the other pointing at the spot where he found the planchette. "Hi, again! Dig here."

Craig blinked. After a moment to adjust and think, he examined the space at which he'd found the planchette. His namesake's body would lie right beneath it.

@ @ @

Dig there?

Experience had taught him never to doubt his visions,

but the notion of finding his own corpse disturbed him, too. With a shrug, Craig headed back to the car, oblivious to Michael's questions in the background, until his companion grabbed his arm.

"Hang on, I'm talking to you," Michael admonished him. "Where do you think you're going?"

Craig grasped the other man's hand, released himself with ease, and continued walking. "Do keep up, Michael. I'm heading to Bunnings for a shovel, of course."

"Why?"

Craig stopped, turned, and handed the planchette to him. "A little ghostie told me."

Michael raised a surprised eyebrow. "Hey, this is mine." His tone softened. "It belonged to my wife, Alison. Where did you get it?"

"On my grave," Craig replied. "Ask your son, James, about it. He and two girls were playing with the Ouija board last night right there."

Michael called after Craig, who was almost to the car. "Wait! We don't need to buy anything. Just check in the boot."

Craig stopped near the Jaguar and regarded him with amusement. "Really?" He pressed the key's remote, and the boot popped open.

Michael pushed past and removed two shovels from the space. He handed one to Craig and strolled back to the grave. "Always prepare, I say," he replied with a wink.

Craig stared at the spade in his hand in wonder. Then another short vision intruded, and he realised Michael's secret. This had been a pebble ten seconds ago, not a shovel. That meant Michael had the power to change things by mere touch!

Chapter 12

High above the trees, the WhisperDrone hovered as its cameras captured the unfolding scene. Not even the most sensitive ears could hear its silenced propellers. Its artificial intelligence guided it to a better vantage point while it broadcast the battle's footage to a mobile repeater station.

From outside the city, Colonel Blaze followed the video with acute interest as the two men dispatched his assassins with ease. As each of his soldiers dropped, he studied the figure of Craig Ramsey.

As unbelievable as it was, and without a doubt, it was his adversary, though something seemed wrong. What was it?

The Craig Ramsey that he recalled was an exceptional boxer, powerful and efficient, as was the man in the video. But the style looked different. Detached, he studied Ramsey's methods, nodding as he defended his centre-line and maintained firm stances. Pretty good, Blaze mused, but inefficient in places. Although Ramsey's technique had showed precision and practice, something distracted him during the fight. But what?

Blaze leaned back in his chair and stared into space as he contemplated his observations.

The Craig Ramsey he remembered could perceive things through psychokinesis. Blaze had first met the super-psychic — as the others in Project Gamma called him — when he approached the firm to test his skills. Ramsey had proven capable of remote viewing, clairvoyance, precognition and telepathy. But Blaze discovered a crucial limit. He had to hold articles, or touch individuals, to gain his impressions. Still, the cocky bastard enamoured Blaze's superior with his talents; the bureau wanted him for special spy missions and reconnaissance operations. But the psychic had refused. There had been a kerfuffle before Ramsey escaped and persuaded the government agency to leave him alone.

The computer's keys chattered as his fingers typed. A moment later, archive footage of Craig Ramsey appeared on a separate screen. In the picture, the psychic battled three other subjects from the Project in the gym. Yes, Ramsey was a boxer, not a martial artist. He next studied the video from the cemetery and watched Ramsey's footwork: quick, sure, and graceful as a dancer. A fighter could only gain that skill after many years. This was a different guy.

Perplexed, Blaze crinkled his brow. If not Craig Ramsey, who was he?

His attention returned to the live footage as Craig Ramsey and the man he recognised as Michael Mach, another escapee from the Project, dug into the grave's earth. With a flick of a control, Colonel Blaze repositioned the camera and zoomed in closer.

He read the headstone's inscription and gasped.

Why was Craig Ramsey digging up his own grave?

Chapter 13

The first foot of earth proved easy to dig. The next two feet, however, resisted their efforts, and soon, the sun's heat forced them to strip off their sweat-soaked shirts.

Craig stopped digging and wiped his brow. Michael swung the pick, which he had 'conveniently found' in the Jaguar's boot. "Wouldn't it be great if we had an excavator in here?"

Michael pushed a lock of black hair from his face. "An excavator?" The look he gave Craig was meant to be incredulous, an innocent 'What the heck are you talking about' expression, but Craig spotted the tell: a quick diversion of eye contact. "That could destroy the grave."

"Possibly." Craig allowed a grin before he stood on his shovel to force it into the hard earth. "Or maybe it would soften the dirt, so we didn't look like Chippendale rejects with the shovels."

Michael grunted and chucked his pick to the side. "We're three feet deep now. That's about it."

"But that is only halfway."

Michael chuckled. "For a guy who spends half his time in cemeteries, you know very little about graves, don't you?" He speared the earth with his shovel. It clanked on something hard. He scraped away chunks of debris to reveal the wooden surface of a casket. "We only needed to dig three feet to get to the coffin."

Craig wondered how Michael knew that and chose not to ask.

Together, they cleared the dirt from the box's lid, the

loose earth growing in height beside the hole. Craig's heart hammered. He'd never unearthed a grave before. Opening his own burial plot was unexpected, too, and he shuddered to think what he would find. When they had finished, the men looked at it, both unwilling to be the first to view its gruesome contents.

After a moment, Michael said, "Well, aren't you going to open it?"

"Pardon?"

"What's taking so long?" Michael urged. "We already know it's empty since you're standing here."

Craig paused. "I don't come from here," he replied. "And it's no fun being here when my wife doesn't recognise me, and my daughter never even existed." He stared at Michael for a moment until the other man broke the gaze. "Do you know how bloody surreal it is to learn I'm standing on my grave, too, or at least the resting place of someone who looked and sounded like me?"

Michael gave a nod and grabbed the pick to attack the box's lid. "Fair enough."

Craig sighed and grumbled. "You should try facing your mortality."

But Michael had already broken through the casket's shell. His head obscured Craig's vision, but his companion's surprised cry caught his curiosity. "Holy schick."

"What?"

Michael scrambled out of the hole. "See for yourself."

Careful to avoid splinters from the shattered wood, Craig reached inside the opening, expecting to feel a face, or even a foot, if they were at the wrong end, but his hands found no human anatomy. At least, it was nothing animate. He pulled out something else and, confused, examined the book.

A blue-covered paperback laughed at him. A male silhouetted figure stood on the cover, surrounded by a series of vortex lines that shimmered. He read the title aloud. "Bootstrap's Journey?"

Craig showed the book to Michael. "I doubt that I'm in the box," he said.

Michael took the novel and flicked through the pages while Craig reached in and grabbed more books from the coffin. He read the novel's cover. "While He Was Sleeping." The hint of a grin appeared on his face. "Whoever did this has a sense of humour." He peered past Craig towards the other visible volumes. "Any other titles?"

"No."

Michael couldn't resist asking. "Is there a body?"

Craig shook his head and stood. "Just the books. They're all the same names, too. You'd think the author had bought them all up to make his sales rank rise on Amazon or something."

A grin flickered on Michael's face. "Whoever did this used them to match your body's weight."

"Which means…" A movement in his peripheral vision distracted Craig, making him glance upward. "Someone's watching us."

Michael followed Craig's gaze and fixed upon the drone. "It figures," he said. "It's Colonel Blaze. If he didn't already know through his goons, then he knows now that you're alive. We haven't much time." He tossed the books back in the hole, and something caught his interest. "Hey, what's that?"

Craig checked the direction in which Michael pointed and, with a surprised expression, grabbed the brown wrapped package. He turned it in his hands and gasped. "It's addressed to me and it has a date on it."

Michael squinted. "That's today! But how?"

A crisp ringing tone distracted them. Michael checked his watch, pressed a button on the side of it, and said, "I'm with him, Sparks. At the cemetery. We'll be back soon."

Sparks' voice shouted in reply. "Michael, come home now. We have a whole Specialist Response and Security Team surrounding us. They've already cut outside phone lines. Hurry!"

"What about Brianna and the kids?" Michael said, and when he received no answer, he repeated the question.

Silence.

Chapter 14

Brianna checked her watch. It was three hours since Michael chased after Craig Ramsey. What the hell was taking so long?

"You needn't worry, Brianna." Sparks' voice gave a slight echo. "His vitals appear fine."

She managed a smile. "He's the one who needs to worry," she muttered.

Hayley had since woken from her sleep as though nothing had happened. How could a little kid get by with such little sleep while Brianna, even after active duty in Afghanistan, needed at least eight hours of uninterrupted slumber? It was so unfair.

The four-year-old was now playing with James, Michael's adopted son, who held her rapt with some silly coin tricks. Okay, maybe not so silly. James knew some pretty cool moves with the coins, which seemed to dance across his knuckles before they vanished to God-knows-where. Then he would reproduce it from Hayley's ear, which made her giggle and beg for more. James somehow pulled a new one from his backside.

"What do you have against Craig Ramsey?" Sparks asked.

"I have nothing against him," Brianna replied, dismissing the idea with a wave of the hand. "I don't believe he is back from the dead either." Brianna sensed puzzlement in Sparks' silence. Was that a tiny sigh or "huh"? It was hard to tell, knowing that Sparks once used to be a flesh-and-blood person before this.

"I don't understand," he said. "The DNA test confirmed

it from a sample we kept before Craig's initial demise."

"And why was that?"

"It matches because it's Craig Ramsey. Human DNA is like a fingerprint. No two people have the same prints."

Brianna nodded, her brow furrowed. Now was the time. "Sparks?" She took a breath. "What was Michael doing last night that was so important?"

"Oh? What do you mean?"

Brianna suppressed a smile at the reply. If an answer carried guilt, this was one. A literal "ghost in the machine", Sparks still possessed the same frailty and vulnerabilities as he did when a human teenager before he had died in the accident that transformed him.

"You know what I mean," Brianna said. "I know James was out last night." She didn't, but it interested her to notice that James lifted his head at hearing his name, and his expression confirmed her bluff's intention. "Michael insisted I look after Hayley at my place."

"He had a date here last night. You wouldn't want kids cramping your style, right?"

Brianna smelled a rat. "Yet when I arrived there were no extra wine glasses." The silence lasted less than a heartbeat, yet Brianna's eyebrow rose at Sparks' response.

"Michael doesn't drink."

Not a flicker passed on Brianna's face when she recognised the almost imperceptible wavering in Sparks' synthetic voice. Her gaze darted towards the sink, now empty since she'd washed the dishes. Yes, there were two standard glasses there before — one for Michael, one possibly for James, though she couldn't be sure it was his — and she nodded upon recalling no lipstick smears on the rims. "A date with whom?"

Sparks replied with the speed of a taipan's strike. "Jealous of your adoptive brother, Brianna?"

"Hardly." Brianna pressed. "He didn't have a date last night. What were the two of you up to?"

Silence.

"Well?"

"Sorry, Brianna." Sparks' voice held a hint of alarm. "We have an intruder alert."

"What?"

"Four vans in the street. One blocking off each end of the street. The other two are outside. Look."

A blue hologram flickered to life in the centre of the living room. The image revealed a satellite view from miles above, showing what Brianna recognised as the tops of steel roofs. It magnified until Brianna recognised Michael's home — the building they occupied. Two vans blocked the street, one at each end, while two more had parked across the road from their house. Men in black commando gear, armed with heavy assault weapons, watched from behind the closest vans, their rifles aimed at the house while three others dashed towards the walls.

"Tell me you and Michael weren't hacking into Project Gemini." Brianna turned to the kids in the living room, her voice urgent as she called to the others. "James, grab Hayley. We have to go."

James dragged his gaze from the video game he and Hayley had been playing, his lips poised to ask when he spotted the hologram image. "Hayley," he said, surprising Brianna with his calm response, "let's go, kid."

The little girl protested and refused to drop the game controller, but James snatched her in his arms and yanked the joystick from her hand. "Come on, Hayles," he said.

"It's time for hide-and-seek."

"No!" Hayley shouted, kicking at James to escape his grip.

Brianna glanced at her backpack beside the sofa, cursed to herself. Having the Glock would have been handy if she hadn't left it at the station. "Sparks," she said, keeping her voice down to avoid worrying the kids, "what did you and Michael do?"

"Later," Sparks answered.

The sound of James opening the trapdoor in the laundry reached her ears. His voice was calm but urgent as he urged her down the stairs. Good kid, Brianna thought to herself, as she peeked through the curtains.

Suddenly, a face loomed at the window. Brianna yelped and stepped back from the blue eyes, outlined with black boot polish, that stared back at her. She settled upon remembering what Michael had told her soon after moving into the house. The windows were not glass. They were tiny monitors and cameras that reflected to the outside a fake interior while allowing people inside a view of the outside. Michael had installed them as a security measure. Brianna could have opened her shirt and bared her breasts and the commando outside wouldn't have noticed.

"You might want to go downstairs too," Sparks said.

A loud thump echoed from the front. The second bulged the door inward.

"That's reinforced," Sparks affirmed, "but it won't hold forever. Go, Brianna!"

A chopping sound filtered into the house. Brianna backpedalled three steps before dashing in the laundry's direction. She'd served enough time in the Armed Forces to recognise it. "They brought a helicopter for a suburban raid?" she shouted.

"It's a news chopper," Sparks replied. "Hurry and get down the trapdoor. Someone's activated a timed detonator."

Confused, Brianna descended into the darkness and was closing the door when the house exploded.

Chapter 15

Blaze lifted the bone china cup to his lips and sipped the tea. With unerring precision, he lowered it back to the saucer without even a glance from the screen where the action unfolded.

Onscreen, Michael Mach rushed with Craig Ramsey close behind him to where the car and motorbike waited. Michael had received a message on his smartwatch that prompted him to hurry.

Had he allowed it, Blaze's face would have reflected a smile. He knew the reason they hurried, and that was enough. The pending results would soon determine if he should celebrate.

He watched in anticipation as the two subjects neared the vehicles. Still, without averting his gaze to glance at the tablet before him on the desk, he hovered his finger above the red icon.

Michael leapt onto the motorbike's seat as Craig reached the Jaguar's driver's door.

Blaze's finger stabbed. Twin fireballs erupted in unison, one from inside the Jaguar, the other from the motorbike. Plumes of flame shot from the explosions and scorched the nearby tree trunks and engulfed the leafy branches. The Jaguar's bonnet blew upwards and flew towards the camera, but the drone's artificial intelligence avoided the missile with ease. Twenty-three seconds later, the roaring conflagration had dropped to reveal the smoking skeleton of what once had resembled a car, its shell a ruin. Michael's ride fared no better.

Colonel Blaze switched the drone to manual controls and brought it closer to the ground level to inspect the charred vehicles for signs of life.

A voice crackled from the screen.

"Sir, we're moving in."

"Proceed," he affirmed. "Ramsey survived death once before. I don't want him popping back."

Six clone commandos appeared and fanned out to surround the blast zone with heavy assault rifles ready for the slightest movement. They split into two groups. One studied the red-hot Jaguar's carcass, gingerly poking his weapon inside to prod for anything amongst the remains; the second checked the nearby treeline. Blaze appreciated their efficiency with a nod of the head. He'd never considered checking the trees. Good men, he thought.

A voice spoke through the speaker. "I found a…" The trooper hesitated before announcing he had discovered a hand. The onscreen vision switched to the soldier's body cam, and Blaze leaned forward to examine the member. He spotted something at once familiar: a ring with a skull symbol he recognised. "Michael Mach's Phantom ring," he said to no one else in the room. His face betrayed no emotion, but his tone carried all the joy he'd allow. Yes, Michael Mach is — was — a fan of the comics. "It seems he isn't the man who cannot die."

Another soldier interrupted. "Second body found and confirmed dead."

Blaze's jaw nearly dropped at the news. His brow furrowed. "Goodbye, Craig Ramsey. Until we meet again." He saw no need to send flowers to the surviving widow and daughter.

Chapter 16

A few minutes earlier, Michael and Craig were dashing through the trees to where they had left the car. Craig's longer legs pumped like pistons, but the wiry Michael kept pace with relative ease.

"Hold up," Michael puffed, and gripped Craig's arm to slow him.

"What?" Craig gave him a puzzled look. "We have to help Brianna and the kids."

Michael raised a hand to his pursed lips as two figures raced past them towards the vehicles. Craig spun to watch them, his confusion growing. Then, he recognised them as exact copies of them. He narrowed his eyes at Michael, who only shrugged. "Decoys," Michael said as he pulled Craig back towards a willow's thick trunk where the dense foliage covered them. He pointed upward. "Listen."

Their doubles' footsteps faded as they approached the Jaguar that gleamed in the post-midday sun. Craig peered through the leaves and, before he detected the spinning blades gentle whirring sound, he remembered the drone. He nodded, but with a questioning eyebrow for Micheal, who placed a hand on Craig's chest to stop him and mouthed the word: wait. Craig nodded, and they watched from behind the trunk, careful not to expose themselves to the drone.

Craig's double had reached the Jaguar's door as Michael's doppelgänger jumped on the motorcycle. A heartbeat later, a brilliant orange-crimson fireball bleached Craig's vision, followed by a roar that shook the ground under their feet.

"What the hell?"

Michael shushed Craig. "Wait."

His mouth agape in shock, Craig's thoughts raced through his mind. "He killed them," he said, and Michael hushed him again. Quieter now, Craig asked, "Who were those two people? Where did they come from?"

Michael shook his head. "They're not killed. It's okay."

"What are you talking about?" Craig hissed. "We both saw them."

Michael held his palm towards Craig and pointed with the other hand. "Keep it down. They'll hear us."

Craig faced the burning wrecks and pulled himself back behind the trunk upon seeing soldiers in black appear from behind the trees like wraiths on the explosion's burning breeze. If he and Michael had followed the dead decoys, they would either have died or been captured by the soldiers.

The penny dropped. "They weren't real people, were they?"

Michael winked. "Decoys, like I said."

"How?"

Michael shrugged with a secretive look, but otherwise ignored Craig's question. But Craig had already figured it out. His companion must have created the couple somehow while he followed from behind.

Together, they spied on the soldiers who searched the wreckage. One picked up what looked like a hand from Michael's motorbike's remains. He laughed as he waved it about for one of his teammates. Another soldier's voice reached their ears.

"Second body found and confirmed dead."

With his back to the tree trunk, Craig slid to the ground

and sat on a thick root. Michael squatted beside him and kept watch on the morbid scene. In the distance, the faint call of sirens floated on the breeze towards them.

"Fire brigade's coming," Michael said.

In the distance, the soldiers picked up body parts from the decoy couple and bagged them before melting away into the trees and among the gravestones.

"I don't understand," Craig muttered, facing Michael. "Who the hell were those people?" He'd already guessed, but it was time for Michael to confess.

A dark cloud masked Michael's expression when he faced Craig. "They weren't real, Craig. That's all you need to know." He stood and strode through the trees, away from the burning wreckage of his motorbike and Craig's car. "That's the least of my worries, anyway."

"How can you say that?" Craig persisted.

Michael whirled and stared straight into Craig's eyes. "How can I say it? It's simple. They weren't real people." His voice chilled Craig as he continued. "Brianna and the kids are probably dead now. Blaze did it, and —" He stopped himself from saying it and took a breath. "Just shut up and move. We have to go home."

Craig glanced towards the burning wreckage of his Jaguar, the fire truck's sirens growing louder by the second, as he considered Michael's words. Yes, somewhere, his Brianna was still alive with their daughter. Meanwhile, he had allowed his selfishness and ego to ignore Michael's words and leave. If they were still at the house, they may have been able to ensure everyone's safety.

Doubt and a guilty conscience gnawed at Craig as he trudged through the grass after Michael's loping form. He didn't know how, but he'd have to do what he could to make things up to Michael, who had been nothing but supportive since his arrival.

"Hurry," Michael called.

Craig hurried until he reached Michael and walked alongside him. "I'm sorry about what happened," he said. "It's my fault."

Michael shot him a strained look. "What are you talking about?"

"For taking you away from Brianna, Hayley and James."

Michael faced forward. His jaw set as he walked faster with determined steps. "You needed to know how you died, I guess."

"Which I hadn't."

"True." Michael pushed a branch out of the way, allowing it to snap back into Craig as he continued. "Oops. Sorry." He allowed a tiny smile. "Not."

Craig lifted an eyebrow. "You know something else, don't you?"

Michael shrugged. "No, I'm hoping they made it to the safe room under the house."

"Safe room?"

Michael stopped and turned towards Craig. "Yes, the safe room." He studied Craig for a moment. "How come you don't know about it? You showed it to me."

"What?"

"Before you died," Michael explained. "You told me about the basement and said the previous owner had kept it as a…" He paused and took a breath as he massaged the back of his neck. "You told me the man used it as a sex dungeon."

"Did I?" Craig shook his head with genuine surprise.

Perhaps something like that happened here, but not where he had come from. "I don't remember that. There's no such room under my house, and I don't see the relevance." The moment the words left Craig's mouth, he paused and hoped Michael hadn't caught his slip by referring to "his home".

But his host never reacted or responded. "You kept it for storage. After your death, I converted it to a secured panic room in case Blaze thought to come sniffing around your house. I'd already created a new identity and scattered a fake paper-trail to throw him off the scent, but I took no chances."

Craig tilted his head in question. "Are you serious?"

Michael nodded. "Yeah, I am. Brianna and the kids are the only ones who know about the room apart from you. How could you forget that?"

"I'm working on the answer to that too," Craig replied, stepping past Michael to take the lead in the direction they headed. "Come on. Let's see if my wife and your kids are okay."

Michael's hand clapped on Craig's shoulder.

"What is it?"

"Look up there," Michael replied.

Craig expected to see Colonel Blaze's drone, but something else loomed above the cemetery's wall: a security camera. "It's facing the other way," Craig answered. "What's the problem?"

Michael tapped his forehead. "Do you remember what happened last night?"

"Vaguely." Craig pondered. "I remember the brick wall, which I guess this is it. I followed it until the fence became the wrought iron one down the end. There was a gate, and

I walked out."

"Colonel Blaze has access to the surveillance cameras all over Statton," Michael said. "He must have seen you. All he had to do was follow you home." Michael punched the tree trunk hard and contemplated his bleeding knuckles. A moment later, the skin healed over and the blood flow ceased. "He set us up by attacking my house. He'd have known my kids were home and attacked, knowing full well we'd probably run to the car."

"How he did it doesn't matter," Craig replied. "It gives us an advantage."

"How?"

"Blaze thinks we're dead."

Michael shook his head. "A Clayton's advantage." He pressed at the buttons on his smartwatch, which beeped back as though protesting at his furious manipulation. "The communication link with Sparks is cactus. I can't check on the others." After a moment, his worried expression had turned to one of futility. "The CPU he's in could have fallen victim to whatever happened there. I have to check the house, but Blaze would expect that."

"Then we'll play it carefully."

Chapter 17

Brianna blinked against the darkness that enveloped her. At first, she could hear nothing but the terrible singing voice in her ears. Her eyes stung each time she moved her eyelids. At last, a voice reached her, calling her name. Dizzy, she shook her head and sat in a crouch, aware of the slight dizziness that spun the world. A soft hand rested on her elbow, tiny and gentle, and she squinted against the gloom.

"Hayley?" She stretched her hand outward until she touched the girl's tiny body. "What happened? Are you okay?"

"Yes." Hayley's voice, innocence mixed with concern, whispered in her ear. "But, James is hurt bad." She stretched the last word to emphasise James' injuries.

Brianna's eyes opened wide in shock as memory returned of the explosion. "James?" she called into the darkness. "Can you hear me?" Her heart thudded hard when James didn't respond. "Hang on, James. I'm coming. Hayley, how close are we to him?"

With her fingers spread in the darkness, Brianna fumbled across the cold concrete floor. Pain from the wounds and injuries she received that morning lanced her shoulders and elbow. She ignored it and inched her way until her hand touched something still and hard. A shoe. Still blind in the pitch black, Brianna fumbled until she touched the sock and recognised the shape. James' ankle.

Careful not to hurt the lad, Brianna patted along his inert body until she found his face and rested her ear near his mouth and nose. She smiled upon feeling his steady breath in her ear.

"Good lad," she said. "Hayley, he's alive."

She checked for obvious injuries and found no broken bones, but what was that smell? Brianna leaned towards his ear and called his name. "Can you hear me, James?" She waited. "Squeeze my hand if you can hear me?" Then a waft of something metallic reached Brianna's nose, and she lifted a hand towards his head, careful not to hurt him with her fingers. The sticky wetness in his matted hair evoked memories from her service in Afghanistan. "Oh, shit."

"You said a rude word," Hayley chimed.

Brianna clucked to herself, ignorant of the little girl's comment as she ripped off her t-shirt. At first, it resisted her efforts, but she at last tore it into strips, which she pressed to the lad's head. "Hayley," she said. "Are you hurt?"

"No." The little girl went silent for a moment. "I tried singing to James to make him feel better, but he fell asleep again."

Brianna was aware of the slippery concrete under her shoes. It was probably James' blood. "How long ago?"

"Ten minutes," a familiar voice said from the darkness near James' hip.

"Sparks!" Excited at finding another voice to share her situation, Brianna reached towards the voice's source and retrieved James' mobile phone from what felt like his back pocket. "How did you get there?"

"Bluetooth, how else?" the cyber-teenager's voice replied with a chuckle. Then he sensed the concern in Brianna's mood. "I patched in barely a nanosecond before the house tumbled."

"I'll ask about that later," Brianna chided him. "We need to check James' condition. Can you tell me if he's alive and stable?"

"Sorry, Brianna. All my bio-sensors died in the explosion. But if it helps, his breathing seems steady from what I can hear through his phone's microphone."

"He's bleeding. It'd be good if we could see what's happening here." Brianna laid James' head on the floor, using the rest of her shirt as his pillow for what it was worth. "We need some light here."

"There's a string hanging just above you," Sparks said. "Pull it."

Brianna passed her hand through the inky blackness until she found a plastic knob attached to a hanging string. She pulled it, and a lightbulb glowed above her. "Let there be light," she said, crouching to her haunches to check the unconscious teenager's vitals.

"Oh, wow!" Sparks' voice quavered from James' phone. "Like, holy…"

Brianna lifted her gaze for a moment to regard the mobile device for a second. "What is it? Something wrong?"

"The closest I have been to — um, nothing." Sparks fell into a silence that carried a hint of guilty amusement.

Brianna shook her head, choosing to ignore the cyber-kid's moods. For a computer consciousness, he was sometimes as immature as a teenager. Then she realised the source of Sparks' mood. He had seen through the phone's camera that she was shirtless, wearing only a bra, and plenty of flesh. *Yep, just like a teenager*, she thought to herself. "You'd better not be fondling your bits,

Sparks," she responded straight-faced, while she examined the wound she found on James. "A piece of debris has gashed James' arm pretty bad." Then she noticed the odd angle in it. "Shit, it's broken too."

Sparks replied, "I'll contact an ambulance."

"Negative," Brianna responded. "If Blaze has the power to set a hit on us, he could also have feelers out through the police. That means they'd hear of suspicious wounds like this." She checked James' head and saw blood dripping from his ear, too. There were no obvious wounds, but he could have hit his head when the explosion's shock-wave hit them. Bleeding from the ears could mean he suffered a concussion, or worse.

"But we have to get him out of here," Sparks replied. "What about a doctor?"

Her heart hammering hard, Brianna turned to face Hayley, surprised to see the little girl looking straight at James without a sign of shock or dismay on her face. Neither could Brianna see a sign of blood or trauma on her. "What about you?" Brianna asked the four-year-old. "How are you, Hayley?"

The little girl said nothing. Could be shock, Brianna thought and reminded herself to keep a better eye on her.

"I've found a doctor," Sparks said, interrupting Brianna. "One of James' friends, a girl named Amy's father, is a doctor. Shall I call her?"

Brianna fought back an urge to vomit as a wave of dizziness washed over her. "What?"

"James needs a doctor," Sparks said, "and Hayley's looking pretty spaced too."

"Sparks," Brianna replied, swallowing some bile, its taste creating an involuntary convulsion on her part. She paused for breath, prompting a worried question from the cyber-teenager, which she dismissed with a wave. "Do we have any bandages in this panic room?"

"Behind you," Sparks answered. "Brianna, are you okay? You're pale."

"It's just the lighting." Brianna found a metal cabinet where Sparks said and opened it. There, a stocked shelf of first aid supplies waited. She cast an impressed eye over the display. "Shit, Sparks, how much did Michael prepare here?"

The cyber-teenager chuckled. "You've seen nothing yet. How about dressing James' gash so we can get out of here?"

Brianna removed the impromptu bandage from the boy's head, applied antiseptic and redressed the injury, so it appeared better. Then she examined the wound on James' shoulder and packed it with gauze, careful of the break in his forearm. "Hang on," she said, her eyebrow raised as a horrible notion occurred. "Sparks, why didn't you mention the bandages before I took off my shirt and tore it up, hmm?"

Sparks didn't answer. Typical male, Brianna thought, hiding an amused smile as she sought something to make a splint for James' arm. Even as a digital consciousness, Sparks had kept enough of his old flesh-and-blood mentality to maintain his humanity.

"I couldn't reach a doctor," Sparks said at last. "The concrete in here has blocked the mobile phone towers. The explosion destroyed the landline connection too."

"I hope you have another great surprise," Brianna grunted and tied off a sling for James, who had just given a small moan. "He's regaining consciousness."

"Easy," Sparks replied. "Have a look at the wall ahead of you."

Brianna propped James in a sitting position and stepped past the table and chairs. There, the southern wall's main point of difference was its pink colour. "What about it?"

"Look for the divot below. You'll find a handle. Pull it."

Brianna knelt and checked. Inside the two-inch wide hole sat a steel ring, which she grabbed and pulled upwards. At first, it resisted, but then lifted out of the ground. The rumbling noise of an unseen mechanism filled the room, clanking and grinding, until the brick wall slid away to the side. Cool air passed her from the tunnel's darkness and caressed her face.

"What's this?"

"I told you I had another surprise," Sparks said. "It leads to the Parklands just above the river. It's approximately five hundred metres; a short walk. At the end, you'll find a service door that opens only from inside. Michael built it as a backup precaution."

A smile crossed Brianna's lips. "That's the best news I've heard so far today. I could just about kiss you."

"Woo hoo, you big tease," Sparks quipped, "but seeing your boobs was enough, thanks." Brianna chuckled and shook her head. "Okay," Sparks added. "One more time."

"In your cyber-dreams." Brianna grabbed the phone, which housed Sparks' consciousness, and went to place him in the back pocket of her jeans, but changed her mind. The cyber-lad would only have jibed her more about being close to her arse. "We have to get out of here," she added, and bent to check James, who was just blinking his eyes as awareness returned.

"James," she said, "are you okay, mate?"

Bleary-eyed, he blinked against the lights and was about to speak when he rolled and vomited against the cold cement beside him. He coughed hard. "That tastes like shit."

Brianna ignored Hayley, who chastised James for swearing, and held her hand before his face. "Watch my fingers." She watched his eyes track her fingertip as she moved it left, right, then back again. "Do you feel dizzy?"

James shook his head and winced when he turned. "Just my arm's sore."

"You broke it," she answered, standing to check the supplies cabinet and grabbing an energy drink. She let him sip some. He kept it down; that was a good sign. "Rest for a bit before we get out of here."

Chapter 18

The throbbing in Brianna's head had worsened, and although James was semi-conscious, he still posed a heavy weight as she carried him along the tunnel. On her own, Brianna could have made it in ten minutes, far better than the half-hour she had estimated.

"How are you doing there?"

James slurred a reply she couldn't quite make out. Poor kid. The sooner he received medical attention, the better. They could both use the rest. Brianna closed her eyes to block the unbearable agony that built in her own head. She suspected she had a concussion too. Sitting underground in a bunker without communication to Michael or other help was less than ideal. The ache returned, bashing a drum behind her right eye.

"Are you okay, Aunty Bree?"

For a moment, she regarded her little niece, the picture of innocence that otherwise contrasted with the intelligence beyond her years.

"I'll be fine, Hayles." Brianna offered her most convincing smile, projecting the best natural expression she could. "James is just a heavy lad. Must be all that Coke he drinks."

Hayley gave her adoptive brother a doubtful look, then checked Brianna too. "Your head hurts too."

"I'm okay." Brianna winked, but the wink she offered doubled as trying to blink back the nausea she fought. "Come on."

Hayley walked by their side, casting furtive glances at

Brianna. "Where's Daddy?"

"Daddy's out, but he's coming." The detective shifted James' weight on her aching shoulder. God, she felt so tired and weak. The early morning motorbike chase hadn't helped; if only the dog hadn't attacked her too. And the other wounds she gained from both the explosion and the road pursuit were taking their toll on her.

But she had to remain strong.

The children depended on her, and that helped motivate her.

After another ten minutes, they reached the iron door.

"Sparks." Brianna panted as she checked the threshold with her free hand. "You're quiet. How are you doing?"

The cyber-lad's reply crackled from the mobile phone in James' pocket. "Just fine, but can we hurry? The phone's charge is down to six percent, and I need to call for help when I get the coverage."

"Can't you boost the battery or something?"

"Negative." Sparks' dejected voice rattled with obvious disappointment. "I've tried, but there's nothing more I can do. When the juice goes, I'll be stuck until you recharge the phone."

Brianna nodded. "I see. The more you talk, the more battery you use."

"Yes."

Sparks' single word said everything she needed to know. All she had to do was to get out so the cyber-teenager could summon help for James. She took a deep breath and fought to keep her balance. Now and then, the room tilted such that she relied on the boys' weight to counterbalance her, but whenever the spinning sensation hit, she had to wait a moment or longer. It was getting worse.

A curious sliding whooshing echoed around her. Earlier, she'd heard it, but it had seemed fainter. Now it was louder, like the hiss of air released from a bike's tyre valve.

"Hayley, where's that sound coming from?"

The little girl gave a questioning look and shrugged.

"You can't hear it?"

Another head shake.

Brianna thought for a moment, dismissed the noise for the time being, and pushed aside both solid steel crossbars that blockaded the exit from inside the tunnel. Although heavy, they proved easy enough to move while holding James upright. "Let's get out of here."

She opened the door, and a fresh breeze washed over their faces. Such a sweet smell. Brianna took a deep breath, and they emerged from the tunnel into the warm early evening that held the final pink and red dying rays of the setting sun. How beautiful it looked.

The Parklands overlooked the Statton River that snaked below them. Like tiny eyes, the city centre's streetlights were just blinking to life from the opposite bank. The sounds of the city's traffic drifted to her ears on a cool summer breeze that kissed the sweat on her face and throat. For a moment, Brianna felt a sense of relief wash over her from leaving the claustrophobic escape tunnel. An outdoors girl since she could remember, including in the Army, Brianna took a deep breath and closed her eyes to enjoy the sweet smell of early evening. She slipped Sparks from James' pocket, pressed the home button. "Sparks, have you —?"

She gaped at the blank display. Damn! The battery was flat. "Sparks?" No reply came.

A wave of agony swept through Brianna's skull as she

released a litany of curses at the dead phone and the consequences that entailed for James. She staggered under the teenager's weight and did her best to lay him to the ground without jarring his injury. A hiss of pain escaped his lips. "Sorry, mate," she said.

Footsteps from behind caught her attention and dizziness swirled her off-balance when she spun to face the sound. Then, she saw the two men, bulky across the upper bodies from the muscles that already strained against the body armour they wore.

"Hey, pretty lady. You look like you're ready to drop." The closest of the newcomers moved forward, his face shielded by the helmet's darkened visor.

Hackles rose on the back of Brianna's neck. These weren't police, as she assumed. Their body armour didn't match the type worn by others in the service, or the soldiers who attacked. This was what the SAS wore.

"Help us." Brianna fought to stand, resisted the urge to shake, despite the growing fatigue and vertigo. To show her physical weakness could prove fatal. "The boy needs medical attention. He's hit his head on a rock and his arm's broken."

The man's didn't even turn, but Brianna guessed he had glanced in James' direction and spotted Hayley too. He motioned to his friend, who moved forward towards the children. She expected the attack from the second man, who advanced.

She realised her error a moment before the leader's rifle butt struck her at full force in the face.

Chapter 19

An alien sense of loss crept through Craig upon discovering the obliterated wreck of his home. Gone were the cacti and roses that once grew there. The bricks and girders lay spread across the bitumen and lawn, the debris scattered into the neighbours' yards, and the streetlight's dim rays drew shadows that stretched long thin streaks across the grey grass. Twice, he reminded himself, this wasn't his actual home but the residence of someone else who was a different translation of him. They shared the same name, physical attributes, date-of-birth and other characteristics, but the resemblances stopped there. Oh, and according to the world, the other Craig Ramsey had died. Still, he couldn't avoid the empty despair of seeing something so familiar destroyed.

Michael sniffed. "Schick, this is a bloody war zone." Craig agreed in silence as Michael waved his smartwatch backwards and forwards across the rubble. A lock of brown hair dropped over Michael's eyes, and he flicked it back as he studied the green display. "No life signs." He muttered something else to himself.

Craig couldn't catch Michael's last words, but he guessed the man, who had proven a helpful host, was not impressed with the day. He looked around for something to do and make himself more useful. "How is it scanning?"

Michael never took his eyes off the screen. "It's a combination of x-rays, magnetic resonance imaging and audio." A warning beep fired from the watch, which now glowed an angry red. He tapped the device and knelt to the ground, holding the gimmick closer to the debris. "False alarm. Just a dead mouse."

Craig released a breath he hadn't realised he held. A rodent. At least it wasn't a child. Being a father, he understood some pain in Michael's mind. He wouldn't want to lose his daughter, either. "That would take some big bucks to buy," he said. "How did you come by it?"

Michael stopped for a moment to look at Craig. "Strange question to ask me." A streetlight's beam glinted from the man's eye before his attention returned to the watch's display.

Craig gave a silent snort. He had asked Michael before about the strange body doubles that had overtaken them earlier in the cemetery before their unfortunate demise. Decoys, Michael had told him, but what kind of distraction? Were they human or spirit? No; ghosts no longer existed here. "It's not such a tough question. You've got more strange toys than I recognise, and I doubt technology has advanced so much in the year since I died."

Michael passed his watch over another section of rubble. "I can understand the disorientation after being away for so long. What I find difficult, Craig, is that you don't know the one thing about me that made you decide to help break me out of Blaze's prison before you died." His voice strained and testy, Michael regarded Craig with a look that appeared accusatory.

"Oh?" Craig stalled, calculating Michael's responses. What did he expect him to know? Could it be?

Michael stopped scanning and stepped across the ruins towards Craig. "I know what you're thinking, Craig." Ah! There it was. He was returning Craig's challenge.

Craig kept his stance, ready for a likely attack, which,

given Michael's attitude to fighting, could prove dangerous. He relaxed, prepared, and fought to remain calm. It was now or never. "I think we're both keeping secrets."

Michael backed off a step, his eyebrow cocked in confusion. "How so?"

Craig pointed at Michael's scanner. "You love gadgets. Some of these things I doubt have hit the market. They appear military grade, but I don't think they have them either. It's like you're some kind of James Bond, but then those people who ran past us in the cemetery. You still haven't told me who they are and where they came from."

"Okay, so you know I have secrets, and you have probably guessed something, which I won't confirm this minute. Shall I guess yours?"

Craig scanned Michael's body with a wary eye. "Go on."

"I believe you're not the real Craig Ramsey."

Craig couldn't stop the smile. "What do you mean?"

Michael pointed at Craig's clenched fist. "You can relax. You're not the enemy, but you're not the Craig Ramsey I met over a year ago either."

Craig said nothing, just looked at his companion while his mind raced for a comeback that wouldn't appear.

Meanwhile, Michael returned to his scanning. "The DNA says you're Craig Ramsey, and you're a dead ringer for him, but you're different, too. I just don't understand how since you're not a clone or android."

"Well," Craig replied, the word stretching, "That's true. This is stupid. We need to talk."

Michael cut him off from saying more. "Not here. We're cloaked from surveillance," he allowed a knowing smile full of irony, "but I'd prefer we find the others. Check out the laundry , about here."

Craig approached the area Michael had pointed at and knelt to touch a clump of bricks and mortar. The vision of a man, whom he didn't recognise, appeared before him. Oblivious to Craig's psychic gaze, he lifted a metal grate from the floor and climbed down a ladder. The hallucination faded. "I saw something," he said, "but it must have been the previous owner."

Michael's shoulders slumped. "Perhaps another brick?" He pointed to the side. "What about that?"

Craig spotted the washing machine's remains that the explosion had crushed like an empty soft drink can amongst the rubble and laid his hands upon its surface.

@ @ @

There stood Craig's other self at the washing-machine, picking pieces of underwear and other clothing from its bowels to place in a laundry basket.

"I don't understand where Colonel Ryan went, Turner. At one moment, he was there. Then he vanished."

Turner? Craig recognised the name that belonged to Tyrone's guardian ghost and mentor. He listened and glanced about the laundry room, hoping to spot the old Cockney's spirit. No, Craig couldn't see him, but that posed no surprise because he'd never seen immaterial beings in his visions before, not even his spirit guardian Emma, only the living.

"I've been pulling my Barnet Fair aht over it too, lad," Craig heard Turner say. "Me old chums `re missing too and don't know why."

Craig cleared his throat and Vision-Craig spun to him and jumped back in surprise. "What?"

"What is it, Craig?" Turner's voice said. "Ya butcher's

loik you've pearly queen a pillar and post." He chortled at his own joke, but Craig caught the concerned tone as he translated Turner's Cockney slang: you look like you've seen a ghost.

Craig chuckled as he realised the event's importance in things. "No, Turner, I'm not a spirit. It's good to hear your voice again, even if I can't see you." He turned toward Vision-Craig. "Listen, Ramsey, let's keep this short. I'm you, well, kind of, and this is the first time you've met me, but I've met you before."

A confused look crossed Vision-Craig's face and wrinkled his brow. "What?"

Turner responded, just as surprised. "Who the bleeding bloody Gypsy Nell said that? Sha yourself."

"Never mind. Maybe later," Craig answered and focused on Vision-Craig. "Listen Craig, I have very little time. I'm in your future and need your help. Do you see the grate in the middle of the laundry floor?"

Vision-Craig turned and nodded.

"Touch it and tell me if you can focus on about a year and a half's time." Craig hoped he guessed the timeframe correctly. "Brianna, James, and Hayley should have escaped down there. Your house has just exploded, and I want to know if they're safe."

Vision-Craig concentrated and searched about him. "Hey, what happened to the house?" Recognition formed as he peered about at what Craig presumed to be his own scene amongst the rubble. "That looks like Michael Mach. What's he doing with you?"

Craig shook his head. Did he normally waste time like, or was this unique to his doppelgänger's traits? "Well... That's a long story which you're going to set in motion, but... well... spoilers. Take your perspective back about four hours, will you? Three lives are at stake here, and Colonel Blaze part of it all."

The name conjured dark clouds of recognition across Vision-Craig's face. "Blaze? I'm getting the picture. Let me see —"

@ @ @

The vision disappeared quicker than a derailed train of thought. "No! I was so close." Craig shook his head. What had interrupted his psychic vision?

"We have to go," Michael whispered, and pushed Craig deeper into the shadows behind the house's ruins. "Soldiers are coming." He rushed ahead into the darkness and beyond the crumpled remains of a garden shed.

Craig touched its surface and realised the Craig Ramsey of this universe had used it as his exercise area, like his own kwoon, except it was a dojo. This Craig Ramsey learned Japanese karate. Another difference.

But he couldn't dwell on that. They had to escape before the soldiers saw them. Together, the duo pressed through a shadow-cloaked hole in the back fence and into the spinifex that Craig recognised bordered with what he took to be the Parklands beside the river. They ducked behind a large rock mere seconds before a torch's beam washed across it.

Craig held his breath and focused on his hammering heart as the soldiers stood at the back fence and spoke between themselves. Their voices floated to them.

"What do you think it was?"

"Don't know. The goggles aren't picking up their heat signatures." A pause. "A bandicoot?"

"Sounded bigger."

A laugh. "They can. Sound travels better at night when other things are quieter."

"Yeah, right."

Footsteps reached their ears, the noise fading with their words as the soldiers left the scene.

Michael's hand tapped him, and Craig followed his companion's silent direction to follow him. They took a direct path through the trees, following the directions on the display of Michael's scanner, as they followed what Craig interpreted to be an underground passage.

"An escape tunnel?" he whispered.

"I should have guessed it before," Michael said. "It's probably easier to trace things from where they could have gone — the end."

Craig nodded. It had been a stressful afternoon. Michael had to keep them alive despite his concern for the welfare of his adopted sister, daughter, and adopted son. Plus, the day had worn at them both. He stifled a yawn and guessed fatigue wore at his comrade, too. "We'll need a place to rest soon."

Michael grunted an indistinct reply.

They were now at the edge of the trees on a high embankment overlooking a grassy area with a path that snaked its way along the river. Craig followed Michael's lead down the side until they reached the ground.

"Here we are," Michael said. "The area's clear. Do your stuff, mate. There's the door."

Craig turned and gaped at the entrance set in the embankment. "A door in the boulder? Doesn't this stand out like a shag on a... rock?"

"Hiding in plain sight." Michael shrugged. "People assume it's a maintenance room."

"Unbelievable." Craig laid his hands on the door's edge.

A moment later, the surface relinquished its story to his psychic touch.

Craig gasped as he witnessed the vision forms of Brianna and the kids leaving the tunnel, and the two soldiers who attacked them. There was nothing he could do but watch in horror, flinch and cringe when the soldier smacked his wife's double in the face with the rifle's butt. Hayley's screams curdled his marrow as one grabbed her and silenced her with a sedative. Then they left the injured woman and boy behind them. Shadows shifted in the psychic vision a moment before footsteps reached his ears. Then a surprised voice spoke.

"Why, there they are, like the message said."

A man approached Brianna. Craig couldn't see his features, but the good Samaritan's hands were smooth, like a surgeon's. They checked over the unconscious woman, examining her injuries, checking for breaks. A stethoscope appeared from his pocket, and he listened to her heartbeat. All the while, he clacked his tongue and shook his head, murmuring at what he discovered. A moment later, he examined James. At last, he looked up and spoke aloud. "This sounds crazy. I don't know why, but I was told to do this. The lady has terrible injuries, including trauma, but she's not critical yet. I think the lad has concussion too. I'll take them both to `my hospital unit'. Do you get that?" He paused, embarrassment obvious in his expression. "I can't tell you the address; I'm not allowed, but the message told me to tell you: check the envelope from the coffin. It said you would understand."

Chapter 20

A sheen of sweat glistened across the exposed skin on Blaze's biceps and neck as his gaze followed his eight opponents. They circled him, relaxed as they assessed him. He took a breath, deep and slow, watchful of where they looked and how they darted from his face, to a point beside him, and back again. A smile flickered, disappearing like a meerkat ducking down its hole.

Blaze dodged to the side, his foot shot backwards and connected with a jaw. A grunt filled the air. Before his stealthy attacker dropped to the ground, the colonel spun and struck a hammer fist into the yielding spongy flesh of another man's groin.

He blocked a kick that had almost slid past his guard and, with a flurry of punches and strikes, knocked out three more men before they could respond. Blood pumped through his temples, the drumbeats throbbing in his ears, as he kept his feet moving with a dancer's precision. Stay still and die. Never give them time to strike. Disappear before they move. Hit hard, fast, and go.

The click of a door opening caught his eye. Ignore distractions. Too late.

The arm that snaked around Blaze's neck drew him into a side headlock. He turned his head into the smelly, sweaty skin of his attacker, and without thinking, grabbed the man's hair on which he yanked downwards, and threw the man to the ground with a thud.

Two men remained, but not for long as he dispatched them fast.

Hands clapping from the side caught his attention, and the room's visitor, whose entry had distracted him, spoke. "Nice work, Colonel."

Standing undefeated, Blaze turned towards the man who had entered the doorway during his workout. "Oates!" He caught the towel the major had thrown him and wiped his forehead while his sparring partners struggled to their feet and dispersed. "What news have you?"

Oates paused, took a breath. "The cleanup team reported back." His words trailed as his brow furrowed.

"Ramsey and Mach." Blaze dabbed his neck with the towel in anticipation.

His subordinate dipped his head in affirmation and waited until the last of the sparring partners had left the room. "It's the grave, sir. There was no body found."

Colonel Blaze's eyes arched as he swallowed hard. "No corpse?"

"Just books."

No reaction appeared on his face as he pondered Oates' words. He had trained himself not to react to surprise, to maintain a facade that poker players would envy, but he still fought to hold back a flicker in his left eyelid. Books in the grave? That could mean two things: Craig Ramsey had never died, or someone else had removed the corpse before the burial. But how? His agents had infiltrated the office of Dr Krootz, the crazy medical examiner, who, rumour stated, had necrophiliac tendencies, and found his notes. The documentation confirmed the psychic's death by multiple internal injuries from being struck by a car — driven by Blaze himself — and massive head trauma. The colonel had witnessed Ramsey's forehead hit the windscreen, the blood spatter, and heard the sickening smash of glass. Even the flop of the body on the bitumen. Then he'd backed over the lifeless flesh and bone, felt the thump like a speed bump, and run over it again before he sped off. The last thing he had seen through the rear-view mirror was Michael Mach racing towards the doomed and still-dying Ramsey.

Oates shifted in his superior officer's long silence and almost jumped out of his skin when Blaze at last spoke.

"Just books, Oates?"

"Enough to simulate Ramsey's body weight in the box, give or take."

Blaze could hide the amusement from his eyes, but not the minute flicker from the corner of his mouth. "But the bodies from today's wreckage?"

Oates lifted his fist and dropped something into Blaze's waiting hand. "Michael Mach's skull ring. DNA results from the body parts confirm the remains belong to Michael Mach and Craig Ramsey. They're dead."

Blaze nodded his satisfaction, his face a mask as he calculated what that could mean in the future. "And what about the house?"

"Obliterated."

"What?" A hideous rage exploded within Blaze at the word. The fools! He hadn't authorised them to destroy an entire house when he wanted just one thing from the raid. That wasn't their aim. Only his extreme self-control held back the obscenities and ultimate outburst. Blaze fought down his dark anger and uttered a crackled response. "Survivors?"

"At first, the teams thought not, but Delta team's equipment detected underground movement, and they intercepted Detective Brianna Cogan, Mach's teenager ward and Mach's daughter at the end of an escape tunnel that led to the Parklands recreational area."

Blaze turned his head to meet Oates' eyes. "And?"

"They confirmed the woman is dead. The boy suffered severe injuries and concussion. We have taken the girl."

Blaze's voice lightened, but only by a semi-tone. Thank goodness for minor miracles, especially this one. "Hayley Mach," he said. "The fruit from the loins of our project's subjects." The smile coloured his voice, but not his face. "Special treatment for her, Oates. Have the doctors prepare the lab for little Hayley and let her rest. Feed her. She needs the strength for our tests."

"Yes, sir." Oates saluted and was about to turn to leave when Blaze interrupted his exit.

"Oh, and Oates?"

The major paused. "Yes, sir?"

"Who led the strike team?"

"Sergeant Tenor." Aware of the sergeant's error, Oates swallowed, the hint of a frown rippling across his brow as he uttered the doomed officer's name.

"You know what to do."

"Yes, sir." Oates saluted and quit the room, leaving his superior officer deep in thought.

Blaze turned and left through the doorway towards his private shower, details sorting through his mind. How interesting. "Books," he muttered. Even a year later, Craig Ramsey was mocking him after death. Or was he?

He was aware of Craig Ramsey's flirtation in the world of illusion. Before the government approached him, Ramsey had enjoyed years onstage in eight different countries as a master magician and mentalist. Blaze had watched enraptured as he witnessed Ramsey perform a guillotine trick. With his limbs shackled and locked in the stock, escape had seemed impossible. Stage lights glinted from the sharp edge of the blade suspended above him. He had only twenty seconds to escape before the blade would drop. Behind a thin screen, Craig Ramsey struggled to escape. But something went wrong. With only 8 seconds left, the mechanism exploded. Sparks showered from the timer. Someone screamed, and the blade dropped. Stage assistants rushed to the scene in panic. But before they could reach the deadly apparatus, the paper screen shielding the horror tore open. There stood Craig Ramsey, triumphant and smiling.

As he turned the tap and the shower's water hit him, Blaze remembered clapping hard at the sight. He'd calculated already how Ramsey had escaped unscathed before the explosion. At least he knew how he would do it.

The death of Ramsey and Mach was an obvious illusion, elaborately cooked to take him away from Blaze. But how did he do it? Or had something else happened? If Ramsey could return from the dead, then could Michael Mach possess the same ability? Or could it be…

Misdirection, he thought. All he had to do was figure out the psychic's intentions before he struck.

After all, Ramsey couldn't have returned from the dead. Could he?

Chapter 21

Sally Green stabbed her cigarette in the overflowing ashtray and looked at the dirty mess of ash. Twelve cigarettes. That was a terrible way to refresh a habit she thought she had kicked with Craig Ramsey's hypnotic help. Sipping gin from her glass, she reached for another cancer stick, poked it in her mouth, and reached for her metallic lighter.

Craig Ramsey.

There was a name she never expected to surface a year after his death. He was the man who revived her journalism career with an exclusive interview after tracking down the Punchliner, a serial killer who had taunted investigators for a year with cryptic jokes. Other major news corporations wanted to speak to him, but he chose her. Ramsey had continued giving her exclusive interviews, including helping her kick the smoking habit with a short suggestion. He'd proven himself as a gold mine until the day a man some alleged held links to dark Government agencies killed him.

Ramsey's death signalled the death knell for her career, which whimpered its way into oblivion. Her employers had delegated her to performing the traffic reports from the local radio station's helicopter.

Then opportunity struck. The pilot was about to steer the craft back towards the airport when he spotted something. Five government vans arriving from different directions to converge upon the normally quiet but affluent suburban area. Luckily, she had her ancient digital video camera, an old habit that never died.

Now she watched the action unfold on the television screen, replaying her memory. The vans closing off each end of the street, a couple more outside the house she recognised as Craig Ramsey's old residence. Commandos dressed in black, bulked by their body armour, hurried towards the home. Some split in opposite directions around the building, which before she knew it had exploded into pieces that showered the surrounding area in debris. The rumbling shock and shock wave of hot air came next and rocked the helicopter, shaking the video camera as the pilot adjusted the flight.

The news channels had lapped up the footage. Sally's face appeared again on television screens across the state. And Craig Ramsey's name resurfaced. The government soldiers disappeared soon. Attempts to question the authorities met either no response or a jumble of sentences that didn't add up: terrorist unit, drug-related, no comment, classified.

But other words echoed in the hardened journalist's memory, spoken by a man who no longer existed. "Watch for the signal." "What signal?" "You'll know when it happens. Stay home that night."

So, Sally did that, her only companions being a resurrected cigarette problem and a pot of black coffee.

Her eyes flicked to the mobile phone's screen when it rang, but she didn't answer it. The man she once trusted had warned her to leave it alone after 6pm. The caller ID displayed the name of Jack Beckman—the head of Statton Communications, the next biggest news corporation in Australia. Most craved a call from him because that indicated the receiver's worth in his shrewd mind. It represented a gold mine to her.

Temptation gnawed as it started ringing a second time. Come on, she told herself, just a few minutes with Jack would mean a new high-profile journalism gig for her. An exclusive interview. But, no, the words spoken a year ago were clear. That man better have been right, or she'd never speak to him again, even if he was dead.

She lifted the cup to her lips, blew across the hot coffee, and took a sip.

The knock on the door surprised her. The drink sloshed, spilling to her bare foot and narrowly missed the toes.

She waited. What did he say about a visitor? Nothing.

Again, quiet but firm, the knocking came on her front door.

Sally stood and approached, pressing a button on the wall to activate the exterior camera, and examined the visitor on the monitor. At once, she recognised the first man but couldn't place his name; the other visitor's back faced the camera. A moment later, she slid the chain off the door and opened it.

There stood Michael Mach, his black hair hanging wet in his face from the night's rain. "Sally," he said. "Are you alone?"

Sally took a short breath, her head cocked at a slight angle. Her visitor regarded her with a searching expression, then glanced inside past her. "Yeah. Why are you here?"

Michael turned towards his companion, who was still watching the street, then back to her. "We need your help. Can we come inside?"

Sally studied the mysterious second person with a growing sense of familiarity. Her eyes opened wide. "Is that–?" She stepped past Michael and towards the other man who faced her, and she gasped.

The familiar sharp face with the laughing eyes took Sally's breath away, and he smiled. "Hello, Sally. I'm Craig Ramsey."

Sally stood still, her eyeballs rolled a moment before a curtain of blackness overcame her.

A moment later, Sally's head involuntarily shook her hard into consciousness in response to an acrid aroma that assaulted her nostrils. Blinking, she coughed and pushed away the offensive item Michael Mach held before her. "What the hell?" She snapped to a sitting position and regarded the second man in shock. "You're alive?"

The man who resembled Craig Ramsey shrugged, his right shoulder rising higher than the left. The corner of his mouth lifted in a lopsided grin when he spoke, eyes twinkling. "Well," he said, letting the word hang, "yeah, I'm alive… ish."

Sally's face screwed up as she studied him. "You're not the same Craig Ramsey."

Ramsey's eyes widened as he leaned back. Michael's head snapped to face him, his mouth miming silent perplexity. The pair looked at each other for a moment before Ramsey's kind, but firm, gaze returned to her.

"Listen, Sally, we don't have time to discuss everything. We need your help."

Sally nodded. "What kind? You know the authorities are looking for you, right? They say you're a terrorist and had been making bombs in your home."

Ramsey and Michael exchanged worried glances before Michael took over the conversation. "Sally, you know you can trust us. Now, we're depending on you. Can we borrow your car?"

Sally fumbled for her phone, flicking the screen for the

voice recorder. "Only if you answer some questions."

Her phone buzzed. Beckman's name flashed on the display. What a time!

"Don't answer that," Ramsey said. "They're bugging your conversations, and they have spoofed Beckman's phone number." He took a breath. "Actually, they're disguising themselves as every single contact stored on your phone and hoping to record your every conversation."

"Who?"

The answer whispered in her ear elicited another gasp from Sally as she listened to what she recognised as the bare bones of the pair's story. And she knew. Her life depended on following their instructions in tandem with those given to her a year ago. But her instincts remained the same.

"It's a deal, but on one condition."

Chapter 22

Sally Green's deal proved simple enough: promise her an exclusive interview on Craig's resurrection and the government. In exchange, she lent them the car and said she would hold off on giving her story to the big media companies. "Keep them wanting more," she told them with a cheeky wink before she handed them the keys.

The instructions in Craig's envelope provided directions to a second address, this one outside Statton. After checking for tracking or listening devices on Sally's Skyline, they drove onwards, their eyes watching for any other surveillance. Michael nodded as Craig read them from the blank sheet. A journey that should have been forty minutes had taken twice as long thanks to three trailing vehicles they had dodged through the backstreets. When at last they were certain they had avoided their pursuers on the road and in the air, they headed for the open motorway until they reached an exit that took them inland.

"The hinterland," Michael commented as the streetlights thinned and only their headlights illuminated the rough dirt path.

Craig yawned and stretched the best he could in the cramped car. "I notice we're on the same route that takes us to the old Army base too."

Michael bit his bottom lip, his eyes fixed ahead of them. "This could be a trap."

Craig shook his head. "I doubt it. The source is too-" He stopped. How could he tell his companion that he was getting messages from himself, or at least another incarnation? "We're fine. What I don't know yet is what we'll find at the other end."

If Michael had noticed Craig's self-correction, he didn't mention it. He feathered the brake and peered through the windscreen at a white letterbox beside a tree with a wide canopy that danced in the breeze. He steered into the driveway, the car's headlights casting ominous shadows to the side as they continued.

"We'll know soon enough," he said, and negotiated the track that led forever in the dark.

At last, a tiny beacon of yellow peeked through the gaps in the thick leafy trees that suggested the path. A house stood at the driveway's end, its front door illuminated by a solitary verandah light around which moths flitted and darted. If not for the car's headlights, the house's outline would have remained a mystery in the moonless night. Craig wasn't sure what he expected, but the building's sky blue walls and white railings were incongruent with the gloomy surroundings. Perhaps the morning sun would present a more cheerful picture.

"This must be the place," Michael said, and turned off the car's engine. He glanced toward Craig, their faces tinged a pale green by the dashboard's glow. "Well?"

Craig bobbed his head and stepped from the Skyline, stretching his legs before shutting its door. Gravel crunched under his shoes. No chance of sneaking up on the place. One of the three front steps protested under his weight as he ascended to the verandah, answered by a squeaky board. Before he could knock, the sound of a sliding bolt came to his ears, and the door opened to reveal a man's silhouette through the flimsy mesh. The house's occupant, silhouetted by an internal light from the back of the house, pushed open the screen-door and peered at him. He glanced towards Michael, who was still standing beside the car, then returned to Craig. "Yes?"

Craig thought for a moment to recall the envelope's message and uttered a pass phrase. "Little Jack Horner sat in a corner."

"And got a square arse," the man replied, his glasses glinting from the shadows.

"With haemorrhoids to match," Craig said, wondering what spy pictures had inspired this exchange.

The stranger humphed, turned on the light inside the house, affording Craig a glimpse of a face he recognised as the man from his vision, who had discovered Brianna and James. "Well, that's two things that matched the message." He called out to Michael. "Come on in. I won't bite, Skids." He looked at Craig and offered another smile. "It's good to meet you. I'm Joseph Maloney. I've been expecting you."

Michael's feet crunched across the gravel as he approached the house. Recognition dawned on his face when the house's occupant pushed open the screen door and stepped into the brightness. "Papa?"

Craig stepped aside, his eyebrow shaping like a question mark. "Your father?"

The man, shorter than the visitors, chuckled as he shook Michael's hand and drew him into a bear hug. "You look good for the years, mate." He stood back and grinned. "Damn, you have barely aged since we were in high school."

A long, absent grin dawned on Michael's face as he regarded the house's occupant. "Craig, this is Joe, an old mate from when we were kids. We nicknamed him Papa."

"Because he thought I looked like a Papa Giuseppe from the pizza commercials," Joseph replied.

Michael introduced the psychic to his friend, who didn't even recognise the second visitor as a long-dead celebrity, which came as a relief. Then he cocked an eyebrow. "Joe, why are you here?"

The bespectacled man allowed a smile, took a thoughtful breath, and sighed. "Come in and I'll tell you." He stepped aside to usher them into the house while keeping a watchful eye in the darkness.

"No one followed us," Michael assured him as he walked inside after Craig, then watched in apparent amusement as Joseph shut and locked the door. Instead of a single bolt, he slid several across into position before again checking the door's deadbolt.

Satisfied things were secure, Michael's friend turned to regard his visitors. "I assume you're here to see the boy and the woman."

"Is Brianna okay?" Craig blurted the words before realising this wasn't his world and he was talking about a different Brianna. He quietened.

Joseph was giving him a curious gaze, otherwise unassuming, and measured Craig's reaction until he realised the person of his interest sensed his attention.

"Can we see them, please?" Michael's voice echoed the same concern, and he craned his neck to peer further down the house.

Joe turned to Michael, offered a smile. "Of course. Follow me. You both must be hungry too."

He led them through the front living room and down a hallway towards the back of the house before pointing into a bedroom door in the house's centre. It looked like any other spare room a parent might convert into a study once the grownup child had left home. A screensaver image of 1980s supermodel Paulina Porizkova drifted across the screen of a laptop that sat on an ancient computer desk in the corner.

"She looks lovely, but I'm hungrier for some proper food," Michael said, which brought a chuckle from their host.

Joseph crouched, poked a finger through a hole hidden in the carpet's pattern, and pulled a trapdoor open. A burst of light shone upwards through the passage to reveal steps leading into a subterranean room. "Voilà!" He motioned to the stairs below. "Come on. It's all good."

Craig followed Joseph and Michael through the trapdoor, and it closed behind them. He gasped while Michael made a low, appreciative whistle. The room wasn't the dingy tunnel he expected.

They were standing in a long corridor of thirty-five to forty metres in length, with a three-metre-high ceiling. The walls arched above them as though they stood under a large sheet of curved corrugated iron. Well-lit and ventilated, it reminded Craig of a past client of his who had built a similar structure in case of a nuclear war.

They had entered what appeared to be a living room with well-stocked bookshelves, a lounge suite against one wall, and a home entertainment system. A sliding door arrangement separated it from sleeping quarters in the next section, with beds against the walls.

"You have a fallout shelter?" Michael's eyes were open wide. "Where did you get the money to do this? And the time?"

A humble smile crossed Joseph's face as he shook his

head. "Later. Follow me," he said and led them through the sleeping quarters that Craig noticed held eight bunks, and through a bathroom area towards a room that looked like a small doctor's surgery.

On the two available beds were Brianna and James, both still and asleep. Michael pushed past Joseph to approach his adoptive sister and son. He smoothed a finger along Brianna's forehead, pushing away a loose strand of hair, and looked across the room where the boy lay. "Are they okay?"

Joseph took a breath. "The message said you would know them. Yes, they're alive." He stepped towards Brianna, felt her pulse in her wrist, and regarded Craig and Michael. "The woman has a severe concussion, and I suspect a fractured skull, too. Unfortunately, I lack the equipment to perform full surgery on her, but she's stable. For now."

A lump lodged in Craig's throat as he approached Brianna. Her close resemblance to his wife troubled him more, and he imagined what he would do if she were to suffer the same harm. He turned away from the sight to regard Joseph as he explained James' injuries: a broken arm and a slight concussion. The boy would be fine with some rest.

"But the woman," the doctor said, his voice making Craig stop still with a jolt and clenched guts. Craig pretended not to notice how Joseph studied him from behind his square glasses before turning to look at Brianna. "She needs surgery."

"Can you do it?" The tension ran high in Michael's voice, cracking it, and he wiped his eye.

Joseph looked down with a slight shake of the head. "I

have an advanced surgery, but some equipment I need… And it's only me here." His voice trailed. "But she is stable for now as long as she remains in the induced coma."

Michael bit his lower lip as though weighing options in his head, then in a voice a shade more hopeful said, "Joseph, you mentioned a message. Maybe it's related?"

Joseph's jaw dropped a fraction as he raised a quizzical eyebrow, then his expression brightened. He clicked his fingers. "Yeah!" He strode across towards a desk at the foot of James' bed and handed an envelope from the drawer to Craig. "Perhaps you should do the honours? It's addressed to you."

Craig's eyes widened as he read the front. "It's my handwriting!" He pressed his fingers upon the envelope's smooth surface and concentrated, but nothing came. No vision. He ripped it open to find a piece of paper, which he unfolded and looked on both sides. No writing. No psychic revelation. "What?"

"Well?" Michael asked.

Craig answered with a shrug. "I'm picking up nothing from it."

"There has to be," Michael said, snatching the sheet then examining it through narrowed eyes. "Maybe you're not doing it right." Suddenly, his face glimmered, and he raised the sheet to his nose. Sniffing the edges, a smile cracked and turned to triumphant laughter. "You cunning bugger, Ramsey," he said. "Have you forgotten something from when you were a kid?"

Craig pondered. Of course! How could he forget? He snatched the paper from Michael and hurried back towards the shelter's entrance until he reached the kitchen.

"Who wants toast?"

* * *

Colonel Blaze rarely mixed with the children at the base. It wasn't the thing to do. To him, the youngsters brought to the laboratories were subjects. If they passed the tests, then they became soldiers. If not, then they were... disposed.

But little Hayley Mach was an exception.

Like a freshwater crocodile in a billabong studying its prey, Blaze watched with patience, observing as the girl ate her fill of dinner: chicken nuggets and baked beans. The way her light caramel-hued hair flicked past her shoulders evoked memories of Michael Mach's wife, Alison, as did her deep brown eyes. But her mouth and jaw, the way it set as she regarded the other boys and girls in the mess hall, that reminded him of Michael Mach.

Never did it occur to Blaze that Hayley missed her father. How could she? The base would be full of toys designed to stimulate her mind. Both hemispheres, particularly the right parahippocampal gyrus. According to the base's scientists, and those from other similar projects, paranormal ability comes from that region of the brain. With custom-made toys and other exercises, disguised as games, he could develop her abilities much better than Michael Mach could have done on his own. Besides, both her parents had powers that measured off the charts, although in different areas. It was obvious that she should be in his special school, a psychic academy where her developed potential would become a powerful weapon to defend Australia and its allies from the growing international threats from China, North Korea, and Russia.

Blaze lowered his gaze to examine the girl's blood test results on his computer screen. Interesting. She had inherited the same anomaly from her father's cells, something seen only in only one other project's subject. He rubbed his chin as he considered the find.

A movement caught Blaze's eye. He looked up in time to see the little girl leave the table and approach the one-way glass. A foot away from the mirror, she glared at him, into his eyes. Without flinching, Blaze stared back, aware of a warm sensation that pooled inside his head. A few seconds later, the feeling stopped.

Hayley turned and returned to her seat at the table, but kept her eye on him.

Blaze returned to studying the girl's report. They would start testing her in the morning.

* * *

Craig, Joseph, and Michael watched the paper as the toaster's heat rose to meet it. At first, tiny light brown smudges appeared as blobs on the sheet. Then the shapes grew to form letters, which morphed into symbols.

Michael shared Craig's grin as sentences formed across the page. "Invisible ink. What did I tell you?"

"You're a genius, Michael," Craig replied. "What can I say?"

"That's what happens when you read enough spy stories." Michael shrugged.

Craig snorted in amusement. For him, it had been his background as a magician, not just reading James Bond novels, but he couldn't remember the British MI6 agent using lemon juice to write a secret message.

"What's it say?"

Craig's eyes widened. The words were in his handwriting, another similarity between him and his double.

All at once, his heart dropped.

BRIANNA WILL PROBABLY DIE UNLESS YOU CAN HELP HER. SHE NEEDS ECTOPLASM TO SAVE HER. THE VIAL SHOULD DO THE TRICK. OH, AND DON'T FREAK OUT, MICHAEL, BECAUSE I KNOW WHERE BLAZE IS KEEPING HAYLEY. IT'S NOT WHERE YOU THINK.

BY THE WAY, WILL THE TWO OF YOU STOP KEEPING SECRETS FROM EACH OTHER? WORK TOGETHER, FOR CRYING OUT LOUD.

INJECT THE VIAL'S CONTENTS INTO BRIANNA'S BLOOD AND WAIT A FEW HOURS.

ALL OF YOU, GET SOME REST.

Craig's signature closed at the bottom.

"Vial?" Michael said, taking the letter to look for himself. "What vial? And what's ectoplasm?"

"Well…."

Chapter 23

Craig searched for the best way to explain it to Michael, aware that Joseph was listening, and he was unwilling to tell just anyone about it. Although his double from this world trusted the doctor, he was unsure yet how much. The secret of ectoplasm could be dangerous in the wrong hands, and with Blaze on their heels, he didn't want to endanger Michael's friend, either. How could he describe it without harming himself or others? At last, he sucked in a breath and dived in to the story. "It depends on which side of the fence you sit. Someone in Joseph's field," he motioned towards the bespectacled man, "will see it as the outer portion of the continuous phase of a cell, sort of like a rigid gelly-welly layer underneath the cell's membrane."

Michael's face remained blank. They would have heard the crickets in the forest fall silent if only the outside world's sounds could penetrate the fallout shelter's walls. Not literally, but that was the effect upon Michael.

Joseph laughed. "Skids, we learned this in high school biology. It's part of a cell, the outer layer before the endoplasm."

"Yeah, thirty bloody years ago, Papa." Michael chuckled. "I barely remember physics."

Papa's eyes rolled as he shook his head. "That's because you thought it was 'Physiques', always staring outside at the girls walking past the classroom instead of listening and learning. But I believe Craig means the other ectoplasm, like the slime from Ghostbusters." He paused upon seeing the psychic nod but give him a surprised expression. "I do watch movies, you know."

Craig nodded, resisting the urge to ask if they really had the same movie in that universe. "Yes, only not green, it's a…" He retrieved the envelope from the coffin, which he had kept in his hip pocket, and unfolded it. He slid a glass vial from it into his other hand and held it on display.

Through the tube's sides, the others saw a teal-coloured phosphorescent fluid that sloshed inside. Light refracted through the viscous material to colour his fingers.

"That's ectoplasm?" Joseph reached for the vial and stopped. "May I?"

Craig allowed the doctor to take the bottle and examine it. "It comes from spirits and ghosts. I don't know what it does for them, but they can expel it like how we spit."

"Gross!" Michael stepped back, grimacing as he eyed the contents. "You want to inject ghost goobers and slobber into Brianna. Why?"

"Because it has healing powers," Craig answered, ignoring Joseph's sceptical snort. "I can vouch for it on many personal experiences." He paused and gazed down towards where Brianna and James lay in the hospital room. "It has saved my wife," he said at last. "Another ghost shot her with it, but it ended up saving her. Sometimes…." He stopped short of explaining the rest, how it only works on certain people. Ectoplasm and its properties were a secret to keep from the ilk of Colonel Blaze, and something told Craig not to tell Joseph everything yet. For his own sake. He eyed Michael. "You should know. I saw how quickly you healed before at the cemetery."

Michael's eyes widened in surprise, but no words came. He glanced at his friend, who was too interested in the vial's glowing contents to notice. Craig gave a slight raise of his eyebrow to Michael. They would talk about it later.

"I need to test the substance first," Joseph said, shaking his head. "I can't inject an unknown property into my patient."

Michael sniffed, and Craig spotted his glimpse down the hallway. They moved in tandem. Michael grabbed Joseph before he could stop Craig, who strode in Brianna's direction. Joseph struggled and implored the psychic not to do it, but it was useless. Michael had applied a joint lock that rendered him immobile long enough for Craig to hunt down a syringe, load it with the liquid, and administer the full contents from the vial into Brianna's arm.

Joseph broke free and rushed towards Craig and grabbed his wrist. "What the hell did you do?"

Craig shrugged. "You saw. I've saved her life."

Joseph's forehead puckered as he kneaded his face with a shaky hand. "I had to test it for toxicity."

"Trust me," Craig said and stared into Joseph's eyes. "She's going to be fine. Now, will you just… Sleep."

Joseph stilled, his eyes reflecting a stunned expression as his jaw dropped, and his head sagged forward. Craig caught him before he hit the floor and, supporting his weight on his shoulder, walked him to a bed in the sleeping area.

"Relax," Craig said. He delivered the rest of his post-hypnotic suggestions to Joseph after resting the doctor's head on a pillow. Once certain the doctor was asleep, he winked at Michael. "That should keep him out for a while."

Michael examined Brianna and noted the bruises on her limbs and face were fading. "She's healing." He turned back to Craig. "But is she going to be okay? Papa said she'd need an operation for her skull fracture."

Craig gave an affirmative smile. "Of course. I wouldn't give anything to hurt someone who is practically my wife in every way. She'll be fine."

Michael's face remained still, his eyes the only sign of the thoughts inside his head. At last, he shrugged. "Fair enough."

"Now," Craig said, his neck cracking as he stretched shoulder to shoulder. "There's the question about the secrets you and I are keeping from each other."

Michael checked his watch. "If you like, but aren't you tired? It's five minutes to eleven, just twenty-six hours since you arrived and dropped unconscious on my doorstep."

"We mightn't get the time when your friend awakes," Craig replied. "Come on. Let's have a cuppa and talk, shall we?"

Chapter 24

They sat in the entertainment area: Michael reclining on the sofa with the leather that murmured under his weight, and Craig in a matching armchair. With a steaming cup of Earl Grey beside him, Craig related his side of things.

He started with the bookshelf and the message he received, how he followed the psychic bread crumbs to the safe in his bedroom, and the Japanese puzzle box. Then he mentioned how he had been conversing with the other Craig, his vision self, who had guided him to visit the cemetery and even told him to dig.

Michael had listened in silence until this point, then interrupted. "Wait. Do you mean to tell me you're talking to your own ghost?"

Craig shook his head. "He's not my ghost. The Craig you once knew is… or was… actually my double." Michael opened his mouth to interrupt, but Craig stopped him. "No, he's not a clone, nor am I. I'm not from your world, it seems."

"Bull schick."

"What is this 'schick' you keep saying?" Craig asked, then shook his head, realising it could lead to a stupid answer. "It doesn't matter. The point is, I can't find the ghosts, as you said, but I saw some at the graveyard. The clones we —sorry, you—killed had ghosts, and my niece collected them." Michael's disbelieving look spoke volumes as he gave his head a slight shake and suppressed a grin. "Yes, I see your sceptical look, Michael. She's my dead niece and now works with the Grim Reaper by collecting souls and sending them where they go. She told me she can travel between worlds herself. I'm not supposed to, but somehow, I ended up here."

Michael stared at the ceiling from where he lay, silent as a stealthy mouse. "So you're Craig Ramsey, but not the one I know, and you're from another world?" Then he shook his head and snickered. "Jeez, I don't believe this."

"It's not so hard to believe," Craig said. "Quantum physicists have talked about the possibility for some time where I come from."

"That's the sort of thing I used to read in comics," Michael replied, shaking his head again. "Parallel worlds, multiplicity, universes where the Americans had won their fight for Independence."

Craig cocked an eyebrow. "But they did where I come from."

Michael reflected Craig's shocked expression. "Not here, they didn't. The British won over them. Of course, they became their own nation in time, just as Australia did, but they're still part of the Commonwealth."

Craig's jaw dropped. "What?"

Michael drained his second cup of green tea. "Yep. It sure helped us win quicker over the Japs when they tried to invade Australia in 1942."

"Really?"

Michael nodded. "It couldn't have happened any other way."

Although he knew different, Craig said nothing as he considered the differences between his world and this one. What other mismatches would he find? This could all take some work to accustom to the new world if he couldn't return. He shuddered at the idea. "I've told you my side,

Michael," he said. "Tell me about yours." He took a breath, and after a slight pause, he added, "Starting with the secret powers you possess."

Michael shrugged, his eye roving across the library of movies in the shelves near the television. "You know about my healing factor. There's not much more I can tell you."

"The shovels," Craig replied, pressing the point. "Fess up."

"Shovels?" Michael effected an innocent expression, his lips forming a firm line as he looked into a corner of the room, but Craig didn't buy it.

"And the androids at the cemetery. Don't play coy."

Michael stretched his arms. "I specialise in creating high-tech," he said, allowing a yawn to distort his words before he wiggled his jaw to suppress it, which Craig recognised as a fake. "There's no great power in that."

"Unless the shovel you pulled from the car's boot was once a pebble." Craig's eyes bore into Michael; his jaw set.

Michael turned his head away. "The real Craig Ramsey would know the answer to that, and it seems you've already picked up the differences." He faced Craig and allowed himself a sigh. "Okay, here it is. In a nutshell, I have a rare ability, which I nickname Polykinesis, that lets me change things into other things."

"How rare?"

"Just me," he replied, the corner of his mouth curling a tad. "Makes me feel kinda special."

Craig rested his chin on his hand and nodded, considering the ramifications. "That's a powerful ability. I bet it was fun when you first discovered it."

Something darker tinged Michael's chuckling reply.

"Yeah. I was just a kid, fifteen or sixteen years old when I accidentally turned a comic book into a school assignment."

Craig's jaw dropped. "Accidentally?"

"Too right. One moment, it was a crappy old comic about a character who could change lead to gold by touching it. I was supposed to be writing an English assignment on Tess of the d'Urbervilles, really riveting stuff—not, and it shimmered in front of me. Next thing I know, I'm reading the assignment in my own handwriting in blue ink. It was written perfectly, as though I'd pondered over it and planned it. Not one spelling mistake, and I used to make so many that my teacher demanded I invest in buying Liquid Paper to save crossing them out."

Craig leaned towards Michael. "How did you get it word-perfect?"

Michael pulled a face and lifted his hands palms-upwards. "No idea, really, but I think my subconscious does most of it. If I have an idea how something should be, how it works, then the result is better. But there was a drawback." He raised his empty cup, which shimmered like the hot air above a scorching bitumen road before Craig's widening eyes. A moment later, the cup had turned into an empty plate. "I can turn a toy into a fully working Lamborghini, but I can't make edible food. It's something about organic material, I guess."

"But what about the organic substances on the android doubles you created at the cemetery?"

Michael gave a dopey grin, his eyebrows raised in embarrassment when he shook his head. "I concentrated on a cyborg body, half-human and half-machine. I don't know what's going to happen if they examine the bodies.

If it worked, I hope Blaze's nice enough to tell me."

"How did you come to know Colonel Blaze?"

"That story's longer than War and Peace." Michael leaned back on the sofa and stared at the ceiling as he released another breath. "After I discovered my weird ability, I had heaps of fun with it. Being a poor lad, I couldn't afford to buy music, so I turned a lot of stones from the front path into cassettes. And later that evening, it occurred to me that this skill could get me into trouble. And what a drama that was. The Russians had discovered an anomaly from my abilities." He noticed Craig's eyebrows lift almost high enough to touch his hairline. "Not like that, mate. Apparently, my brain emits a special radiation. The Russians accidentally picked it up, realised they were delta waves, only stronger, and sent a KGB agent to track the source. The Americans caught wind of what the Ruskies were doing and tracked me too, and pretty soon, I was up to my eyeballs in it. The KGB wanted to bring me to Russia, and the American officer who found me figured I needed protection, but I didn't trust either side. Down the track, I learned they knew nothing about my power, only the energy emissions."

"Is that how you met Colonel Blaze?"

Michael's nostrils flared, and his temples pulsed in tandem with his clenched jaw. He shook his head. "Blaze found me and caught me by surprise. He spotted me at a kung fu tournament when I was twenty-two. I had won the championship against contestants from other styles, and he requested lessons from me. He wasn't a bad student, but the man's intense. I reckon he has Asperger's or OCD. For him, everything has its place. Anyway, after a while, he invited me to trial an experiment at the Army base. It turned out to be the psychic camp, like the MK ULTRA project they had in America during the–" He paused. "Have you heard of it?" When Craig nodded, he continued. "It started off tame. Guessing shapes from those Rhine cards. I did okay at that. My girlfriend Alison came with me, too, and did better. We could communicate with each other well by telepathy; Blaze said it was probably our personal connection. He loved it. Then we tried remote viewing. I was average at that." Michael stopped and stared into space for a moment. He swallowed. "Then the tests changed. They became rougher. Got me to try thought projection." He snorted, shaking his head as though recalling something. "They tried getting me to kill goats by staring at them. People would have come next."

"So you wanted to get out," Craig said, stopping Michael there, his voice brimming with understanding. He recognised a similar parallel in his personal experience.

Michael broke his staring at the blank television screen as though waking from a dream. "You've seen it before, haven't you? Even in whatever universe or planet or wherever you come from, there's another one like it, right?"

Craig nodded. "Project Gemini. Australia's answer to the USA's MK ULTRA."

Michael raised an eyebrow. "USA?"

Craig smacked his palm against his forehead. "I mean what you call America. Where I come from, it's the United States of America."

"Ah, okay." Michael nodded, his thoughts elsewhere a moment before he returned to the conversation. "I got out of it. Told Blaze that I wanted to concentrate on my martial arts, get married and have kids. He accepted it. Even came to the wedding. Then I never heard from him for years. I thought it was over." Michael paused, wiped his eye, missing a bit that glistened from his cheek in the overhead light. "Alison died a couple of years after Hayley was born. I nearly lost it. She was my high school sweetheart, you know."

Craig murmured an awkward apology and sat forward, wanting to place a comforting hand on Michael's foot, but stopped short and waited. Michael sniffed and wiped his eyes with the back of his hand.

"I imploded, Craig. Part of me wanted to die, to be with Alison in death, but I couldn't do that to my daughter. She was all I had... still is... and now Blaze has her." He lifted his face, and Craig shuddered internally at the dark, baleful glare from Michael's eyes. "And it's all my fault. I shouldn't have gone back to him."

Thoughts came to Craig of his own daughter and Brianna. He wondered if he would ever see them again or if he would be trapped in this world, so similar yet so alien. And he realised he was as good as a visitor from space here, too. He sat beside Michael, his arm resting across Michael's shoulders in as brotherly a gesture as he could manage. "Michael," he said, fighting back his own tears for his new friend's sake. "We're going to rescue your little girl."

Michael uncrossed his arms, took a deep breath, and exhaled in a faint whisper. "Never you worry about that. I'm not giving up on her."

"Hayley was the target this morning before the attack on the house, wasn't she?"

"Yeah." Michael lifted his face, a thoughtful expression

glimmering in his eyes. "She was."

Craig glanced at Michael. "Are you thinking what I'm thinking?"

"Duh." Michael clicked his fingers. "She's been the target the whole time, not you and not me. Blaze is tracking her."

"Why?"

Michael leaned to the side and reached deep into his pockets before retrieving an object, which he placed in Craig's hand. "Hayley's brain emits the same radiation as mine, maybe even more, and as she grows, it's likely to increase."

Craig examined the hairpin Michael had given him. A metallic clip with a pink heart on it. The pin looked like anything his own little girl might wear in her hair. Then his psychic vision came to play, and he realised. "It's a dampener to stop people picking up on the brain radiation that she inherited from you."

"You got it," Michael said. "I found it this morning just after Brianna and Hayley arrived home. She's supposed to wear it all the time to cloak her energy, but she'd left it at home when she visited Brianna's place."

"What cloaks your energy?" Craig asked, checking Michael's head and spotting nothing out of the ordinary.

Michael winked and pointed to his shoulder. "Implant. I made it myself, same as the hairpin, but I didn't want to put one in Hayley since she's so young." He sobered. "I didn't count on her pin falling out."

"But what about the other girls Brianna found in the van with Hayley?" Michael's eyes narrowed, and Craig continued. "They have been kidnapping other children too. Hayley's not the only one with the energy."

"Holy schick! You're right." Darkness and light showed

in Michael's expression as he contemplated the purpose. "Blaze is recruiting children as his psychic spies!"

Chapter 25

In the dream, Hayley's mother was alive, her lips curled and stretched to reveal shiny white teeth under eyes that sparkled with joy whenever she spoke to Hayley. They were sitting in a yard that looked like the one their new house had. But it was different. The extensive building in the back didn't look like the Japanese house in the Karate Kid movie that her father made her watch. It looked similar, but something told her it was different. The garden was greener, too. And there were others. Aunty Brianna sat beside another man she'd seen once but a long time ago; he was tall with long legs, a little thinner than her father, with brown spiky hair. Her daddy was there. But he looked different, brighter, but his muscles were just as big. Then there was the other little girl who looked straight at her, with brown hair tied back in a ponytail and eyes so blue they sparkled like sunlight in the ocean. She didn't know the girl, but she called Hayley's Aunty Brianna "Mum".

The little girl dropped from Aunty Brianna's lap and approached Hayley, who dared not move. "My name is Louise. What's your name?"

Hayley replied with her name. "Where am I?"

Aunty Brianna looked up from the table at which they sat. "Who are you talking to, Louise?"

Hayley's mum and dad glanced in her direction too, their faces full of curiosity. The tall man gazed at her, too. But Louise took no notice of them. She held out her hand. Hayley accepted the gift and was about to look at it when another woman appeared beside her. The lady's fiery tresses bounced in waves from her shoulders as she knelt beside Louise to gaze at Hayley with friendly eyes.

She spoke funny with Rs that bounced from her words like tiny growls. "Hello, there, wee one," she said to Hayley. "You're a long way from home, aren't you?"

Fascinated with the way the woman spoke, Hayley remained silent and watchful.

"Who is she talking to?" one grownup asked again.

"Whoever it is, Emily sees them too." Aunty Brianna said.

The lady with the funny words smiled at her. "It's time to wake up, Hayley. Your daddy is coming soon, but someone else needs you right now."

Then she heard it. Someone was crying. It sounded like a little girl, but it wasn't the girl called Louise, who was now waving bye to her. Everyone else seemed happy enough at the Christmas dinner.

Suddenly, the ground dropped from beneath her, knocking the breath from her chest, and the bright sunlight faded to black. Hayley woke in the hard bed. And the crying was louder.

In a heartbeat, Hayley knew this wasn't her bed or her room in which she sat. She wasn't alone either. Her eyes adjusted to the dark through which a dim nightlight glowed. By its faint light, Hayley spotted a lump in one corner of the room and stepped out of her bed to approach in her bare feet. There, in the gloom, she recognised this as another little girl about her age.

"It's okay." Hayley drew her roommate into a comforting hug and held her until the sobs disappeared. "My mummy died, too, but my daddy will come."

The other girl sniffled and wiped her nose with the back

of her hand. In the half-light, her skin looked a faint blue. "How do you know?"

"Emily said."

* * *

When Hayley woke next, it was to blinding white light from above. The girl, who had told Hayley her name was Beaulah, clung tight to her, pleading the woman in black to leave them alone. It didn't help. The lady in the dark soldier's clothing pulled the girls apart and took Hayley by the hand with a firm grip.

"Come on, Hayley," she said. "It's time for games."

By the way the woman urged her on, Hayley figured these weren't games like Hungry Turtles or the video games James played with her. The woman strode with long legs along the hallway so fast that Hayley had to run her little legs to keep up. She protested at the speed, and the lady slowed her steps, but the pace remained brisk.

Hayley opened her mouth to ask when Dad would arrive. Memory of the dream she had after Beaulah fell back to sleep stopped her from talking.

Don't tell the men your dad is coming. It's a surprise, the lady had told her.

Hayley loved surprises and didn't want to spoil it for these men, even if she didn't like them much. But could she tell the woman? Maybe not now. The lady was quiet, as though she didn't like kids either. Hayley shut her mouth.

A smile grew on her face as she thought of the surprise her daddy would give these wicked men who had hurt Aunty Brianna and James. After the ride in the lift and another walk down a hallway to a room full of other children sitting at tables, her grin was broad enough to hurt her cheeks.

"What are you smiling at?"

Hayley's train of thought derailed, its passengers vanishing to ether as she faced the lady soldier. She looked at the woman who was leaning close towards her the way her daddy did if he guessed she was hiding something from him. "Nothing." She pointed at the children in the room. "Look! Kids!"

The uniformed lady glanced at the room's other occupants and then at Hayley. "Yeah, lots of them to play with." Then the lady nudged Hayley forward with a firm hand on her shoulder. "Go on."

* * *

Over the rim of his teacup, Blaze watched from the hidden den through the one-way glass as the little girl entered the room. He placed the drink exactly in the spot where it normally sat on his desk, its handle at the precise three o'clock mark.

He suppressed a gasp. The way Hayley Mach flicked the hair from her face was the same as he remembered her mother, Alison Boldman, used to do it. And her eyes, so full of quiet intelligence, absorbed everything in the room.

She passed one little boy hunched over the table before him, staring hard at a spoon. No words played between them, yet he raised his head and gazed at the four-year-old. Another girl sitting opposite to the lad turned to watch Hayley, too.

The newbie, Blaze figured, suppressing a nod. Why not? She has all the best physical features between her parents. Something caught Blaze's eye. A pattern never seen before in fresh recruits was weaving itself in the laboratory. He stood from the desk, a knot twisting in his stomach, and stepped closer to the glass to observe.

One by one, each child watched Hayley. For anyone else, their interest was momentary, a fleeting glimpse before they resumed their psychic games. But the subtle differences piqued the colonel's notice as the children's gazes lasted longer. Oblivious to the attention received from boys and girls alike, the new girl followed the white-garbed scientist towards the isolation test chamber. When she reached the open doorway, she paused, rounded to face the youngsters, who were all returning her gaze, and nodded. Each went back to their seats or activities without a word, as though nothing had happened.

Blaze lifted a trembling hand to the glass, his eyes wide open as he processed the event he witnessed. He diverted his focus from Hayley, who pivoted and entered the test chamber.

* * *

An hour later, after Hayley had completed three tests, Blaze gazed at the little girl on the large screen before him. The leather murmured as he shifted on the seat.

Hayley Mach had proven herself proficient as a psychic, and so young. His eyes played over the printed data from the first test, which involved a guessing game with Zener decks: a collection of 25 cards comprising 5 sets of squares, circles, wavy lines, stars, and crosses. By running through four decks to make one hundred possibilities, the testers could measure the girl's ability to read minds, foretell the future, and maybe past events. She had passed with flying colours with ninety-five percent accuracy when an assistant, seated behind a screen, drew each card and attempted to transmit the shapes to her.

The second test used colours, letters, numbers, and pictures on a 100 card deck. No cards repeated themselves, and the girl did not know what each card's graphic could show, yet she scored high with ninety-seven percent accuracy. They classed the eight incorrect guesses as near misses, such as mistaking a clown wearing a conical hat for an upside down ice-cream cone. The negative attempts could have showed a lack of recognition of the graphics. They needed to investigate that possibility further.

The third test proved more amazing. It involved fifty identical boxes, one of which contained a random object picked by a computer. The person who placed the target object inside came nowhere near any other staff, therefore he couldn't communicate its contents to the woman who collected it, along with the other empty containers.

Hayley not only detected which box contained the mystery object, but she described its object with unerring accuracy. A double chocolate biscuit.

Now the little girl happily swung her legs like pendulums from the wooden chair as she bit into the treat.

Blaze suppressed a smile as he watched her on the screen. Only her parents had scored this high; Hayley's results beat theirs by three percent. With practice and training, that would improve further. Of course, he would have to play his cards right with this little one. What other traits had she inherited from her family?

Blaze leaned back, his eyes losing focus of the scene before him as he reminisced about Alison Boldman. The last he'd seen her was when he tempted her into visiting the other project base. He didn't think she'd agree to come. But they had been friends before the disagreement he had with Michael. If only it hadn't occurred the way it did. The poor girl. Why did she have to do that? She was not meant to have died.

Blaze blinked. What happened? His gaze locked on Hayley, who was staring in his direction through the one-way glass.

Slowly, she rose from the chair, then walked in a direct line towards the mirror, slapping it with both palms hard enough to rattle the heavy pane. For a hellish second, her eyes glowed, then dulled to their normal colour.

Blaze jumped back from the glass by instinct before he realised it. His hand touched his racing heart as he recomposed himself.

Then her voice, so filled with disgust and hate, too much for a child to hold, filtered through the transparent barrier.

"I know who you are. You killed my mummy."

And Blaze's blood chilled his chest.

Chapter 26

The first thing Craig heard was the groaning from the bunk opposite him. His eyelids snapped open as he sat up in a flash, banging his head on the bed above him before he realised he wasn't in his own bedroom. A second later, he landed back on his pillow, stars dancing in his vision.

The groan came to his ears again, and Craig turned to see Joseph stirring. The doctor wiped his tired eyes, then squeezed the bridge of his nose. He squinted at his wristwatch and stopped. With a puzzled expression, he angled his head to regard Craig. "What happened?"

"Good morning, Joseph." Craig rolled out of the bunk, blinking away the pain in his forehead. "These bunks are more comfortable than they look, aren't they?"

Eyes scrunched, Joseph patted the bedspread until he found his glasses on the small bedside table. "The woman!" He sat up, avoiding the same head-banging accident Craig had suffered, and scrambled towards the treatment room.

With a grin, Craig bounced out of bed and followed the doctor. He chuckled. "See? She's still there."

Joseph held Brianna's wrist, checked her pulse against his watch, then leaned close to study her sleeping face. A surprised gasp escaped from his mouth as he swung about to confront Craig, his jaw gaping and eyes blinking. "Where did her bruises go?"

"Out the door, I presume?" Craig fought to suppress his amusement as Joseph returned to examine his patient.

After checking Brianna's vitals with a stethoscope and

other equipment, the doctor turned his attention to Craig. His eyes flickered to Michael, who had just arrived in the room, then back to the psychic investigator. "The blue liquid you showed me last night. Ectoplasm. What is in it?"

Craig offered a wink and waggled a finger. "Nuh, spoilers, Joe." He nodded towards Brianna, who was still asleep on the bed. "What's her current condition?"

Joseph glanced back at the motionless detective's body. "I don't understand how, but from what I can tell, the lady has almost fully recovered. I'm just unsure for how long she'll remain unconscious." He shook his head, sighed, then pinched the bridge of his nose, and blinked in puzzlement. "Even her skull fracture has shrunk to being a minor bump on the scalp."

Michael released a relieved sigh and approached Brianna's inert form. He stroked her forehead and leaned in and delivered a brotherly kiss. "Thanks, Joseph." Then he whispered something to his adoptive sister that the others couldn't hear. A moment later, he stood. "Joe, when will she wake?"

Joseph shook his head. "I don't know," he turned towards Craig, curiosity caked like bad makeup on his face. "If the current results mean anything, it could be sooner than I expected."

While the doctor continued conversation with Michael, Brianna's only next-of-kin in his mind, Craig placed a gentle hand upon his wife's doppelgänger. A smile crossed his lips. He may not have studied medical science, but Craig knew enough from the touch to say, "Brianna will be fine." He checked his watch, closed his eyes, looked again. "2:10am tomorrow morning." Then he chuckled. "She hates waking early on Sundays, too."

Joseph looked in disbelief at Craig. "2:10am, you say? How can you be so sure?"

"2:09am, to be precise." Craig gave Michael a wink. "I rounded it. The bruising around the skull fracture will disappear in," he counted on his fingers, "fifty-five seconds. It's just her mind that needs healing and rest. She'll be 100% when she wakes."

Craig stepped aside as Joseph returned to Brianna's side and checked her head at the fracture's site.

The doctor glanced at his watch and gasped. "The bump's gone. Incredible!" He spun to face Craig. "What is in that fluid?"

Craig shrugged. "Vitamins, a spot of protein—maybe— and amino acids?" He flashed a cheeky grin and winked.

Joseph sputtered and gesticulated. "Do you understand the importance of that substance?" He glanced at Michael, who couldn't help smiling at his schoolfriend's frustration, then glowered back at Craig. "This… ectoplasm could revolutionise medicine. Think about it, man. AIDS, broken bodies, victims with motor neurone disease, acquired brain injuries. These could potentially be cured by that blue liquid." His eyes searched the room. "Where's the bottle you had it in?"

Craig hid a smirk as he shook his head with the most innocent expression he could muster. "It's gone."

Joseph would hear nothing of it. "I need it. Just a tiny drop is enough to…" Then his pupils dilated for a second, his voice trailing.

"Forget the liquid." Craig leaned in close to Joseph, whose eyes had set in a blank stare as the psychic continued his hypnotic suggestion. "You gave her vitamin shots. Brianna's a fast healer."

Joseph remained standing, his head hanging towards his chest. "Yes, of course. Vitamins are more amazing than most doctors give them credit, you know."

Amusement glinted in Michael's eye as he checked Joseph was okay. "Craig," he said, "can I make a suggestion?"

Craig smirked. "You want him to cluck like a chicken?"

Michael thought for a moment, a grin crossing his face at the idea, then he shook his head with a chuckle. "No, seriously, stop hypnotising my friend, will you?"

Craig waved a dismissive hand. "Oh. Joe's going to be fine." He approached the bed where James still lay and placed his palm on the sleeping boy's arm. "So will he."

Michael fluttered his fingers in front of Joseph's eyes, which remained still and unblinking., and an amused curl formed on his lips. "How long is he going to stand here?"

Craig shrugged with a conspiratorial grin. "I haven't decided. Listen, Michael, I like Joe. He reminds me of someone I know on my world, but I can't have him asking questions about the ectoplasm. If the wrong people get it, it can—"

Michael held up his hands. "Chill the beans. It's okay. We both have secrets we keep from Joseph." He cocked his head. "Will he remember everything we're saying now?"

Craig leaned closer to Joseph's ear. "Wait for exactly five minutes before you wake. When you wake, you will forget about the blue liquid and think nothing of Brianna's quick recovery. Nod if you understand." He winked at Michael when Joseph nodded and signalled for him to follow.

Craig led the way as they released the trapdoor's lock and climbed up the stairs into the house above and out the front door. Outside, the early summer morning was a comfortable temperature, thanks to the shade provided by the surrounding eucalyptus trees and their thick foliage. Two pine rocking chairs swung gently in the breeze, their rockers talking against the wooden floorboards.

"What I've always wanted, a home among the gum trees," Michael quipped, checking the seats, before plonking himself into one. "In me old rocking chair. Want a seat, grandpa?"

Craig snorted good-humouredly at the song reference, shook his head and sat on the verandah's railing, his back against the post. He tossed something to Michael, who caught it in a neat motion and gave him a questioning look. "It's James' mobile phone. I thought you might like to give it a quick charge. You'll be interested in the result."

Michael regarded the phone, shrugged, and closed his eyes for a second before pressing the power button. The device chirruped, booted to life. "There," he said, and winked at Craig's surprise. "Charged. What am I looking for?"

A familiar voice replied, "Skids! You're alive."

Michael's mouth opened in bewilderment before turning into a grin. "Sparks!"

"In the chips, mate," the electronic consciousness buzzed. "Hey, what happened to Brianna and James?"

Michael gave a summarised explanation of the recent events and how they had found James and Brianna. For a moment later, his cyber-friend remained silent. "Are you still there, Sparks?"

Sparks' voice replied from Michael's watch. "Just moved location, Skids. You wouldn't believe half of what I discovered while I was inside James' phone."

Message notifications chirruped on the mobile phone,

filling the screen with previews of the contents. Michael glanced at them but didn't open the device. "What? This is my adopted son's privacy we're talking about here."

"The message you're seeing now came from Amy. You know her, right?"

Michael shrugged. "Yeah, I teased James about her having a crush on him. He doesn't believe me."

"Check your watch," Sparks answered. "That way you can always blame me for invading James' privacy."

Michael checked the screen. "This is Cooee 360, Sparks. I don't have time for this schick."

Not a fan of social media either, not even blogs, and what he felt was a corporation bent on manipulating public perception, Craig snorted to himself as he listened to the exchange between cyber-consciousness and man.

"This is James' Cooee 360 account, but I've hacked it, so now you can see behind Amy's profile's privacy settings. Check this photo."

Craig moved around to view what Michael saw on the screen as the latter's jaw dropped.

"That man's Joseph."

"Yep," Sparks answered. "That's Papa alright. A lot older than I remember from thirty-odd years ago. He's Amy's father."

"I didn't even know he married," Michael answered. "We haven't had much of a catch-up yet." He mocked a cranky look at Craig, then winked. "Who knows when or how that'll go. Craig has hypnotised him twice since we arrived." He shook his head as he scanned the screen's contents. "How is this important?"

"While we were all trapped in the tunnel under the house," Sparks replied, "I tried to get help. I knew I couldn't contact you, not just because of the poor coverage, but I figured Blaze was watching anything you were doing."

"But you have encrypted our phones," Michael answered. "There's no way he could do that."

"It's a precaution," Sparks said. "I sent a text from James' account to Amy, asking for her father's help. I played it safer by following the message to Amy's phone because James' battery was about to die."

"And?"

"Check this out."

The screen on Michael's watch flicked through Amy's Cooee 360 profile page until it reached another photo. Michael squinted to peer at the image on the tiny display, then he gaped, eyes widening again as he looked at Craig. "It's Colonel Blaze!"

Craig couldn't contain himself and took a closer look. "What?"

"Blaze is Amy's uncle," Sparks answered.

"Bull. Schick." Michael shut his eyes and leaned back in the rocker, pressing his lips together until they turned white. "Why didn't we know sooner? He's been on to us longer than we knew."

Craig stepped away towards the verandah railing, thrusting his palms against it and leaning forward, rocking on his hands before facing Michael again. "We have to move fast."

* * *

James woke with a start and looked about him. He glanced from side to side, taking in the unfamiliar surroundings. Where am I? He struggled to lift his hand and stopped upon discovering the cast on his arm which sat in a sling. Shocked, he tried to sit up and allowed the room's spinning to slow before attempting to move again. He spotted Brianna across the room, sleeping.

"Brianna!" He stumbled to her, leaning on whatever furniture he could to check her. But his aunt was dozing, and something told him it wasn't a normal slumber. She needed the rest. The teen spun, a little too fast, and almost jumped out of his skin upon seeing Joseph, Amy's father, standing behind him.

The man had his glasses in one hand while the other rubbed his temples. "James," Joseph said, a hair's breadth from dropping the lad as he stumbled. "It's okay. You're safe. How are you feeling?"

James motioned towards his arm in a sling. "It's broken."

The man nodded, a kind expression on his face. "It is, but it's a clean break. I've set it for you, and you'll need rest." He took James by his good arm and guided him back to the bed. "Come on. I'll get you something to eat."

James assented and lay back on the bed. "Is this a hospital?"

Joseph shrugged. "Sort of."

"It's not like any I've seen before, Mr Maloney," James said, noticing the room's compactness and its strange walls and curved ceiling. "How did I get here?"

"Amy received your message and told me. I came as quick as I could. But…" A puzzled look appeared on Joseph Maloney's face as the words left his lips. To James, it looked as though something else had happened, too. Whatever the man was about to say, he changed his mind. "You must be hungry. Perhaps you'd prefer to eat upstairs in the fresh air?"

James raised a quizzical eyebrow. "Upstairs?"

"Yes." Dr Maloney headed down a passageway past several beds towards something that looked like a kitchen at the end.

James craned his neck to get a better look and stood again to follow. "Where are we?"

"We can talk about that later, James. Head upstairs, if you like. There's someone wanting to see you." Joseph urged him with a nod. "Go on. I'll bring some breakfast."

Someone to see me?

An image of Tamsin appeared in his mind, standing next to Amy, who had brought his crush with her. A dream, he knew, but it might happen. Men's injuries always seemed to conjure sympathetic feelings from the fairer sex to make them realise what a great guy sat under their nose. At least, that's what the movies made him think.

His heart skipping, James ascended the stairs to discover what resembled a small home office with a computer that displayed a picture of some hot vintage babe from ancient days——the 1990s. At first glance, she was adorable to him. Except her jaw. That was too wide for him.

Then a familiar voice reached his ears. His lips whispered the word in disbelief. "Dad?"

James' face sagged as the image of a loving Tamsin fled his imagination, but only for a second as he realised he'd missed his father too. He hurried the best he could; the voices grew more distinct as he followed their words. Then something caught his attention, warning him. He stopped. Listened.

His father's words froze him in place. "It's Colonel Blaze!"

James slowed, standing just inside the door where he could hear the conversation without alerting them of his presence.

The new guy's voice: "What?"

Then Sparks' voice: "Blaze is Amy's uncle."

James smiled to hear Sparks' voice. He had been worried about Sparks, but to hear the name of Blaze, his father's enemy, and his connection to Amy made him freeze.

"Bull. Schick," James' father said, his voice a mixture of worry and anger that James recognised and felt. "Why didn't we know sooner? He's been on to us longer than we knew."

The voice of the other man, who James suspected was Craig Ramsey, a fact he couldn't be sure about since the man had died a year ago, reached his ears. But the words didn't penetrate the feelings coming over him. A spidery sensation crawled over James' skin, skiing a fiery trail of guilt that spread flames of shame across his chest and stomach as he considered what he had heard.

Amy, his best friend, had betrayed him?

Chapter 27

"So, the question is, what have we got to help us rescue Hayley?" Craig held up his fingers as he counted: Brianna, who lay comatose, and would remain so until 2:09am; Sparks, for electronic surveillance; Michael, for his polykinetic abilities, which he still wanted to keep a secret from others, including Joseph; and Craig. "What about James?"

Michael frowned at the mention of his adopted son's name. "James? He's injured, broken arm, and just a kid. Younger than when I first encountered the Russians and Americans." He pondered it, then shook his head. "No way. I don't want him hurt more."

"You know James might surprise you." Craig stretched his shoulder, pinning his arm against his chest with the other, then repeating in the opposite direction. "Anyway, he's not coming to the base with us." His neck cracked into place with a slight jerk.

Michael leaned back, his arms crossed and foot tapping on the floor for a moment, before shaking his head. "Nope." He unfolded his limbs and stretched some more. "I can't involve him."

Craig remained silent, thoughtful, as he watched from his perch on the railing and reflected upon the past day and two nights. "We're just going in for a snatch-and-grab to rescue Hayley, right?"

Elbows on knees, Michael leaned forward to rest his face in his hands, his fingers tangling in his black hair. "Craig, I know you're trying to help, but you have to understand.

When Alison died, I found myself a single dad. I promised to keep her safe. Then just before I met your namesake, I had rescued James from the same place."

"Yeah. But the kid has no psychic powers. They were trying to do something else with him."

Michael shrugged. "They had him in a cell there. They'd shaved his scalp as bald as a baby's bum. My guess is they were going to operate, but to do what, I don't know. He remembers nothing more than faces and needles, but he knows I adopted him. All I want is for him to be happy with Hayley and me, but Blaze is like a pit-bull terrier and won't let go. No way." He looked up, the whites of his eyes tinged red. "That bastard will follow us to the ends of the earth." He pulled back when the psychic leaned forward to lay a comforting hand on him. He sniffed, wiped away a stray tear. "Yeah, let's do it."

Craig rubbed his hands together. "Is the base still twenty kilometres out of Statton along the Cunningham Highway?" When Michael raised a disbelieving eyebrow at him, he said, "This isn't my world, remember? I'd like to get a handle on the place."

Michael pressed a button on his watch. A holographic map image opened in the space between them as he marked its position. A smile appeared on Craig's lips, relieved to learn the army base looked the same in the satellite vision as that of his world. It made it easier as Michael highlighted the base's weak spots and points of entry. Their basic plan involved masquerading as uniformed soldiers to enter. Once inside, they would locate the entrance to the warehouse that covered the secret lift leading underground to what they recognised as the torture labs.

Approaching footsteps from indoors reached their ears. Both men fell silent and looked towards the doorway from which Joseph emerged, carrying two breakfast plates, each stacked with juicy bacon, English sausages, tomatoes and baked beans.

Saliva welled in Craig's mouth as the aroma teased his nostrils, and a wave of guilt for his merciless hypnotising of the poor man washed over him as he accepted the plate of food. "Joseph!" he said. "You didn't have to go to the effort."

Michael thanked Joseph and inhaled the delicious smells. "Papa," he said, slipping a piece of the crispy bacon in his mouth, "you'll make a good wife for someone someday." He winked as he crunched the meat.

Joseph chuckled and shook his head. He glanced past Sally Green's car in the driveway and then toward the side, his eyes searching. "James is awake. He's eating downstairs." He rubbed his neck, winced, and mumbled something about not sleeping right.

Plate in hand, Michael excused himself from the verandah and headed inside to see James. Another pang filled Craig as he thought about his own family.

He missed Brianna, his Brianna, his wife, the woman who entered his life through unexpected events: the death of Debra. Brianna was an investigating police detective on the case when his adopted niece had died in an accident deemed unexplainable in everyday terms because of the bizarre circumstances. Craig had visited Brianna's office in search of clues that he could use in his own quest, and their personalities clashed. The sceptic and the psychic. Somehow, they became friends in their hunt for Debra's killer, then soon they were lovers. He couldn't explain how effortlessly the relationship developed and flowed. Never before had that happened; not even with his first wife. And when he and Brianna made love, the experience was unlike anything he had encountered with the tiny list of women he had known before. For one, furniture moved and floated. He had never heard of that happening before, especially the bed and other loose objects during the act. Then along came Louise, his little button of a daughter, who carried so many of her mother's traits.

Yes, he missed his family after only two days. What made it harder was seeing this world's Brianna, a dead ringer for his spouse, who didn't see him the same way. To watch her injured and unconscious downstairs had left an odd sensation in him. The emotional spark from her resemblance to his wife frightened him while the logical side of him fought to remind him: she's not yours, Craig.

Craig's thoughts returned to his own family. What if circumstances prevented his return to his loved ones? While marooned in a universe not his own, would he remain alone forever? If this universe's Brianna eventually drew to him as his own had, would it be cheating? He would have asked Emily, his spirit guide, but she was in his world, and all the ghosts on this planet had gone missing. Another puzzle to consider while he was here.

He choked back the concern, wiped a tear, and pushed aside the worries in time before Michael stepped outside to join him.

Michael cleared his throat, distracting him from his misery. He blinked and gave a nod. "How's James doing?"

"Groggy." Michael plonked himself into the rocking chair. "He'll be fine once his arm heals." To the psychic investigator, Michael looked like he was about to say more, but changed his mind.

Craig controlled his expression, allowing empathy for James' situation to show without betraying the other concern that rang alarm bells inside his head. There was something in the way that Michael's gaze flickered when he mentioned James' state. "What is it?"

Michael looked up from his plate, which Craig noticed held more food than before, a second helping, and shrugged. "The kid looks like something's stuck in his head, haunting him."

Craig nodded. "Don't forget he's been in a war-zone, Mick. Both kids were there when Blaze's men attacked and blew up the house. That's something I'd have trouble with now, let alone as a teenager."

"Maybe." Michael resumed his second helping of breakfast, ignoring Craig's watchful gaze as he chewed on the bacon.

He's thinking about how he coped with the KGB when he was a kid, but doesn't think James is as resilient. Craig considered voicing his concern, then changed his mind. Perhaps later.

"I know what you're thinking," Michael added, giving a wink. "Don't worry. I'll watch him."

"Mm-hmm." Craig allowed his head to move in agreement. But his gut said something else.

* * *

Ever since the four-year-old Hayley had stated her feelings to him, with an eloquence beyond her age, Colonel Blaze decided it was best to keep tabs through other means. So he watched from the comparative safety of a flat screen monitor.

But even through the cold, unblinking eye of the camera,

Blaze's nerves prickled whenever the little girl glanced in its direction. During a game, which involved guessing the face-down shapes, Hayley glanced above her handler's head and into the glass lens. Blaze could have sworn she winked, just a subtle one at him. As soon as he realised, he blinked and squinted closer at the screen. But it was too late. The little girl had refocused her attention on the cards. The colonel switched to another angle. This time, Hayley looked backward over her shoulder and straight at him with a cheeky grin.

Blaze was now on the fifth camera viewpoint, picked randomly from the nine available. There was no way she could guess he was back at the first angle. A smirk crossed his face as he considered his cleverness and watched intently. The microphone by their desk picked up every word.

"What shape is this one, Hayley," said the handler.

The little girl wiped a strand of hair from her face. "A star."

"Very good," the female officer replied, turning the card to reveal a matching yellow symbol. The young girl allowed a smile to cross her lips, but it didn't hide the bored expression in her eyes. The handler shuffled the cards and picked another at random, this time underneath the table so the child subject couldn't spot any flashed symbols or markings. "And now?"

Hayley didn't even think. "Flower. A rose."

The woman turned over the card, which she had not seen herself until that moment, and gasped. "Wow! You got it! How did you do that?" She continued to gush at Hayley, who merely shrugged.

Then, slowly, she lifted her face towards the camera

through which Blaze watched. "I know a rhyme about roses."

"Really?" The handler humoured her. "What is it?"

"Ring a ring a rosie, a pocketful of posies, I'll get you, then hurt you, and you'll all fall down."

Tea erupted from Blaze's mouth in a violent spit as he heard the words, his cup smashing on the floor. His fingers shook like a leaf as he picked up the broken pieces. Through the monitor's speakers, the handler's surprised voice came. "That's a terrible rhyme. Why would you say such a thing?"

"I won't get you, Stacy," Hayley replied, angelic now, minus the coarseness her voice had held a moment ago. "You play fun games with me."

The handler paused, regained her composure, unaware that her superior officer was experiencing his own issues in his own office fifty metres away. "Okay, then. Let's play some more."

"Okay."

Blaze switched off the live feed. He had heard and seen enough for now. Too much. And little Hayley Mach's words echoed through the tightly ordered compartments of his mind.

Fingers still shaking, he clutched at reason. This had to be a coincidence, some trick the mind played after working on this project for so long. Kids come up with all kinds of rhymes that shock adults. What was the one his classmates used to tell when he was in fifth grade?

On top of Old Smokey, all covered in blood. I shot the teacher with a 44 slug. I went to the funeral the very next day. People threw flowers, but I threw grenades. The teacher went up, the teacher went down, and the teacher went "squish" all over the ground.

He remembered smiling to himself at the rhyme, although he never dared tell his parents because his father used to be the hardest headmaster in his little town's only school. The old principal, a man whose father had emigrated from Germany to Australia, was a hard man with an iron hand. He would never have accepted it.

Blaze pushed the memory back into its little box in the dark room of his head and shut and locked its door. The key, he shoved deep into his mental pocket under the other keys to the other doors of his mind. Lost.

Then he cleaned the spilt tea from the floor and the desk, wiped it from the monitor, before checking the video feed from all cameras at the same time.

He had to know. Had to reassure himself.

And as he stared at the tracks simultaneously, the realisation crept over him and fought hard at the locked door in his tortured mind. It was no coincidence. The little girl hadn't just been checking each camera and looking at them. The only cameras she had stared at were the ones through which he watched... at the same time that he had. She knew! He couldn't deny it. And her voice carried more authority than he imagined possible from a child. Could it be-?

He yelped in surprise at the sound of the knock on the door. Strict self-discipline and conditioning barely helped him regain control before Major Oates entered the room with a concerned look on his face.

"Sir?"

Colonel Blaze's heart hammered in his chest, but he willed it to a slower pace as he looked up at the new arrival. "Major Oates." His eyes flicked towards the binder in his visitor's hand. "You have news, I gather."

Oates reached forward to hand Blaze the folder, then stepped back and took in the surrounding scene. On the outside, Blaze remained aloof to his subordinate's behaviour and said nothing. To say something would betray his fearful thoughts to Oates; a superior officer should never reveal weakness.

The major cleared his throat. "We set the plans according to our previous conversation, sir."

Blaze looked up from the folder of results for Hayley Mach and another child. "Conversation?" His brow crinkled for a second. Oh, yes! He'd been so preoccupied with Hayley's actions that everything else had slipped his mind. A smile curved. Perhaps he could turn things around. "Of course. Yes, very good. Thank you, Oates."

The major hesitated a moment. "Is all well, sir?"

"Yes. I was just thinking about our results here for young Hayley. Excellent. And this other subject intrigues me too." He paused, glanced at his watch. "But I must go. I have a family commitment to keep. I mustn't be late." Standing, he smoothed down his jacket and started towards the door with Major Oates. "Oh, one more thing. Keep me informed of any developments while I'm away, won't you?"

* * *

The summer sun set after 6pm, its parting rays spraying the clouds and sky with an assortment of pinks, oranges, and reds—a painting to inspire Van Gogh's envy. But Craig and Michael were too busy downstairs, tucking into their butter chicken dinner, to notice.

In two hours, when darkness would fall, they would take off on their journey to rescue Hayley. All their preparations were as complete as they could be. Weapons and equipment installed and packed in their lightweight camouflage suits—all created by Michael.

Craig stretched back in his chair, his stomach full. "Are you sure you don't want to wait for Brianna to wake?"

Michael finished polishing the dregs of his second helping with a piece of naan bread. "I'd rather not."

"But she'll be fully fit and alert." Craig glanced down the shelter's hallway to where Brianna was still sleeping. "And she has skills we might find useful."

"Do you mean her techniques as a sniper?" Michael suppressed a burp in his fist, and patted his stomach. "Damn, that was a good meal."

He stood from the table and removed his shirt to change into the uniform he had created earlier. A figure-hugging uniform with an intricate pattern of green, black, and grey, with pockets sewn in strategic places to hold tools and weapons.

Craig picked up his own suit, idly fingering its strange fibrous mesh. "I meant her skills in Krav Maga, too. We could use the backup, don't you reckon?"

"I agree. She's a fantastic fighter, but we need someone here to watch after James."

"To babysit, you mean." Craig indicated with a glance upstairs where they could hear Joseph pottering around in his study. "What about your schoolfriend?"

Michael gave Craig an incredulous glance, then refocused his attention on his gadgets as he distributed them in the different pockets of his uniform. "Joseph is hardly fighting material. We're not taking him along."

Craig chuckled, recognising Michael's attempt at humour to distract him. "That's not what I meant, and you know it."

Michael raised an eyebrow, a mannerism Craig now recognised as his friend's mimicking of Roger Moore's characterisation of James Bond in the films—his boyhood idol. "It's not?"

Craig took a long, slow breath, then shook his head. "Whatever. I think you're doing yourself an injustice, that's all."

Michael gave a quick shrug, patted himself down to ensure he had everything. "You'd better get changed now too," he said, heading to the stairs. "I'm going to check on James before we go."

As his friend clambered upstairs to the house above, Craig picked up his uniform. While dressing, he heard Michael's voice calling for the teenager, but no reply came. Then Joseph's words in his calm yet surprised tone, followed by Michael's, angry this time. Soon the sounds of hurrying footsteps passed the study towards the front door. Michael swore with the usual "schick" that Craig had become used to. A moment later, he was back downstairs, an exasperated expression on his face.

"Is James down here?"

Craig looked down the hallway towards the hospital room and hurried down there, but saw only Brianna's sleeping form. "James," he said. "Are you there?" No reply.

"Shick and gimcrackery!" Michael stormed, pacing back and forth, his fingers tangling in his hair. "Where the hell has that kid gone? Craig, can you check for clues, please?"

Craig looked around the fallout shelter, his eyes searching for a starting point, and gave a nod. The stairs. He laid a hand upon one of them. A few random visions flashed past his consciousness—Joseph bringing supplies into the shelter; the doctor and a larger version of himself, his brother, struggling to take a hospital bed down the stairs— then he saw it. James ascending the steps.

Craig pointed at the step which had provided him with the psychic vision. "He heard us, every word."

A puzzled eyebrow rose on Michael's face as he pondered Craig's words, then his mouth gaped. "Everything? Do you mean?–"

"Yep, the lot. We were talking about Amy's relationship with Colonel Blaze."

"Where?" Michael lifted his watch to talk into it. "Sparks, track James' phone and tell me how far away he is now."

A moment later, Sparks responded. "His phone is in your pocket, Skids."

"Schick! Not good, not good." Michael acknowledged Craig's questioning look. "I rescued James from Project Gemini a few years ago. He was an orphan, and he hates Colonel Blaze, even if that is all he remembers."

Craig sighed, bobbing his head with understanding. "I see. Hormones and over-reaction go hand in hand." For a moment, he pondered the possibilities before an idea came. "Mick, relax. I'll find him."

Michael crossed his arms. "What about the mission?"

"We've got an hour and a half. We'll be back in time." Craig took the stairs a few steps at a time, remembering to duck his head at the top, and was almost out the front door when he stopped. For a moment, he considered using Michael's favourite swear word, and turned to find Michael just behind him. "He's taken Sally's car."

"Schick, schick, and... crap." Michael barged past Craig to look around outside, as if expecting to see the Skyline elsewhere. "How the hell did he do that with a broken arm?"

"I said he'd surprise you." Craig placed his hand on the ground near where they had earlier parked Sally's car. "You've taught him to drive in the Jag, and it didn't take him much to figure how to operate her automatic. Shame I don't have the Jaguar now, since it blew up."

"That's it." Michael clicked his fingers. "The Jag! I'll get you your Jag, and you go after James. I'm going for Blaze myself."

Chapter 28

Pelting rain lashed hard against the ground and trees, turning hardened dirt to slushy puddles that gusted into rivers that soaked through almost everything. With a hand raised to protect his face from the stinging drops, Michael leaned against the gale that threatened to blast him along the bitumen road and away from his target. He had left his motorbike on the other side, hidden behind a billboard advertising something that passing motorists would be lucky to read in the weather's chaos.

Another powerful wave of wind and water slammed into him, almost knocking him over. He staggered, pressed his shoulder into the airborne water that stabbed the skin on the back of his hands and chilled his bones, fuelled by the dream of seeing his daughter again. Nothing would stop him.

As Michael pushed onwards, he remembered the pledge made over his wife Alison's grave. He would protect Hayley with his life and keep her safe from Blaze.

But he hadn't, had he? No. He shouldn't have allowed Craig's arrival to distract him, chased him on a fool's journey and left his daughter unprotected. He trusted that Brianna's capabilities could have helped the mission, but her injuries from the previous morning took her out of that game, not to mention those from the explosion that had ripped apart the house.

Now, Blaze had his daughter, and Michael couldn't afford to allow Craig, Brianna, or even James to be hurt while he regained his honour as a father.

Somehow, the anger inside Michael towards his nemesis steeled him, fired his focus and determination until the storm affected him less, so he soldiered through its wailing winds.

Michael almost didn't realise it until too late. For a hellish second, a sense of weightlessness swept across him and his feet lifted from the ground until he was on his toes. Then the backwash of the semitrailer shifted. Michael flailed to stay upright, to fight the turbulence as the truck passed him, the blast from its horn rocketing through his body in a wave that set off his adrenaline. Still off-balance, he willed himself forward, challenging his endurance to overcome the deadly breeze, until he reached the other side at last.

An amused "huh" escaped as he turned his head and watched the juggernaut continue its journey, its taillights blinking like a demon's eyes as it disappeared into the maelstrom.

"Hayley won't rescue herself." Michael leapt across the drainage ditch beside the road, the storm waters already filling it to capacity and rushing along its canal, his foot almost slipping on the other side. Three feet later, he reached another mini forest, eucalyptus trees and vegetation that he knew formed a visual barrier between the highway and the base.

Something above him cracked, the mighty ripping noise loud enough to hear above the fierce storm. Michael didn't look. He dashed towards the thick-trunked ghost gum tree and dodged behind it in time to hear the large branches crash to the ground. A chilling wind wound through the trees when he glanced at the carnage, but the battery-powered automatic heating coil inside his suit shielded him from the worst. Yet a shiver tickled up his spine at what could have been.

Michael changed his pace as he weaved his way between the remaining trees until he reached the edge, then crouched behind a trunk to survey his target. There stood the base beyond many protective barriers. Rain still belted the ground, bouncing from its airstrip's bitumen and the hangars nearby, scattering into a fine mist that further reduced its visibility.

He grabbed a pebble, closed his eyes and concentrated, turning it into a pair of goggles, and put them on. The lenses afforded him a new vision and allowed him to tune out the rain as he crawled on his belly towards the chain-link fence that outlined the base's perimeter.

From an earlier examination via a satellite feed hacked by Sparks to view more of the base than Google Earth allowed, Michael knew the boundary would be a piece of piss to pass. Crowned by coils of barbed wire, the top curved outward to stop people climbing over from the outside. All he had to do was snip some links and bend back the strands to crawl through the hole. The military hadn't installed them with vibration sensors in case an animal—a kangaroo or a wild pig, for example—brushed against it. For the same reason, the military hadn't electrified it, either. Two minutes later, he had created an opening with his snips and crawled inside the base.

Then he stopped.

His reconnaissance hadn't revealed the next security layer. He'd learned it on his last visit over a year ago when Craig Ramsey had rescued him. To all appearances, it was an unfinished fence with its poles thrust into the ground, but no chain mesh joining them. An unsuspecting intruder would walk right between them, unaware of the trap they presented. Just as Craig Ramsey did years back.

There were two lines of poles that could have created two fences. Each line's poles stood equidistant. But what Michael's goggles revealed were crisscrossing paths of microwave beams between them. Anything bigger than a magpie that crossed them would set up an alarm.

Michael scratched his chin as he assessed the situation. He couldn't go through without alerting the guards. Any attempt to disrupt the beams could trigger another alarm, too. Digging underneath them wasn't practical. Maybe over them?

He pressed a pocket on his thigh, pushing out a smooth pebble from its safety, and concentrated on what he needed. It became a metal cylinder, three inches long, which he squeezed until it popped out to form a long pole suitable for vaulting. He spent a moment to ponder the next step. Running straight at the invisible fence wouldn't work because the pole could fall through the microwave beams and activate the alarms. But perhaps he could run along it and vault? He took a few deep breaths in preparation.

"Stop right there!"

Michael halted as Sparks' voice screamed through the earbud. "Okay," he replied, rubbing his ear to ease the shock on his eardrums. "There's no need to shout. What is it?"

"Look down."

Michael obeyed, focusing his goggles on the slushy grass before him. "What is–?" Then he noticed the slight mounds that a casual observer would have missed. Pressing the display on his watch, he focused the goggles to find a mosaic of red dots; some were small, like pebbles; the others were the size of paving stones. "Are those mines?"

"Pressure sensors attached to the alarm systems." Sparks' voice was now at whisper level in his ear.

Michael swallowed a curse word. If not for this extra little twist, he might have taken a quick run-up and vaulted over the next obstacle. Now he couldn't run up to it or along it. "Can you override them, Sparks?"

"Negative."

"Fat lot of good you are, mate." Michael sat on his haunches and studied the pattern of red dots and ignored Sparks' reply as he planned his next move. "Actually, some of those dots have enough space between them to—"

"Still set off the alarms, Michael. They're set to detect movement between them, too."

"Schick, schick, and crap." He rubbed a hand across the stubble on his face, brow furrowed. Underground or overground? Perhaps if he rigged something that could let him float past the barriers and into the centre? No. Radar would pick up his mass. If he were small as a single bird, there would be no problem because that wouldn't show. "What if I changed them into something else?" He shook his head. "No. It might still trigger the alert. If only I could…" He clicked his fingers. "Easy!"

He closed his eyes, concentrated, and transmuted the vaulting pole into a scaffolding. He stepped back to check and grinned at the result. The ladder arrangement neatly stood with a frame that bridged the underground sensors, instead of standing on them, and it crossed the invisible microwave fence. "There we are!"

"Nice work, Skids," Sparks' voice answered in his ear.

"No wonder the girls all love you."

"Long time ago, mate, long time ago," Michael replied as he climbed the ladder and shimmied past the barrier on his stomach to avoid radar sensors detecting his bulk.

Just then, the rain beat harder, and a ferocious gale blustered across the yard. Michael felt the structure tip under his weight perilously close to the invisible microwave beams. He stopped still as a statue, but it didn't help. The powerful wind's force, in combination with his mass on top, had overbalanced the scaffolding.

Instinct compelled Michael to dive forward and down the other side, his hands catching him on the slushy ground. One hand slipped in the mud; he almost lost his handstand, then he saw it…

… The scaffolding was still toppling. Another two inches, and the pieces would interrupt the beams.

Confetti floated through the lines of light, but not enough to set off the alarms.

And Michael sighed. His fingers had just brushed the scaffolding and allowed him to transform it before it could activate the alarms and attract the guards.

With his heart still hammering, he took a breath and guided himself safely to the ground from his handstand.

"Bugger me, that was close." Sparks' voice betrayed the concern he felt even as a being of electrical consciousness.

Michael said nothing. The rain fell heavier again now as powerful gusts dumped more water from the sky, reducing the visibility. While no one could see him through the veil created, neither could he without filtering it. He pressed his watch's screen, adjusting the filter on his goggles until he eliminated the interference from his vision like killing static on a radio. Apart from the odd dancing speckles, he could see better now.

He need not have worried. The heavy rain had confined most of the guards to their barracks, with only a few at the hangars. It turned out easier than expected as he skirted them, avoiding their gazes as he headed around the base's inner perimeter towards a warehouse at the other end.

Michael stuck to the shadows, blending with the darkness as he approached. His uniform's sensors had detected he was out of the rain and kicked in with drying units, increasing his comfort further as he sneaked closer to the warehouse's entrance. Then he stopped.

A uniformed guard was standing beside the large doorway, face turned towards the barracks. Sloppy, Michael thought to himself as he glided across on noiseless feet until he was directly behind the unsuspecting soldier and rendered him unconscious with a precise nerve pinch. He surveyed the interior from the doorway and gave a quick nod of satisfaction. Nothing much had changed since his last visit. To most of the soldiers on this base, this building served to store firefighting equipment, including three fire engines. But Michael knew better. Still keeping to the shadows, he darted from one vantage point to another, approaching the door that he knew opened to a lift that would take him down to the secret levels.

At last, he reached the lift's entrance and stopped upon recognising something new. A hand print and retina scanner.

He whispered in a barely audible tone, aware that the heavy rains outside still made it noisy as it bashed the building's tin structure. "A little help, Sparks?"

"Onto it, Skids."

Two seconds later, the lift's door opened. Michael slipped

inside, pressed the close button before anyone might notice, and dropped unexpectedly into darkness… then unconsciousness.

Chapter 29

It wasn't his Jaguar, but Craig found the silver Toyota Corolla sedan responded better than he had expected. Had Michael souped it up when he created it from a nearby fallen tree trunk? It was hard to tell, but it wouldn't stand out the same as Craig's favourite car. With Colonel Blaze's soldiers potentially watching for him, and the police, he needed to avoid unnecessary attention as he cruised Statton's roads to reach Amy Maloney's house.

The GPS directed him until he reached the suburb of Woodland Grove then through the narrow, winding streets. He saw Sally Green's familiar looking Skyline ahead before the guidance system chirruped to say he had arrived at his destination.

Although he wasn't adept at seeing the future, unless it played out in a psychometric vision, an uneasy feeling slithered in his stomach. Psychic precognition or not, he listened to it and surveyed James' friend's house as he passed.

It looked innocent enough. Three tall lilly pillies growing inside a dark green picket fence obscured the small brick home with the red colourbond roof from the road. The foliage provided a thick cover through which he couldn't properly spot the front door, but he caught sight of what appeared to be white-painted security bars. But that hid a clear view of the footpath from the house's occupants, too. Opposite grew a eucalyptus forest beyond ferns and bushes with a concrete path by the street, a nature walk for the locals. A nice quiet neighbourhood, even if the next suburb was rife with crime like the one in his universe.

Two blocks away, Craig parked in an empty spot near the forest walk, stepped out and headed back towards Sally's Skyline, which James had "borrowed". Upon reaching it, he placed his fingers on the bonnet, still warm from the engine, not the sun's heat. The teenager hadn't been here long. A moment later, the vision came to him.

@ @ @

Craig was standing in front of the car, illuminated by the streetlight from the corner twenty paces away, when they arrived. Their shared features matched those of the clones he had fought in the cemetery the previous day. Biceps and chests threatened to burst through their black t-shirts as they approached the vehicle.

Craig held his breath as one appeared to look straight through him, although he knew the clone couldn't see him. The leader, who had slightly more hair than his balding companions, took a mobile phone from his pocket and scanned the Skyline's registration plate. A moment later, he harrumphed. "Belongs to Sally Green."

"Who? The journalist?" said one of the other two.

The leader flicked through the data on his phone. Craig stepped round to better see the display and gasped upon viewing Sally's photo, her name and address on the screen. "Yep. Car's not reported as stolen."

"Then she knows the kid has her car."

"Probably where Michael Mach and the Ramsey guy are too, I bet."

Still in the vision, Craig placed his palm on the clone's arm. Instantly, the scene changed. He was now standing in Sally's home and facing her as she watched the television. The psychic investigator desperately wanted to warn her, to shout at her, but it was no use. This insight was about the future. He could touch the people and objects, but Sally wouldn't feel his hand, nor could he move things in it. All he could do was watch as the front door splintered from the clone soldier's kick as he burst inside. He could only stand there passively in mute horror as the soldiers questioned her, interrogated, and tortured her until she died from the rough treatment.

And tears flowed from Craig's red eyes as he watched the journalist's corpse dumped face-down in the river to be found three days later by a shocked angler and his son.

@ @ @

Thunder rolled in the distance, and the vision faded. Craig stared at Sally's Skyline as he contemplated what he had seen. It had only shown what could be in three hours' time. He could still change it... maybe. An idea came to him.

The psychic tested the door handle and grinned as the car opened. Thank goodness teenagers forget simple things, like using locks!

He reached inside and under the dashboard to pull the bonnet release. It had been a while since he used this technique, something he had learned from the ghost of a car thief, but surely it would work here too. Ah! A psychometric flash told him where to find the next thing. Jumper cables. Sally kept them in the car's boot. He grabbed them and a flat blade screwdriver, then checked the engine, connecting one cable to the battery's positive terminal, then to another section of the vehicle's body. A moment later, he found the starter solenoid and unlocked the steering wheel with the screwdriver. After three minutes, the starter cranked, grumbled, and brought the engine to life with a satisfying purr.

Grinning, he drove round the corner to the end of a cul-de-sac and parked outside another house. The clones wouldn't think to look here, he hoped. But he had to check. This time, touching the rearview mirror showed a police officer checking the abandoned car's registration before reporting it. No clone soldiers. No mention of Craig or Michael. Sally would live.

He gave a sigh of relief, wiped the bonnet, the steering wheel and everything else to erase his fingerprints, and hurried back to Amy's house.

Craig's head sparked with ideas and concern. Although he had adjusted the possible future of Sally Green's demise, hiding her car in a different location wouldn't have removed the inevitable. Colonel Blaze's clone goons would still arrive, maybe even sooner. Craig's best chance would be to find James and escape together before Blaze's minion's arrival.

Craig carefully opened the driveway's metal gate to avoid any squeaks and followed the path to the front door. He was about to knock when instinct stopped him. Voices reached his ear from inside. One was a boy, James, and he guessed the girl talking in a haughty tone was Amy. But who was the man's voice? It sounded familiar.

Placing a finger on the front door's frame, Craig's heart jumped a beat at the vision. So that's who it was! He should have guessed. Cursing to himself, he took a breath, ran the next scenario in his head, and lifted his hand to knock, vaguely aware of the approaching thunderstorm. If he played everything right, he might be out of here with James before it hit.

The voice inside stopped. He moved against the wall to

prevent the person inside from checking through the curtains to see him. Surprise was his only ally. A shaky one at that.

The young teenaged girl's voice quavered from behind the door. "Who is it?"

Craig hurried to think of a good name, not wanting to give his own yet. "Khan."

"Khan who?"

Craig paused. Was this a knock-knock joke?

"Khan, and open the door, will ya? It's hot out here."

A long silence followed. The sound of curtains moving came from the front window. Whoever was watching wouldn't see much of him in the corner, and Craig had also blocked the peephole with his finger to prevent premature recognition. A chain slid aside. Something scratched on the doorknob from the inside before the lock disengaged with a sharp click.

Then the girl's voice. "Come in. It's open."

The hackles rose on Craig's neck. Yes, it was a trap. Although hasty and impromptu, he had to be ready. He lay a hand on the wooden door's surface and snapped a couple of different visions. One ended with his death by a bullet in the back of the head while fleeing with James. A second resulted in the boy's demise. But there was a third option, the outcome of which eluded a definite result. Perhaps survival meant being caught? It couldn't be worse than the other alternatives.

He took a breath, closed his eyes and mouthed a silent prayer to the universe before reaching with tentative fingers towards the brass doorknob to check the psychic vision. Perhaps he could learn more that way.

Spasms threaded up his arm and forced convulsions

through his body. He dropped to the ground, heart racing, and shaken close to insensibility. A moment later, the door opened, and a man loomed above him, silhouetted by the light from within the house. A familiar figure.

"Well, well, well." A lightning flash strobed his features. Colonel Blaze. "There's someone I haven't seen in the flesh for over a year, Mr Ramsey."

Craig fought back his disorientation from the electric shock and tried to move. Too slow. Blaze kicked down on his chest, knocking him to the ground, winding him. Shaky visions spiked the psychic's mind, painting a confusing picture.

The colonel grabbed Craig's feet and dragged him inside, letting his head hit the doorstep. A moan escaped Craig's lips as the world tilted and gravity overpowered him. His captor moved fast and tied his wrists behind his back with something he figured was a cotton rope clothesline. Craig studied his surroundings through the gloom as lightning cracked and thundered, illuminating the scene for a second: a lamp lay on the ground, its power cord ripped from the base. The broken and frayed line, its bare wires exposed, was still plugged into the outlet. Craig snorted. So that's how Blaze had electrocuted him through the doorknob.

Blaze tightened the knots and re-examined them. "That should keep you snug, Mr Ramsey." He lifted the psychic into a sitting position. "I remember your escape-artistry skill and how it works."

"What a charmer." Craig shook his head and blinked more to clear it. "Here's me thinking you'd forgotten me, Nigel." He glanced to his left and spotted James nearby, restrained similarly, although uncomfortable with his plastered arm. Craig gave him a quick wink. "It's time to come home, James."

"Exactly my thoughts," Blaze replied. "James, I still have unfinished business with you too."

Craig raised an eyebrow, glancing at James' angry but frightened face, then back at Colonel Blaze. "What's the boy got to do with you?"

Lightning struck the trees across the street. Thunder cracked and rumbled, and a loud crash reached their ears from outside. The house and street fell into darkness. Craig struggled to take advantage of the distraction. Blaze was quicker. Booted Craig hard in the face. "Not so fast."

He didn't even know he had been unconscious until he heard the voice beside him. "Are you alright, Craig?"

Craig spat blood from his tooth, aware for the moment of the irony that it was the same one knocked askew years ago by a sniper's bullet he'd caught. "Yeah." He coughed more bloody sputum, feeling the tooth with his tongue. Still in one piece. Good. "Just getting my kicks. How'd he catch you?"

James sighed. "He was here when I arrived. Amy must have set it up."

Nearby, a girl's voice huffed. "I didn't do it, James. You have to believe me."

"How can I? You never even told me your uncle was Colonel Blaze. For all I know, you–"

"James, that's enough." Craig moved himself next to James, whose hands had been tied in a similar manner on the floor. "You're safe."

Rain teemed down from outside, hitting the colourbond roof hard enough that Blaze's sadistic laughter sounded little more than a whisper. "Amy's a good girl, James. She's my favourite niece." He waited as the teenage girl hurried past them in the darkness, the only other sound her bedroom door slamming. A moment later, Blaze chuckled again.

"Let it go, James." Craig took a smooth breath and spoke in a calm voice. "Trust me." He appraised their tall, chuckling captor and considered his next words. "Blaze, tell me, why are you flip-flopping about in the last forty-eight hours?"

Blaze sneered back at him and lowered himself on his haunches to stare into Craig's face in the gloom. "Flip-flopping, Mr Ramsey?"

Craig suppressed a shudder as he stared into the familiar icy eyes, illuminated only by the reflecting lightning from outside. In his memory, on his world, Colonel Nigel Blaze was dead, killed by his own hand when he pulled the trigger of the gun he held. This was a different version. Craig swallowed. Should he say it? Ah, to purgatory with it. "Backwards and forwards. One moment you want me dead, and you hit me with your car. Then you miss me so much that you keep watch for me for over a year until you finally see me on camera." Craig paused, noting the subtle movement in Blaze's cold eyes despite his immobile eyelids. A grin crossed Craig's lips. "Yes, I know what you did because when you found me in the cemetery, you sent your goons to bring me back alive. Then you watched and tried to send me to hell with your drone."

The corner of Blaze's mouth twitched enough to elicit hope in Craig. The colonel leaned forward. Aware of the colonel's clenched fists even in the semi-darkness, Craig added. "You still haven't killed me. Admit it, Nigel." Craig stared hard into Blaze's angry eyes, then chuckled. "You want to kiss me right now, don't you?"

Craig expected an outburst. Not the stinging pain on his cheek from Blaze's slap a moment before James' surprised yelp. He raised his eyebrows and lowered them with each blink, a smarting tear welling in the corner of his eyelids, and grinned back at his captor. "Such a fiery temper."

Blaze readied for another strike, but a knock at the door interrupted him. "Enter."

Two soldiers entered, their glances darting about in the darkened living room at the broken lamp and Blaze's captives. One of them sneered in Craig's direction as if in recognition of the psychic investigator, his fingers flexing. "Sir, we came as soon as we could."

Blaze stood, readjusted the legs of his pants and pointed at Craig and James with a toss of his head. "Take them both away." The soldiers advanced, ready to grab them by the shoulders, and Blaze stopped the one behind Craig. "Wait."

The psychic didn't have a chance. Blaze's boot crunched into Craig's face before he could dodge, sending him to the ground in a groaning heap. The coppery taste of blood filled his mouth. Would his tooth jut out again like last time?

Hands as strong as a vise lifted him to his feet until he was level with Blaze's face. Craig narrowed his eyes as he regarded the colonel's stony face. "You're going to regret that... Nigel No-friends."

Blaze sneered. "I doubt it, Mr Ramsey."

Blaze's subordinate moved forward. A sharp pain exploded in Craig's neck. Blackness fell.

Chapter 30

The voice was familiar, one she had not heard for a long time. It reached to her through the darkness, coaxing her to wake.

"Brianna."

Her eyes fluttered. A flurry of confusing images and sounds from memory flickered through her mind as she blinked against the light. Couldn't she just sleep a little more and recapture the dream, whatever it was, and stay there longer? She crinkled her brow upon realising it wouldn't come.

"Brianna." There was the voice again. She hadn't dreamed that. "Are you awake?"

Groggy, the disorientation keen in her skull, Brianna turned towards the source of the insistent talking. Her voice, coming from a throat as dry and crackly as autumn leaves, rasped. She shook her head, fought to swallow. "Water."

Darkness lifted from her vision, faded, and gave way to shapes that made sense to her. Nearby, a short, balding man turned to retrieve a pitcher of water, which he used to fill a glass, and he offered her a drink. "Sip it." His voice exuded a firm kindness and calm. Where did she know that voice?

With fumbling fingers, she clutched at the glass and brought it closer to her mouth. Ah! A few sips of the cool water felt like a draught. Her eyes widened as the fluid washed away the cobwebs in her head, and she took another gulp.

"Slowly." The bespectacled man guided her with a firm hand as he held the glass and withdrew it from her grasp. "You have been in a coma. Do you remember your name?"

Brianna hesitated, her eyes skimming over the white walls and the bed on the opposite side of the room, which looked more like a section of a corridor to her. "Coma?" Then her gaze settled on the stranger again, his expectant gaze reminding her of his question. "I'm Brianna Cogan."

He nodded, a kind smile illuminating his features. "I'm Dr Joseph Maloney." He glanced at his watch and raised his eyebrows, his mouth open in surprise. "2:09am! Just like he said."

"Who said?"

The doctor reached for her wrist, his fingers resting lightly on her pulse as he counted. He gave an approving grunt and scribbled something on a nearby chart. "Your vitals are fine." After checking Brianna's eyes and asking her to track his finger as he moved it side-to-side and up-and-down, he nodded again. "Your friend told me you would wake at 2:09am. He also said you'd make a full recovery. No sign of a concussion." His head tipped towards his shoulder, an eyebrow raised in surprise as he made a "huh" sound. "Which surprises me. You looked terrible when I found you."

Brianna repeated her question. "Who?" Then memory returned to her of the soldiers in the park and the beating she'd received, the explosion before that. She winced at the mental image of the rifle butt slamming into her face. Caught in the memory, she grimaced, stopped herself from flinging her arms up in defence. She lifted her fingers to her nose, wincing in anticipation, and was surprised. "No pain?" Brianna threw a questioning look at the doctor. "No bruises. Nothing. How long have I been here?"

Joseph released a short laugh, one filled with as much disbelief as Brianna felt. "Would you believe you've been here since around midday Friday? That's when I found you and the boy in the park."

"How many days?"

"Nearly two days. It's now Sunday morning, just after 2:09am, when…"

"You were told when I'd wake?" Brianna raised herself to a sitting position and checked the rest of her limbs and torso. No pain, not even dizziness. "You said that before. How come I'm so well now? Those guys beat the shit out of me when I was already half-dead."

"Nearly killed you," Joseph replied with a brief nod, examining her over the top of his glasses. He stood to his full height and took a deep breath; his brow furrowed as considered his answer. "All I know is that two gentlemen arrived hours after I had brought you here. How I found you is another story, but I assume you know Michael Mach and Craig Ramsey?" The doctor paused and waited for Brianna's confirmation before he told her about the blue contents of the vial that they had injected into her bloodstream. He clucked his tongue, shaking his head in disappointment at being overpowered, but admitted his surprise at her complete recovery. "He said it was something, but I can't recall its name. How it worked, who knows? I've seen nothing like it before."

"He?" Brianna asked. Impatient with the doctor's rambling, she swung her legs to the side to sit up, but Joseph protested straightaway.

"Wait," he urged. "You're—"

"Fully recovered." Brianna placed her hands on her chest, resisting the urge to cup her breasts, then patted down her limbs and torso before touching her head. "No pain. That's amazing," she said, and flexed her fingers and shoulders. Her eyes settled on the bed opposite the one on which she'd been. Its sheets were a mess, as though someone else had slept there. Then she remembered. "James. What happened to him?"

"He has a broken arm and a light concussion." Joseph's gaze dropped, his brow furrowing. "He woke yesterday morning and vanished soon before Craig Ramsey went searching for him."

"Disappeared? Where's Michael?"

"He's looking for Hayley."

Memory of the rifle butt slamming with brutal force into her face made Brianna shudder again, but this time Hayley's screams rang through in the background. One of the last things she'd heard before unconsciousness overcame her. "The soldiers took her."

A sound caught Brianna's attention, and she spun to face the new arrival: a man whose angular features looked familiar yet confusing to see then. "Craig Ramsey!" Brianna couldn't hold back her surprise, but she sensed something wasn't right. Her eyes narrowed. "Where's James? Weren't you searching for him?"

A puzzled look flashed across the man's features for a second. "Oh, you mean the boy. Don't worry, I'm still looking for him." He paused, his keen eyes checking her responses, then changed his tone. "Well," he added, stretching the word, "kind of. Isn't he here now?"

Annoyance heated Brianna's face. How flippant! If not for this Craig Ramsey's cockiness in jaunting off elsewhere, prompting Michael to give chase, things may have turned out better when the soldiers attacked the house. Hayley would have been safer. James wouldn't be hurt and missing. Concern for the children's whereabouts and welfare, and this man's apparent disregard for them, sparked an anger for this man who claimed to be the Craig Ramsey she had once known. "*Kind of* looking?" She stepped towards him and would have pushed him backwards if not for his quick response to counter her attack. "Where do you—"

"Let's not dance, Brianna." He regarded her, his eye twinkling, and chuckled at the daggers in her fiery eyes. "Don't you remember? I told you about this before." He saw Brianna's puzzled face, then sighed. "Oh, damn. I forgot to tell you the code word."

"What?"

He lowered his voice, leaned his head closer so that his breath warmed her ear. "Moonbeam."

Brianna froze in confusion for a second. Her brow crinkled, then random images sparked to life in her mind. Memories or dreams? She cocked her head at a slight angle as thoughts reassembled and coalesced into a tangible sensibility. A kiss in a darkened storefront's empty doorway, the moment designed to provide cover when hiding from an enemy. A chase through the streets of Chinatown for an elusive assassin of non-human origin. The discovery of a plot dangerous to herself and many others. A hushed conversation with Craig Ramsey in the dark that segued into an intimate occasion, and the words that rocked her before the curtain closed over her mind for over a year: "To solve everything, I have to die first." Then the memories swirled, parted, and returned to sequence with the realisation of Moonbeam's meaning. It was time to wake.

"Oh my God," Brianna whispered in surprise. "Is it really happening?"

Chapter 31

"Right, let's go!" Ramsey spun on his heel and strode towards the steps that led upwards into the house. He paused and nodded at Joseph. "Thanks for your help, Joe," he said. "Hold the fort until we return." A moment later, he had ascended and disappeared from view. She gave Joe a quick hug, "Thank you for everything." She smiled at his crimson blush, then clambered up the stairs and hurried out the door after the psychic, who had already reached a waiting blue Mini Cooper.

"Come on!" He called to Brianna. "Bad guys don't catch themselves, you know."

Brianna choked back a laugh as she opened the passenger door and folded herself inside the compact car. The smirk, familiar as an old pair of comfortable jeans, remained as she shut it.

Ramsey spotted her expression as he turned the ignition key. "What?"

"A Mini Cooper?"

"Well, someone else had totalled my Jaguar," he replied, with a hint of sadness in his voice. "How could you let him —you know, the other guy—take it? Lucky that Michael made this up for the mission."

Brianna chuckled. "Never mind, moneybags. You can afford another one. Now, how about you tell me what's been going on?"

Ramsey bit his lip as he negotiated the twisting dirt road by the dim headlights. "How much do you remember?"

She shook her head. "Not a lot. I know that you've been

sitting underneath Colonel Blaze's nose for most of the time. You told me I'd see you again and that I would hardly miss you."

Ramsey steered the car onto the motorway heading towards the other side of the city, then allowed himself to look at his passenger. "And?"

"We all missed you," Brianna replied. "We thought you were dead! It devastated Michael, especially after you died in his arms." She stopped for a moment. "By the way, how did you die and come back?"

A devilish smile crossed the psychic's countenance, silent and secretive, as his eyes twinkled. "With a little help from my friends, you included."

Brianna's head cocked at an angle. "I don't remember that, yet."

A satisfied expression crossed Ramsey's face at those words. "That will pass in time, when the time's right. You probably recall before my demise what I said. To catch Blaze, I'd have to die first. Yeah?" She gave him an assenting nod, although the full details remained hazy in her recollection, and he continued. "Well, that was it. I told you and Michael about it before I hypnotised the two of you into forgetting my plan until I returned."

"But I don't remember everything."

"Well," Ramsey allowed the word to hang a moment as he appeared to consider his words. "I hypnotised you both with a double-bind."

"Why?"

"For this to work." Ramsey shook his head as he overtook a few cars on the motorway, ignorant of their annoyed horn blasts as he cut one of them off. "I couldn't risk the chance of you or Michael accidentally blowing my cover before I was ready. Do you know how hard it is to get myself into Blaze's base without them realising my real identity? That's why I faked my death. Take me out of the equation, then Blaze stops worrying about where I am."

"But you could have died when he hit you with the car."

"Well… yeah." Ramsey shrugged with a sigh, as though he had explained it all so many times already. "That happened. But the ectoplasm in my blood helped me regenerate. According to–" He paused as he nearly said the name, which Brianna realised he avoided to protect the other party as a precaution. "I hear that my heart slowed down enough that the machines couldn't detect my brainwaves or heartbeat."

He fell silent a moment and Brianna guessed he was reflecting on the event. "Michael turned your house into a fortress and even altered the street cameras to cloak his existence. He was grateful to you for giving him and Hayley, and James, a place to live."

"Part of the hypnotic suggestions," Ramsey responded with a smug grin. "But I've had a year to work everything out. Michael's suspicions about Blaze were right, by the way. He's planning something bigger than we originally thought. Building an army of psychic children to be tomorrow's paranormal soldiers of the future."

Brianna raised a questioning eyebrow. "Oh? What's bigger than that?"

"Try a psychic attack on the Communist countries." He glanced at Brianna and nodded slowly at her incredulous expression. "First, he finds the kids locally. I hear he's been using a subliminal device attached to a van. It plays sounds that only psychics can sense, and it works best when they're asleep. They–"

"They walk out like zombies and straight into the van?" Brianna asked. "I heard the same music. It was like Mr Whippy's tune that played when we were kids."

"What?" The steering wheel slipped in Ramsey's hand, jolting the car when he regained control to avoid smashing a car in the neighbouring lane. "You heard it?"

Brianna nodded. "That's how I found Hayley getting inside it. They were right outside my house and had two other kids inside."

Ramsey nodded. "Were any other parents out on the street at the time?" When Brianna shook her head, he grunted in appreciation of the issue. "You must have already had latent powers before then. That's why you heard the sound." Brianna tried to ask what he meant by that, but Ramsey kept talking. "So, anyhow, onto the rest of this. He's picking out the best psychics from this group for something bigger. They only need three to power it, mind you. But they have to be really strong."

"What?"

"The weapon he needs to wipe the minds of all other psychics in the Communist countries. You see? The Communists are training their own armies in psychic technique, too. Blaze cottoned onto that. Well… his superiors did."

"The Australian government?"

Ramsey shook his head. "Bigger."

"The Americans and British?"

"Bigger still."

"Who?"

"Another organisation. It's older than the English, been around since… well… a long time."

He turned off the motorway and into the outer suburbs

on the other side of Statton.

"I thought we were heading for the base," Brianna said, noticing they were entering a built-up industrial area. "Where are we going?"

Ramsey steered into a fenced-property's driveway, wound down the window, and waved an ID tag at a nearby sensor. The gates clanked and slid aside for Ramsey to drive the car inside towards an adjacent warehouse that lit up upon their entry. "Movement sensors and a security chip device on the windscreen," he explained, and twisted the wheel to spin them into a car parking spot next to others in the lot. "This is the help's entrance."

"Do you mean this is the base? A warehouse in the middle of the industrial area?"

Ramsey nodded. "Hidden in plain sight. It's great, isn't it?" He stepped out of the car and shut the door and waited for Brianna to exit before he locked it. "Cameras are watching us. Microphones, too, that can pick up the sound of a flea's cough. So watch what you say, yeah? Come on… Linda."

Linda? Brianna opened her mouth to question who Linda was, but Ramsey had slipped something into her hand, and she looked at it. An ID tag with her photo on it, and the name Linda Carey. She peered at the picture and realised it had come from an old ID file from when she once worked in the Army.

"Come along, Linda," Ramsey quipped. "We're cutting it fine." He led her through the rows of parked cars towards a set of closed lift doors. "Use your tag here." He pointed towards a nearby scanner and swiped his own pass there. The door opened and slid shut after they entered.

A woman's voice filled the lift's car. "There are two

people in the lift. Please identify yourselves by retinal scan."

Ramsey looked into a nearby receptacle from which a green network of lights passed over his right eye, scanning his eye twice before a crisp tone made its affirmative approval. "Your turn," he told Brianna, and stood back for her to try the same. She hesitated. The ID label she understood was forged, but her retinal scan? How could she get by on this? "Come on," Ramsey chided her. "We don't have a year." He granted her a meaningful look and pointed at the scanner.

"Person number two," the woman's voice chirped. "Please scan."

Brianna's gaze jumped between Ramsey and the scanner. She peeked through the sensor, keeping her eye open as the green light examined her retina, until at last it beeped.

"Person two confirmed. Choose a floor."

Ramsey winked at Brianna and pressed one of the lower level buttons. With the merest hint of a motor whine, the lift's car descended, the only sign of its movement being the floor numbers changing. Brianna had never seen them move so fast in a lift feeling nothing before. She asked Ramsey, who shrugged. "Something to do with inertial stabilisers. Top science stuff that I couldn't quite follow." Then, a moment later, the door opened outward. "Here's our stop."

They had barely stepped foot outside the lift when a klaxon's raucous tone filled the sterile corridors with its hullabaloo. Brianna tensed, her eyes skipping ahead and to the hallway on the left, at the sound of running feet. "What's that?"

Ramsey shook his head, his expression reflecting her

concern. "Something's happening." A lab assistant hurried past, worry painted on her face, and he put out a hand to ask, "What is it?"

The base employee looked at Ramsey and blurted her reply. "An accident! No, an incident. Something's going down in the testing rooms. The uniforms are in there now." She raced down the hall, away from the sound of further commotion.

Screams ripped from the throats of at least two people, followed by shouts. The hiss of rushing air, a muffled explosion, and then more cries of surprise mixed with terror. "Move around." "Watch out. Get Hobbes out of there." "Use the gas." "Fire in the hole!"

A slam of a large security door rumbled moments before another muffled explosion. The floor swayed under their feet, disturbing the electric lights which dimmed, then everything fell still.

"What the hell was that?" Brianna wanted to know, but Ramsey only shook his head. He removed his arms from around her, which she hadn't realised he'd wrapped round her during the excitement, then he strode down the hallway towards the sound. Brianna followed at a trot to keep up with him. "What are they testing?"

Concern and curiosity coloured Ramsey's voice. "The children."

"The…" Brianna choked as the gravity of Ramsey's words struck her. "Children? Is that where?"

Ramsey stopped, his hand out to halt Brianna as paramedics wheeled three gurneys past them. Brianna glimpsed a body, noticed its height, and breathed relief upon realising there were no children's bodies among those trundled past. Then her guts rolled when she spotted a new casualty. A young brunette woman. Barely twenty-five, by Brianna's guess. A layer of ice covered the side of her face, reflecting a pale blue under the lights, and her blackened lips pulled taut to reveal her teeth, straight and white, with the surrounding tissue bleached light and grey. Brianna averted her eyes only to stare at a different casualty passing, but where the first had fallen victim to intense frostbite, this man was ancient, the muscles wasted to an atrophic state where the soldier's uniform was wrinkled and flat instead of filled. It was as if someone had deflated the clothing. And his face's skin had become as thin as paper.

"What the hell?" Brianna swallowed a burning drip of bile that had risen in her throat. A surprised whisper escaped her lips. "Are you seeing this?"

Ramsey shook his head, eyes fixated on the victims as they passed. "I knew all these soldiers. Clones," he said, his voice lowered to a stunned hiss as he absorbed the carnage.

"Clear out. Give us room!"

Brianna and Ramsey stepped back from the hallways into an open door to allow a small crowd of soldiers the space to race past, two of them carrying a stretcher upon which lay a young girl. A four-year-old. With hair disarrayed, to form a scattered halo on the pillow. An arrangement familiar to Brianna.

"Hayley!"

Instinct pushed Brianna to move towards the girl's inert body, but Ramsey halted her. She tried to brush back his hands, but he held fast and muttered something that made her look again. And she saw them. Straps buckled around the child's chest, arms, and legs. So Hayley wasn't dead.

Just sleeping. Sedated. She crumpled in relief, fighting her emotions, knowing that to run to her niece would only further endanger the little girl and themselves further.

Ramsey held Brianna until everyone had gone, and the klaxons silenced. When a presumable normality arrived, he finally spoke in a shocked whisper. "Well, that was unexpected."

Chapter 32

The knocking on Colonel Blaze's quarters' door would have woken him had he not already been awake. He rarely slept longer than four hours, anyway, and he had a conundrum on his mind to prevent him from sleeping. Now dressed in uniform, he pressed the unlock button for the entry, which hissed open to reveal Major Oates looking the little worse for wear from fatigue.

"It's 4:30am, Oates."

The major paused a beat before entering the room, keeping his eyes averted from Blaze's gaze for a second, and saluted. "My apologies for interrupting you so early, sir."

Blaze waved a hand at his subordinate's words; everyone knew the colonel's strict habits. "I assume it's important. Tell me your report."

"Last night, we proceeded on the somnambulist experiments with the Hayley Mach girl." He pulled at his collar with a finger as though it were too tight. "And an incident occurred."

"An incident." Blaze echoed, and leaned back in his desk chair, fingers steepled and his eyebrow arched high as he fixed the major in a steely gaze. "Do tell. Is the girl well?"

Oates swallowed and gave a nod. "Yes, but we lost six men."

"Lost, Major?" Blaze drew a breath and subdued his impatience. "Do you mean you can't find them?" He ignored his subordinate's sorry attempt to disguise his indignation at the grammar correction.

"I mean they're dead, sir."

"Dead?" The word whispered from his mouth in awe a second before a heavy sensation filled the pit of Blaze's stomach. Hayley Mach's remarks echoed in his mind, the warning that she had given him—big words for a tiny squirt of a child, but the memory of their tone still quaked his heart. A giddiness spun Blaze's sanity, and the blood left his face. He turned away to hide the fact from Oates. "How did they die?"

The major shifted his stance. "Terribly, sir. Three succumbed to severe frostbite. Within seconds at most, although we believe it was instant. Two of them died—" He choked and coughed on having swallowed saliva down the wrong way. "They were old. Really old."

Blaze moved the chair round again to regard Oates, his eyes asking the question. Oates' voice cracked as he continued. "Extreme old age, sir. They aged fifty to sixty years before our eyes." The colonel said nothing. He stared ahead for seconds as he fought to stop his fingers from trembling. Instead, he settled for tapping a tattoo on the armrest of his desk chair before he finally blinked. At last, he spoke. "That's five people. What happened to the sixth?"

"Went mad, sir. He attacked another private who had no choice but to kill him on the spot."

Blaze's head bobbed back and forth as he considered the importance behind the news. On the one hand, he felt awe and jubilation; Hayley Mach had shown abilities they hadn't expected or thought possible in a psychic; she would prove to be a valuable asset in his mission to build an army of super psychics. No more silly experiments like the Americans and their staring goats to death crap.

Hayley's powers would piss over anything they had and more. But, if he were honest with himself, the information was horrific enough to chill his blood because he knew that the little girl hated him with a passion. That's what last night's incident was really about. She was throwing a tantrum, something he must treat with extreme caution and careful handling. If only he had a means to regulate it and live.

Blaze wiped a bead of sweat from his brow, oblivious to Major Oates watching him, then he realised. A tantrum. What does a parent do to handle their children's outbursts?

"Major," he said, a dark smile curling a corner of his mouth. "I believe we need to ground the little bitch. Place her in Lab 41. It's time I give her a good talking to."

Chapter 33

The first thing Hayley realised when she woke was she couldn't remember any dreams from the previous night. Dizzy and uncomfortable, she lay there and tried to coax any memory of a dream to life. But none came, not even a nightmare. She was alone with her thoughts in a bare room different from the other cell. She raised her hand to touch the centre of her face, just above the nose, where a strange headache throbbed. It hurt to turn her head.

How did she get here? She stopped to think, but the ache in her forehead crunched every image, like when she would stomp on the meat ants that she loved to watch at the park where her father used to take her. Dad! The recollection of his dark hair and laughter and how he cooked her favourite breakfast, pikelets lathered in butter and golden syrup, twisted and turned in her mind. Even the idea of the aroma made her mouth water until she realised it wasn't real. Hayley's bottom lip jutted out. Dad wasn't here; he was just a memory, which he said her mother had become, something we keep in our hearts when they visit heaven. Is that where Dad lived now? She wondered. He may as well be since he hadn't come for her like the lady with the funny way of talking had told her in the other night's dream. But why did he feel so close?

She stood to look around the cell. This room had only one bed. Where was Beaulah? Had she been naughty and taken away?

Or had she been the bad girl?

No, you weren't bad, Hayley. We were.

Hayley crinkled her brow and looked round the room. Seeing no one, she crouched to peer under her bed and found only a bare cement floor. "Where are you?"

I'm here.

And I'm here too.

Me three.

We're all here, Hayley, but don't tell the man in the jacket where we all are.

That's right. It's our secret.

The young girl lifted a petite hand to her hair and scratched the scalp in the spot where she heard the other children's voices. "Is that you, Beaulah?"

I'm here, Hayley.

We're all here, the children answered. *We can talk to each other through our heads.*

And we also see the man in the jacket is coming, Hayley, an older boy's voice intoned in her mind. *Keep our secret.*

Hayley's head bobbed fast in agreement and, instead of asking aloud this time, she spoke through her inside thoughts. *I'm scared.*

A clicking from the door distracted her, a sound she associated with a card swipe, then six beeps of a number entered on a keypad. An image of the wicked man in the uniform, the one responsible for her mother's death, intruded in her mind. At once, she sensed the other children's shocked voices in recognising him and his connection to her. A couple of them expressed outrage and stopped when the wall in front of Hayley lit up to reveal the face of evil before her. She gasped and almost fell upon the bed when she took the backward step.

"Good morning, miss Hayley." Oddly, the man reminded her of another she had seen on one of the cartoons on

ABC Kids. On the show, he was friendly and smiled at the camera when talking to the children, but this person's scornful expression was like someone who looked down his nose at people. The kind who loves to hurt others. "Did you sleep well?"

Hayley said nothing. Just nodded. That seemed the sensible thing to do.

"Good." The sardonic grin disappeared, became like the look her father gave if she'd been naughty, like when she drew on the walls, or the time she had used scissors to cut out the pictures of her mother to make something nice. Her dad had yelled at her for that, said that they were precious, that he hadn't wanted them lost; then he'd cried. But this man in the green jacket shed no tears. He made her want to cry the way he looked at her, though. "Now, young lady, tell me about what happened last night."

Hayley didn't know what he meant. The last thing she remembered was Miss June taking her out to do some testing. Nothing else came to her knowledge.

Voices spoke from the nether regions inside her head. Words of recognition. *He means how we hurt the people. Say nothing.* She had hurt someone?

The little girl's face broke into shock at the thought. But the dangerous man's eyes hardened further at her response, his gaze tipping forward until his gaze burrowed into her from beneath his stern eyebrows. "Yes," he said. "You remember, don't you?" Hayley shook her head hard. No, she couldn't. Not Miss June! She was kind to Hayley.

He doesn't mean Miss June. He means the others, the ones with the guns and the hard stuff on their clothes. We hurt them with cold and time and fire and other things.

"No," she mouthed in a faint whisper. "I didn't —"

"You certainly did, young lady." The wicked man's voice was quiet, controlled, and reminded her of a snake she had seen at a park her father had taken her to visit. "You can't keep doing that. It's not becoming of a lady. What do you say?"

Shocked at the revelation because she couldn't recall hurting anyone, although she desperately wanted to hurt the man himself, Hayley felt the weight of responsibility crushing upon her little shoulders. "I'm sorry."

"You should be." The man stared hard at her for what seemed forever. "What would your father say if he knew you had hurt someone? Even killed them?"

Hayley's hands balled into fists, her nails biting into her palms until they stung. "No." She shook her head. "I didn't mean to do it." Then she remembered something. Her daddy was coming to rescue her, anyway, and he would hurt this man a lot. She knew that because her daddy hated this man and nothing would stop him. "And my daddy will know I did nothing wrong."

"Really?"

"He's coming here to get you, you *bad man*!"

A smirk twisted itself to life on his face before he tossed his head back in laughter, his mouth opening wide as the mirthful peals escaped his lips. His chuckles vibrated the speakers in the walls, hurting her ears, until he stopped to wipe a tear from the corner of his eye. "Hayley," he said, his amused grin disappearing. "I know about your father. He's here." A picture of her dad, chained by his wrists and ankles to a stone wall, appeared on the screen before her. Blood ran from a cut in his head and face.

"No!" Tears, hot with hate and anger and frustration, sprang from her eyes to blur her vision at seeing her helpless and hurt father. "What did you do to him?"

"Nothing yet," Blaze replied, his tone caustic as the words flowed from his lips with flowing precision. "That depends on you and something I want to talk to you about." He waited for her to stop screaming, then continued. "My doctors will come to do more tests with you today, and you're going to do as you are told because if you don't, I won't be able to stop my friends from hurting your daddy more." His face dropped in a sad expression that she sensed made fun of her. But his words still scared her.

Hayley turned to look away from the screen on the wall, unable to see through her flood of tears. "No. He doesn't want me to help you."

"And he won't be happy if you let them hurt him, either. It will be your fault if they do. You don't want your dad to be unhappy or sad with you for letting others hurt him, do you?"

Hayley shook her head, the thoughts conflicting in her mind as she wondered why her father would be angry at her for something she couldn't stop.

"Then you will do as you're told, won't you?" Conflicted, she said nothing, unable to put her words together.

"I'll let you think about it, Hayley," he answered a second before the room plunged into darkness.

Chapter 34

Images of corpses remained fresh in Brianna's thoughts as fragments of dreams until she realised they were real. Her eyes snapped open with a start. The new surroundings appeared bleak by comparison to her minimalist bedroom at home: bare walls, a simple IKEA desk to the side, and a single bed, cramped by its other occupant.

"Ramsey?" she uttered, unfolding herself from an uncomfortable position to better see the man who everyone had presumed dead for the past twelve months.

Ramsey was sleeping against the wall, his face planted hard against the unforgiving surface to make room for her. "What? What time is it?"

Brianna checked her watch. "Six o'clock am on the Play School clock," she replied with the realisation she had watched too much children's television shows with her niece Hayley. She shifted and rolled out of bed, her forehead glancing slightly against the desk beside it. Rubbing her head, she sat up and stretched into a yawn. "I don't believe how tired I still feel."

Craig sat up, untangled himself from the sheets, and stood to peer at the bedraggled face that returned his stare. He rubbed his hair a bit, the spiky bits popping back into disarray. "I think my pillow reincarnated from a 1980s hairdresser."

Brianna made an amused snort. "That's the first time we've slept together." Then in a mocking tone, "I can hardly wait for next time."

"What? All we did was sleep," Ramsey replied, opening a

desk drawer and taking out a packet of Woolworths glazed doughnuts. He ripped open the plastic and handed a pink one to Brianna. "Breakfast."

With two fingers, she gripped the doughnut, her face pulled in disgust as she regarded the sticky mess over the day-old baked item. "You've got to be kidding." She took the plastic packaging and dumped the inedible mass back inside. "Don't you have an eating area here at least? It *is* an army base."

Ramsey shrugged and took a large bite from his own doughnut and chewed with a satisfied smile and joyful sounds. "You don't know what you're missing, but yeah, there's a mess hall here. I just figured you would want to discuss events more before we plan our next move."

Brianna raised a quizzical eyebrow. "But I thought you had worked out everything already. What have you been doing for the past year in this place?"

"Things changed last night." A pained expression of embarrassment spread over his face as he spoke round the food in his mouth with the eloquence of Rambo talking through a mouth-guard.

Brianna had to concentrate to catch everything he said, but still couldn't interpret his words. "What?"

Ramsey swallowed. "I said things changed last night. Those corpses we saw the soldier boys carrying didn't happen in any of the eighteen different scenarios." He coughed, paused and punched his chest to dislodge something, and continued. "In fact, I still have to find where they're keeping Michael and the other Craig Ramsey. That wasn't supposed to arise."

He checked his watch. "James should be at the shelter while the rest of us would by now be halfway home with

Hayley."

"And after that?"

Craig gave a dismissive shake of the head. "It doesn't matter. Things have changed."

Brianna stood from the bed, patted down her clothes to remove the wrinkles and pinned her ID tag to the collar. "Then it's time we started doing something."

"But what about breakfast?" Ramsey said, offering her a doughnut.

Brianna's nose scrunched at the gooey sight and shook her head. How could Ramsey have been living like this while undercover? "I'm on a diet. Come on, let's go see if we can find where everyone's being kept and plan our next moves." She headed towards the door, but the wall beside it flickered and came to life.

Brianna took a step back, eyes widened to expose the whites, for there on the wall appeared a live image of their current antagonist—Colonel Blaze—which spoke in a voice that reminded her of an angry king brown snake.

"Detective Sergeant Cogan, how lovely to see you again." The cold steely eyes regarded her for a second before aiming a death glare towards Ramsey. "And Craig Ramsey... there's someone I have not seen in some time. It's wonderful of you to return."

Chapter 35

Brianna yelped before she realised it and backpedalled away from the door towards the room's centre next to Ramsey, whose jaw dropped at their antagonist's face. "How long have you known?" Ramsey asked, as bold as brass but with a slight tremor that Brianna caught.

Blaze's magnified countenance twisted into a sardonic leer. "Long enough. Mr Ramsey." It stared at them for a second before the image flickered, the face morphing into that of a sixteen-year-old thin-faced boy with brown hair. The lad laughed as Brianna and Ramsey looked at each other in shock. "Surprise!" Animated tears of laughter rolled down his computer-generated features. "You should have seen your faces. Brianna's all 'oh, my God,' and you were pretending you didn't need to scoop out your undies, Ramsey."

"Sparks?" Brianna thrust her hands on her shoulders and glared at the youth on the screen. "How long have you been there?"

The Sparks image checked a watch on his CGI self's wrist, invoking a memory to Brianna of when she knew him three decades ago before his death. "I've been here with Skids since about eight o'clock last night. By the way, did you know they have captured him?"

Ramsey chuckled, sweeping his hand across the screen's length. "Is this what you used to look like?" Sparks gave a nod and the psychic detective continued. "I can't believe I never knew that before. It's good to see you." Brianna nodded beside Ramsey, who answered Sparks' question. "I didn't know for sure about Michael's capture, but I'm guessing that since he and Craig went in —"

Sparks raised an eyebrow. "Just checking. How can I tell the difference between you both? Your DNA matches his."

Ramsey thought for a moment, then gave a shrug. "I'm the one you knew before I died, old friend. Don't forget, I couldn't hypnotise you, right?" Sparks nodded. "Anyway, I'm guessing that Blaze has captured the other Craig."

"And James, too." Sparks shook his head in apparent embarrassment.

"How?" Ramsey wanted to know. "Everything was going well until I arrived back here with Brianna. We should have made it to this room and the others in this hall, which I prepared, then met in here this morning."

Brianna's incredulous look and gasp interrupted him. "You had other rooms prepared for us?" She cast a disgusted look around at the cell and the single bed.

"Never mind that, Sparks," Ramsey replied. "Something changed, and it had to be on a monumental level if I couldn't pick up on it until now. What happened?"

Sparks gave a cheeky grin to Ramsey from the screen and winked at Brianna. "He's getting old and doesn't want to admit it slipped past him." That made Brianna giggle and Ramsey's mouthed an "Oi," before the digital teenager continued. "To cut it short, I hitch-hiked in Michael's electronics and stayed with him after his capture until they plonked him into his cell. It's about two levels down from here." A schematic of the base appeared on the LED display with labels on their rooms and the cells below. A bar of red highlighted Michael's cell. "By the way, while you both slept, I hacked into other parts of the system—

piss easy when you're already inside—I found a heap of stuff."

"Where are they keeping the other Craig Ramsey?" Brianna interrupted before Sparks could get carried away with himself. "And James and Hayley."

"Ah! Craig's on the other end of Michael's level. From what I've seen, he's unconscious still. Hayley's being kept separate to the general population of psychic trainees. There are a lot of them. And James is in the cell next to hers."

Ramsey, who had been pacing back and forth while Sparks explained everything, was shaking his head, his lips pursed. At mention of James' name, he stopped. "That boy should not be here. I gave implicit instructions to keep him away from here." He dismissed Brianna's questioning glance. "But tell me what else happened. What was it with the disaster movie scene we witnessed last night?"

Sparks' face returned to the screen to shrug with his hands held palms-upward. "No idea. Oates had acted against Blaze's orders from what I can gather. Hayley should have been in her cell all night — ("As I originally surmised," Ramsey muttered) — but Oates removed her and took her to a testing room." The scene changed to video footage taken from a fresh vantage point above Hayley in the room's corner.

Brianna and Ramsey watched as the little girl's demeanour shifted from the tame four-year-old that they remembered, to a cold, vicious vixen's visage. Her tone drifted, taking on a distorted note as though the words had transposed a tenth of a second on either side of each other, quivering, machine-like, or monotone. To Brianna, it was reminiscent of when she and her schoolmates gathered for assembly and greeted with, "Good morning, teachers," except the preschooler's remarks were profane, forceful, and demanding. Almost demonic. "Let me go. Let my daddy go, and my friends, or we will kill you." Hayley's harsh voice stabbed through Brianna's core, and a shiver wormed up her spine at the message. Then she gasped as the video's events escalated. A ball of light exploded from within Hayley that bleached out the display for a moment. When the image returned, they saw a lab-coated assistant grasping her chest before dropping to the ground, her body glowing yellow before collapsing and turning to a dust pile on the floor. Pandemonium followed, as the technicians scattered in all directions. Before, there were four scientists, but that became three when one man quit the room before the door slammed shut after him. The remaining trio weren't so lucky and were frozen as glistening ice statues, lifelike even in death. The soldiers, recognisable to Ramsey and Brianna, as those whose corpses they had seen the previous night, rushed inside and met their grisly fates. Screams reverberated from the video display's speakers, muted thanks to Ramsey's deft finger on the remote. Despite the lack of volume, the victims' screams echoed in their souls, cut short by their deaths, and demon-Hayley's horrible laughter played accompaniment to their dying symphony. A hissing sound resounded through the laboratory, and clouds billowed across the camera lens. Hayley's cursing voice slurred, softened, then fell silent.

The video faded. Ramsey turned from the screen and wiped his brow, apparently to disguise the worry in his eyes. "Sparks," he said, "you mentioned that Hayley's in a new cell now." He paused. "Is she alive?" A ball of light exploded from within Hayley. It bleached the display for a moment, then faded to reveal a lab-coated assistant grasping her chest before dropping to the ground. The woman's body glowed a brighter yellow before collapsing, leaving nothing but a dust pile on the floor.

"Yes, right after her Linda Blair routine, they put her in a lab modified for her. She's under observation."

A fresh shiver shuddered through Ramsey, and Brianna hugged herself to ward off the sick chills. "This is not right," she said, choking on her words. "Hayley's possession will devastate Michael. What can we do?"

Ramsey screwed up his face as though thinking. "No, she's not possessed." He paused. "Well… not how we think. Did you hear the voices all mixed with her own? Something else is going on that not even Blaze expected."

"What?"

Ramsey shook his head as though struggling to find the right words. "I suspect she's a conduit of some sort. Turner told me about them, but I can't remember what he said, and he's not here to help. None of the ghosts or spirits are here." A hopeless chuckle of disbelief escaped his lips. "Another thing to solve."

Sparks interrupted Ramsey's speech. "We still have to get Michael and Craig out of here. Along with Hayley and James, I mean."

"No." Ramsey stood and faced the screen and Brianna. "We can't. The visions have changed. We can only save one of them. Michael. Craig. Hayley. Or James."

Brianna's eyes flashed, her gaze hardened on Ramsey. "Fuck you. I'm not giving up on any of them. Not even the other Craig Ramsey. This isn't even his fight."

Ramsey rose to his full height, feet set in a firm stance as he confronted the shorter Brianna Cogan. "What? You're crazy. There are five probable outcomes that I've seen. We can recover any of them, but only one, and have barely enough time to escape alive. The moment we try to save a second, we all die."

Brianna advanced and shoved the psychic, who stumbled into the concrete wall, his shoulder blades crunching on the surface. With one hand, she pressed on his chest, holding him fast against it. The other poised, ready to strike if needed. Hot breath exploded from her nose as they eyed each other like jungle animals sizing up the other. "It's not as if your every vision has turned out to be correct, is it, Mr Craig Ramsey? You didn't predict this happening, or James' capture. Nor did you see—"

The lights in the room flickered, distracting them both and making them look towards the door. But no one entered.

"Now that I have your attention, lovebirds, will you calm your farm?" Sparks said. "We can't afford to fight ourselves. First, I would say to save Hayley, but it's a shitty life for her without her father, even if he would tell me to focus on her survival instead of his." Brianna nodded, still keeping her grip on Ramsey. "Second, same for James. Michael would kill us all, including me, if we rescued him and not her."

Ramsey scoffed. "So we save my doppelgänger instead? And screw the others?"

Brianna studied the psychic investigator through half-closed eyes, an idea brewing behind them. "You told me once that your visions were sometimes changeable. When did you last check them?"

Hesitation registered on Ramsey's face and his jaw

relaxed as he considered Brianna's question. "Yesterday morning."

"Then you need to check again." Brianna grabbed his wrists and, before he could respond, thrust his open palms upon her breasts. "Oi!" he responded, and Sparks interjected, "Hey, get a room, you two. Oh, this is it. Never mind me." Ramsey's eyes glazed for a moment, his consciousness lost in a vision, then a smile appeared on his face.

"I like the way you think, Cogan."

Brianna pushed the psychic away before she could lose control of the cheeky grin she suppressed. "And?"

Ramsey's eyes twinkled, his teeth showing as the corners of his mouth sought his ears. "What's your plan?"

Chapter 36

A warm sea breeze washed across Craig's sun-kissed skin, the white sand reflecting the rays against his face as he watched his little girl playing in the Pacific Ocean's waves. Her wet hair waved like a horse's thick tail as she plunged into the water with her kick-board and paddled along the shoreline. And Brianna's hand moved to his. "Do you remember when we first dated, and you took me here?" his wife said. He turned to look at her, tanned flesh darker through his Ray-Ban lenses, and smiled at the memory. He reached for her, but his hands refused to move. Something restricted him. And he realised. It was a dream, images played by a subconscious mind to remind him of a greater desire.

And he woke.

Craig blinked away the fog from his eyes, his vision rolling like the picture on an ancient television's faulty vertical hold setting, then took in his surroundings.

A plasterboard ceiling, painted a clinical white, greeted him along with what resembled a trolley laden with medical instruments, metallic and sharp, between him and the concrete wall to the right. Besides the paraphernalia, including a drip attached to his arm by a canula, a toilet in the corner near the large mirror on the left, the room was bare.

He strained his hands to move, and the same paralysis he encountered in the dream manifested itself as restraining straps around his wrists, chest, legs, and feet. And what was that on his scalp? Electrodes! Then he remembered.

Colonel Nigel Blaze! Déjà vu washed over him upon recalling how his alternate world's namesake had been as twisted and single-minded as this one, right down to the bondage techniques. Craig stretched his neck to see and better appraise the situation. Judging by the little wires stuck to his forehead and face, tickling his skin, Blaze couldn't resist testing the psychic again—probably to determine how he could still be alive.

Craig turned towards the sound of two beeps on the left, and the cell door opened inwards to reveal his alternate nemesis, who strode inside with a mocking leer.

"Mister Ramsey!" The uniformed officer regarded Craig's restraints and the medical equipment to the side. "At last, you have woken."

Craig glared back at Colonel Blaze, staring straight into his cold eyes for a second. Then a smirk crossed his face. "You're looking chipper for a man who lost his testicles." Blaze's mouth gave a single tiny twitch. Craig smiled to himself at the response, knowing the other man practised extreme self-control. Even more amusing to him was the knowledge that this Colonel Blaze had suffered the same unfortunate injury as the nemesis from his own world. Craig pushed his luck a little further. "Do your underlings still call you Colonel Castrati?"

Blaze's self-restraint proved strong, but not enough to prevent a slight reddening around his throat's skin. He remained silent, his eyes icy slits that regarded Craig the way a cobra might watch its prey before striking. But he stopped when another man appeared in the doorway.

The new arrival didn't appear special—at least not in authority. He sniffed upon entering, his shoulders rounded and neck poking forward like a turtle. The man's beady blue eyes gazed at Craig with a casual interest, his thin lips pressed in a straight line above a sunken chin. He reminded Craig of a cartoon vulture he had watched as a child. At Colonel Blaze's nod, the silent man circled the slab and regarded Craig with curiosity for a second or two. He stopped, tapped his gladstone bag, from which dropped a four-foot pole that snapped outward to form a tripod stand for the portmanteau. Practised fingers flicked open the satchel and retrieved a set of blades. They glittered in the light from above, dazzling Craig, who looked away to see what else the silent one did.

"Nice table," said Craig with a sincere node. It reminded him of a magic table he once owned, and he couldn't take his eyes off it. But the mute remained silent and waited for Blaze's instructions.

The superior officer regarded a sheaf of papers that Craig had failed to notice earlier in the officer's hand. He licked a finger and used it to turn the pages, his eyes flicking across the contents with laser efficiency. Now and then, he allowed an interested murmur, or nodded, then turned another page.

Meanwhile, the serene mute watched his superior as intently as a cattle dog keeps a keen eye on its master, awaiting a command. It was a ploy to make Craig uncomfortable in suspenseful anticipation of what came next, and each excruciating moment stretched for an eternity. At last, Blaze stopped, looked up at the second man, and said, "Please start, Willard. Don't let me hold you from your work."

It happened fast. Craig didn't even see the stranger move until the knife flashed, its stainless steel sinking into the flesh of his bicep as if it were soft butter. And the pain! It scorched through his nerves, rocking up his arm to the shoulder, which simultaneously paralysed and flared at the same time. The tears sprung to Craig's eyes and gushed down his cheeks before he could release his pained yelp amidst a flurry of swear words. Then Willard jerked his hand downward towards his victim's elbow, dragging the scalpel along by two inches. Craig couldn't stop crying in bitterness as the blood welled and ran from the gash. For the next minute, he could hear it splashing on the cell's floor.

Neither Blaze nor Willard flinched at the sight. Not a sound did they make.

Yet their eyes remained glued to Craig's wound, which turned crimson at the cut's edges for two minutes; the blood's pulsing flow ebbed and stopped before the gash closed and healed as if nothing had happened.

"You're a fast healer, Mister Ramsey." Blaze nodded in appreciation of the miracle. "I can't believe I didn't notice that earlier." He looked at Craig's assailant. "Willard, aren't you impressed?"

Willard gave a non-committal shrug at what he'd witnessed. Shocked, Craig took a deep breath, slow and controlled, and willed his heartbeat to a gentler pace. There was no point complaining because he was familiar with Colonel Blaze's nasty streak, a trait the tyrant shared with his namesake from Craig's world. A self-confessed fan of Hitler, who believed many of the Nazi horrific experiments on the innocents had contributed much to modern medicine and scientific knowledge. Madness incarnate.

Willard apparently enjoyed his job a lot. He tore the blade back along Craig's upper arm, opening a fresh wound from the elbow to the shoulder. Craig winced as he felt the cold steel touch bone. Then the pain shuddered through his body again, raging through his mouth in anger as new tears sprang forth in hitched sobs. Yet Willard's face remained stoic, impervious to Craig's pained cries, and as empathetic as a shark to its meal.

Craig glared at the man who delivered his pain, his gaze promising a slow death if he had been free of the restraints.

Blaze tut-tutted and asked in a deadpan voice. "No more smart words, Mister Ramsey?" Craig said nothing. He didn't dare yet. He stretched his fingers, hoping to gain traction on some part of the slab, anything that the colonel or one of his minions might have touched, so that his psychometric powers could reveal something, any clue, to help. But it was no use. "I see what you're doing. My staff have taken the precaution of ensuring you can touch nothing useful."

Willard gave another shrug for Colonel Blaze's benefit and received a head shake in response. He stood back, eyes settled on Craig's arm, which by now had healed from its second wound.

Blaze bent until his lips rested close enough to Craig's left ear. "I know how you survived. You're a fast healer, aren't you?" Craig's eyes flickered, suddenly aware of Blaze's interest in the current events. "You recover so quickly that Willard will struggle to kill you with a thousand cuts," Then he looked up towards the torture expert. Craig shuddered as he sensed the unseen grin on Blaze's face and felt the next words. "A man with your capabilities would prove... quite useful in the field, don't you agree? I'd like to learn your limits." He stood and beckoned to the torturer. "Care to try, Willard?"

This time, a smile crossed Willard's visage that haunted Craig's soul. He nodded, reached to his knife belt and retrieved another three blades, which he placed with measured care on the slab beside Craig's legs. Choosing one, he turned the surgical steel back and forth in the air, mesmerised by the light that danced on its edge, before staring into Craig's face. His thin lips opened to reveal teeth blackened from excessive coffee or strong antibiotics.

Willard's shrewd eyes twinkled and narrowed as his grip tightened on the scalpel's handle. Craig knew what was coming next as the other man's knuckles whitened. In a moment, the hand would slash downwards toward his chest. Perhaps he'd survive the stab to the heart, or maybe not. Craig didn't know the full extent of the ectoplasm's healing properties that flowed through his veins. But soon, he would –

"Wait!"

Disappointment coloured Willard's face, an angry sneer crossed his lips in a silent snarl. Craig's heart hammered so hard he nearly passed out, but he held on to learn what stayed his execution.

Craig turned his head towards Blaze, wondering what had caused him to stay Willard's sadistic hand. There beside the colonel stood a different technician. This one, a mousy young man, whispered something to the army officer who was reading what appeared to be a new sheet of paper. Blaze scanned the sheet's contents, his eyes opening wide. A smile stretched across his face, filled with glee, an emotion Craig wasn't certain he liked on the colonel.

"Mister Ramsey, you are a man full of surprises, aren't

you?"

Craig drew a slow, painful breath. "I'm glad you approve."

The colonel humphed. "Willard, your services are no longer required at this moment" The torture specialist made a questioning voice, and Blaze added, "For now."

Willard's disappointed sigh reminded Craig of Lurch from The Addams Family and packed his knives away. As he did so, his superior officer approached closer. "You have earned yet another reprieve, Mister Ramsey."

Willard snapped the leg of his makeshift table back into the base of his gladstone bag, clicked his heels together, and glided away and out the door, followed by the new lab technician and Colonel Blaze.

"But don't go anywhere. I have more plans for you."

The cell door slammed with an echo that bounced in the room. Craig remained still, thinking, curious about the turn of his fate. He raised his head to check his arm, which, despite the lingering pain, had healed back to smooth skin. Not even a scar. His eyes flicked to the mirror on the wall. It had to be a one-way glass panel, an observation area from which Blaze would probably watch his every move. It was likely that's how his nemesis knew Craig had woken. He pondered the chances, decided that Blaze wasn't in there now, then allowed himself the flicker of a smile before looking at his right hand.

Blaze had thought Craig couldn't reach any object likely to give him a chance of escape. But he was wrong.

Craig's fingers, dexterous but slightly out-of-practice since he hadn't practised sleight of hand in some time, reached under his backside to reveal one of Willard's blades he had sneaked there. Earlier, his pained cries and faces had distracted everyone from his quick action. A ploy to help him escape.

With a light fingertip grip on the scalpel's handle, he manipulated the blade into position against the leather strap on his wrist. Craig's brow wrinkled. It wasn't the ideal position to cut the leather, risky and slow, but no other choice existed in his thoughts. His fingers were long, but not enough to remove the strap.

Two beeps from the door caught him by surprise. It opened inwards and Craig briefly wondered if it was another vision.

"Well, fancy meeting me here!"

Craig looked in shock at his mirror image. "You took your sweet bloody time in coming here."

"Just in time, I'd say." A broad grin appeared on the other Craig Ramsey's face, then he spied the scalpel in Craig's hand. "Unless you want to do it yourself?"

Craig dropped the scalpel and managed a shrug. "I'm out of practice, I'm afraid. Be my guest."

The other Ramsey gave a nod and began removing the straps from Craig's limbs. For a moment, a curious expression crossed his face, then Craig experienced a new vision. When he recovered from it, Craig regarded his doppelgänger. "You know what I saw?"

"I think I do," said the other man. "At the same time."

"Then we have the same idea."

Chapter 37

The world swirled for Michael when he opened his eyes to find Blaze's steely gaze returning his stare. Blinking his eyes, Michael groaned. "This had better be a bad dream."

Blaze's face remained still as he returned Michael's stare. With a flick of his finger, he stepped back as the bed on which Michael lay tipped upward. Thick leather straps held Michael fixed to the bed as it moved into a vertical position that allowed him to face the colonel, who kept a close watch on him. Was that a flicker of amusement in the officer's eyes? Michael couldn't be sure, but a sick sensation sat in the pit of his stomach.

"Good morning, Mister Mach." Blaze glanced at Michael's restraints. "Does this help fill your James Bond fantasies?"

Michael shrugged.

Blaze's gaze lowered to the skin-tight suit Michael wore. "Interesting attire you have there. We found a couple of throwing stars, but every other pocket held pebbles." He paused, the closest to a chuckle Michael had ever seen his enemy make in a long time. "Planning on invading a glass house?"

"More like returning the rocks to your head," Michael replied, drawing a deep breath and releasing it. His gaze shifted, eyebrows raising in curiosity at Blaze's off-sider. To the side stood a silent companion in his forties or fifties with black hair plastered to his scalp with too much hair gel. Blue eyes that narrowed and reminded Michael of a rat's calculating stare looked back at him. "Who's the goth?"

Blaze turned his head toward the other man. "Oh, you haven't met Willard, have you? You might remember his predecessor Klaus."

Michael rolled his eyes at mention of the former torture expert. He had never experienced the full extent of Klaus' abilities, but he knew the man's reputation to inflict pain with a capital P. "Do you want me to talk?"

Blaze tilted his head, a puzzled look on his face, until recognition dawned. "A pop culture reference to James Bond?" He gave an appreciative nod. "Very well. No, but I do want something." With precise movements, he circled behind Michael's upright slab as he spoke. "First, Mister Mach, I–"

"Will you stop calling me Mister Mach?" Michael blurted, fighting a rising anger. "You have no right to use that name."

Blaze paused and returned to his previous spot before Michael, then leaned closer to his captive's face. "Does it bring back terrible memories, perhaps?" When Michael responded with his own baleful glare, temples pulsing, Blaze gave a nod. "Perhaps I am stirring enough torture by reminding you of your father, the man my associates… terminated when you were a child." He gestured towards Willard. "I hope that doesn't disappoint my pain specialist too much."

"Not that you'd care what others thought," Michael muttered.

If Blaze had heard the comment, he showed nothing. "Michael," he said, his voice quiet but definite in emphasising the name, "I discovered something interesting about you in recent times. A secret you no doubt want kept from others because of what it can do."

Michael's eyes widened. "A secret?" He had tried to sound casual, but his mind raced for words, anything to say. Only panic came. Did he know about the–?

"You have a powerful brain. One with a high energy yield, yes?"

Michael released a silent breath of relief, but did his best to appear disappointed. At least his real secret was safe. He hoped.

The colonel lifted a folder. "The Russians first discovered this in 1987. You would have been in high school then." His voice trailed as though he had posed a question, but Michael said nothing. Blaze said, "The file we uncovered shows that a KGB agent approached you and even attempted to take you to the USSR to power a machine they intended to utilise in crippling the British Empire's defences and society. Do you recall anything about that?"

Michael offered a non-committal shrug. "You can't believe everything the government tells you."

Blaze spun about-face and glared at him. "I know my history…" Something in the army officer's eyes warned Michael about making an outburst. "I checked the facts for myself. You see, when I read this just over a year ago, I followed through with the data provided by our friends across the ocean." Michael fought to contain his amazement at the depth of his captor's knowledge. However, the colonel was watching him like a hawk. He must have noticed a reaction; Blaze's tone deepened, and he spoke slower to press each word. "I watched you, or at least your energy, and built receptors that aimed at Statton. Even your old hometown of Banksia Grove. At first, I picked up the wavelength of the signature at the same frequency the Russians did. It seems you're not the only one. Lots of children have it. But you remained hidden. How?"

Michael's poker face came easier. "Like I said–"

Blaze interrupted. "But the other night. Now, that was an interesting time. Out of nowhere, our satellites detected a massive jump." *Oh, shit*, thought Michael as he realised what would come next, and he waited as the monologue continued. "We found an energy source that moved from (He pointed at Michael) your place, Mister Mach. The deceased Ramsey's former residence. And it ended up at Brianna Cogan's home. And that is how we learned of Hayley's special gift of inheritance from you, my old friend."

"My friends know to leave my daughter alone."

Blaze's eyebrow raised as he gave a nod. "Wise advice. If I had a daughter that pretty, I'd protect her with my life too. There's just one thing missing." The way his tone came made Michael narrow his eyes in question. "You failed to discipline her."

Blaze faced the opposite wall, raised a small device, and pressed a button. A flat screen monitor came to life and displayed a picture of Hayley performing ESP tests. "Your daughter is a whiz at the psychic experiments, particularly those related to remote viewing, but she has become somewhat… insolent." He gestured towards Michael. "I apologise for sounding like a schoolteacher when I say this, Mister Mach… Michael… but she has a discipline problem."

Michael laughed. "She's a bright kid, and I will not spank her for you. Forget it."

Blaze pressed the remote button again. This time, it

showed the destruction wrought by Hayley's fury. The picture was worth one thousand words, and each echoed death, chaos, and mayhem on a scale that inspired Michael's jaw to hang in shock. "What the hell?"

"I need your help to discipline her."

"You've got to be kidding. No way," Michael answered. "I don't know how Hayley did that, but I bet they had it coming."

"Then you leave me no choice, Mister Mach." Soon, the screen's display changed. The scene resembled another cell with similar decor to Michael's room, except this had a proper bed with a mattress, sheets, and a blanket. Laying there with her face buried in the pillow, tiny shoulders shaking with sobs, was Michael's daughter.

"Hayley!"

At the sound of her father's familiar voice, the girl turned and looked directly at the lens. Relief flooded Michael to see she was still well and healthy, just upset, her face wet with tears. "Daddy?"

Blaze's voice was gentle but firm when he spoke to her. "Hayley, I have your father with me."

The little girl's features hardened. "Let me and Daddy go. I mean it."

Michael couldn't hold back the smile. She was so much like her mother when her brow crinkled in anger. It amused him to see his brave daughter stand up to the colonel.

Blaze's tone reflected a serene but deadly intent. Authoritarian. "I've been speaking to your father about your terrible behaviour, Hayley." He paused. "Have you thought about what I said to you earlier?"

She stuck out her chin, squeezed her lips together, and

shook her head.

"When a child does such naughty things, Hayley, it shows your daddy did a bad job of raising you. Did you know that?"

Hayley remained silent, defiant, and her nose screwed up more. "No!"

"It's not your fault," Blaze added, his tone softening. "Your daddy is at fault, and I will punish him for you."

Too late, Michael realised Blaze's idea. He tried to yell, to tell her to stop, to look away, to cover her eyes and ears, to sing her favourite song in her head. But he could only scream as Willard's knife slashed over his chest, through his suit, penetrating flesh to scrape along the ribs in a long jagged line that erupted with blood that ran in rivers across the abdomen. Hayley's frantic cries echoed. Willard sliced and diced again and again. And when the little girl tried to look the other way, another flat screen monitor popped to life before her to display the terrifying, bloody images to her widened eyes. And her daddy's screams repeated over and over, even when she covered her ears. She didn't see her father's wounds shut and heal by themselves like the mythical Prometheus of Ancient Greece. All she knew was that Blaze had hurt her father, and the pain engulfed her heart. The torture dragged by for five long minutes, which may as well have been five days, an eternity to the child. And as suddenly, it stopped.

The monitors switched off. Blaze examined the wounds on Michael, observed how his captive continued to breathe, his chest rising and falling. And with the sound of Michael's sobbing and cursing echoing from the cell's walls, he left without further word.

Later, his breathing steadied, Michael spat a ball of blood

from his mouth that splattered on the floor. He stretched his fingers towards his bonds. Just the slightest touch. That's all he needed. But he couldn't reach any part of his restraints or even the table.

But he was damned if he would stop trying.

Chapter 38

Brianna cast an eye around the corner, her ears pricked for any other signs of trouble, as she approached her next aim.

The first part of her plan—rescuing the children from their cells—had finished without a hitch. Ramsey's psychic prowess with psychometry, although quite accurate on many accounts, came with one big flaw. His ego. He didn't always accept that other options existed beyond what he sensed. Here, Brianna's military training and her ability to think laterally topped Ramsey. He hadn't considered saving the children first.

They were the actual victims. Being in a centralised section, it proved a snap to spirit the kids from the cells to two armoured vehicles waiting upstairs from them. Ramsey had get the transportation and positioned them ready with the help of three "sleeper agents" he had recruited through hypnosis from under Blaze's nose. And their secret weapon, Sparks, handled the security camera footage by planting fake computer-generated loops through the network. Anyone watching the cameras would have seen nothing as the children disappeared up the lifts to the transport. By now, they were long gone, which meant Brianna and Ramsey could concentrate on their next objectives: rescue Michael, Hayley, and the other Craig Ramsey.

"Just another ten metres to go," Sparks' voice whispered through the Bluetooth earphone connected to the phone in her pocket. The cyber-teenager had assured her no one else could listen since he altered its software from inside the device. "You'll find Skids' cell there. There're two guards outside it."

Brianna couldn't believe her luck. "Only two?"

"Affirmative."

They didn't stand a chance. Without fear of detection from the hacked security cameras, Brianna dispatched the sentries with well executed Krav Maga moves before they noticed anything. As the second guard dropped unconscious, she caught sight of his familiar face. "Sparks," she said. "This is the same driver from the van that kidnapped Hayley the other morning." She rolled up his sleeve and noticed the same tattoo of the kangaroo as before. "It is!"

"No," Sparks replied, obviously following the real footage from the cameras above. "He's a clone. A database search shows the original soldier died during the Afghanistan campaign. He probably didn't even know they'd captured his DNA."

Brianna let the sleeping sentry drop back to the floor and rifled through his pockets for a key pass, which she held against the cell door's sensors. It opened with a hydraulic hiss. "I'm in."

"It's just Michael in there. You're clear to go."

Brianna ducked inside, shutting the door behind her, and gasped upon spotting Michael and the blood on his clothing and the floor. "Michael!" She hurried to his side and saw the bruises on his wrists. Her adopted brother had put up a fight by the looks of things when they tortured him, but couldn't escape. Her glance fell upon the clamps, and she nodded. His shackles held him down such that it proved impossible to touch anything with his fingers.

Otherwise, she might not have needed to rescue him. His eyes remained closed, his body unmoving, a pained expression colouring his features. "Michael?"

Brianna gave his face a gentle slap. Michael's eyelids took a few agonising seconds to flutter to life before his body jerked into action. He struggled, shouting, then stopped when he noticed he had friendly company.

"Brianna?" His voice was raspy and dry as autumn leaves blowing along a street. "Is–?"

Brianna's hands moved fast, fingernails picking at the clamp and unlocking it. "Relax, mate. We're getting you out of here."

He coughed and spat a dried ball of blood. "Hayley! What about Hayley? The bastards tortured me to get her to do what they want."

Brianna flinched at the image in her mind. Physical torture of the father to manipulate the little girl! Angered, she removed the rest of Michael's restraints. Somehow, Michael quipped something about being out of bondage, another reference to one of his boyhood idols, as he collapsed into Brianna's arms. "Come on, Mick," she said, struggling to hold his dead weight. "Move your legs, won't you?"

A cacophonous shriek filled the corridor outside and echoed into the cell. Its wails deafened them at first, and Brianna shouted, "Sparks, what the hell is going on?"

"They've discovered us, Brianna. I'm sorry."

Brianna swore under her breath. "Do I want to know how?"

"Looks like a faulty hard disk sector. The video loop I saved for the security guards is corrupt." Sparks went quiet, then added, "Some boffin in Blaze's cybersecurity found it and re-patched the cameras. We're cactus, guys."

"We might be, but you aren't," Brianna puffed as she supported Michael with one arm around her shoulder. She urged his feet to move and regain circulation. "You're wherever you are. Get us out of here."

Michael's legs regained their coordination, but wobbled like wet noodles as he limped beside Brianna. He appeared groggy. Had they kept him drugged?

They hurried down the corridor, but Brianna's ears picked up something else. Stomping footfalls. Lots of them. They stopped, turned and headed the other way, and halted at the next sight. Another group of soldiers, armed to the teeth with their weapons levelled at them.

Brianna checked Michael's state and realised he still wasn't ready for a fight. The odds proved too great.

Swearing to herself, she whispered for Sparks' benefit as she and Michael raised their hands. "How are the others?"

"You mightn't want to know."

"Sparks," she uttered under her breath. "Tell me."

"We're cactus."

"Not that."

Chapter 39

Two soldiers, decked in standard tiered body armour, trained the F88 Austeyr rifles on Michael and Brianna while a third strapped their wrists behind them with zip ties. Brianna spotted one man's stare centring on her breasts as the other pulled her arms tighter behind her back. She cleared her throat, and when his focus lifted, Brianna recognised his face.

"You're the man from the park!"

He shook his head, an amused smirk twinkling in his eyes. "Someone else."

A clone, she realised as the third soldier spoke from behind. "All sorted. The colonel wants this guy in Lab 42."

The familiar soldier with the rifle looked past Brianna, gesturing to her with his weapon's barrel. "What about the chick?"

"Bring her too, he said." The soldier beside Brianna patted her down for weapons, fingers lingering between her thighs for a second too long before bringing his hands higher up. "Hey! What's this?" He reached towards her ear and removed Brianna's Bluetooth device, which he held near his ear for a moment before dropping it to the ground. It crunched as he stomped upon it. "Don't need any of that here."

"Okay, move along." The armed guards forced the two prisoners to turn the other direction and walk along the corridor and round the corner.

Brianna glanced at Michael, noticed his gait still seemed wobbly, but something wasn't right. Her eyes flicked to his face and met Michael's. Relief filled her upon seeing him give her a quick grin before he peeked to ensure the captors hadn't noticed, then he gave a wink. Brianna wished she could read Michael's mind to know what he was planning, or was he faking his weakened condition the way a mother bird fools the predator to misdirect from something else? Whatever he planned, Brianna figured it best to wait for his move, but she couldn't keep herself from checking through the corner of her eye. Ah! His fingers were stretching, testing their reach inside. Any moment now, the zip tie would touch his palm or fingers and change into something weaker. Yet nothing happened.

Michael coughed. She glanced again at him, and he shook his head. He had changed his mind.

Then she realised why. For ahead of them stood an open doorway. Michael spotted a sign outside the door a few steps before they entered. "42, eh? I don't think it means life, the universe, and everything. What do you think, Bri-?" A rifled nudged between the shoulder blades silenced Michael, but that didn't stop his jaw hanging open at the sight within. Michael had visited an older version of the Project's base before and was no stranger to the environment. But to Brianna, this appeared-she hated to admit it-like something from a James Bond movie.

For within, the lab featured more than a mainframe with blinking lights and cheap noises. The chamber was larger than the 11,700 square metre interior of the Duomo di Milano Brianna had once visited on a European trip before joining the police. Above them, encircling the room's perimeter, sat many cabinets outlined by blue led lighting that contributed to the spooky atmosphere. She didn't need to hear Michael's whispered commentary that this must have been one of the most powerful supercomputers in the world after China's Sunway TaihuLight. The soldiers ushered them down a ramp that gently sloped towards a lower level in the middle of which waited Colonel Blaze, whose eyes flashed with a smugness as they approached.

"Hayley!" Michael stepped quicker to meet his daughter standing beside the colonel with another guard's hand on her shoulder.

"Hold it!" his guard warned, but the colonel gave a quick shake of his head.

"Let them hug."

Hayley ran to her father and into his arms, her legs curling around him like a koala. He gave a small groan. "Daddy, are you hurt?" she asked.

Michael ran his fingers through her hair as he looked into her eyes and smiled. "I'll be fine, angel." He pointed to Brianna. "See? Aunty Bri is here too." The little girl squeezed him hard, murmuring something that Brianna couldn't catch. "That's a good girl. We'll be fine."

"That's enough," Blaze barked in an impatient voice, and Hayley's guard separated the father and daughter.

The ground vibrated under their feet and a panel in the room's exact centre slid open, creating a hole in the floor from which a gigantic structure rose. It took less than two minutes before it locked in place to reveal what resembled a box structure like a supercomputer's cabinet. Attached to the sides of it were three egg-shaped structures. The clear perspex shells contained what looked like seats or backrests. Brianna couldn't tell which, but they could house one person each.

"We call this the Neurolyser," said Blaze as the machine flickered into life, maroon-coloured LEDs bathing him in a sickly light that made Brianna think of the alleged flames of Hell. Appropriate, she figured. A sound behind them all caught his attention and everyone turned to see two guards leading Craig Ramsey into the chamber. "Ah! Mister Ramsey! So glad you could join us. I was just about to explain this machine to everyone." To watch, it appeared more as if Ramsey hadn't a care in the world and was leading the others inside, not the other way round.

"This machine…? That explains why everyone's awake!" Ramsey quipped, his straight teeth shining in a cheeky grin despite the scarlet light shining on him as he stood next to Brianna. He nodded to her, then Michael and Hayley. "Hello!" Brianna raised an eyebrow and looked back at Ramsey, who turned towards the machine. "So what did I miss?"

Blaze's brow furrowed, narrowing his eyes, as he assessed Ramsey. A distracted look appeared but soon disappeared before he resumed talking, with an occasional curious glance at the newcomer. "We first tested it this week but had to fix a bug in its software. Still, we improved it further and no longer rely on the power grid to run it."

Brianna tensed when, without warning, the soldiers levelled their rifles at Ramsey, who had reached inside his jacket. He stopped, watched the barrels, and cocked an amused eyebrow. "Jumpy boys, aren't you?" Ramsey said, removing a pair of spectacles, which he placed on his face to peer at the lights on Blaze's new toy.

The colonel resumed. "With this, I can quickly find psychics, those with the greater gift, and avoid the trial and error when testing them."

An intrigued expression crossed Ramsey's face. "How?"

Blaze considered the psychic investigator's question as

though deciding how much to say. "Over the past three years, we have launched several satellites into orbit above the southern and northern hemispheres. Each satellite scans for a particular frequency of brainwave activity in humans." He paused as though expecting Ramsey to interrupt. When none came, he said, "Not every human is blessed with this wavelength, and so far, we have found only three people with it." He gave a grand sweep of his arm toward the Neurolyser. "This will help us find more in Australia and, soon afterwards, the world."

Something about Ramsey piqued Brianna's interest. He seemed too blasé, too obvious, as if he were enjoying every moment. Then she noticed it and wondered if her discovery should require concern on her part.

Ramsey's gaze froze and hardened as he watched Blaze. "And when you find these psychics, will you recruit them?"

A twisted smile curled across Blaze's face. "You're a quick study, Mister Ramsey. Yes."

"And those in enemy countries?" Michael asked, his voice rasping from a dry throat, which he cleared.

Blaze shrugged in a hasty manner. "We kill them."

Ramsey and Michael looked at each other with matching expressions of horror. Even little Hayley understood and stared hard at Blaze. "I won't let you," she said, her voice as calm and cruel as it was when she had confronted Blaze the previous day.

For a second, the colour drained from Blaze's face. He nodded to a nearby soldier, who aimed his rifle at Michael's head. "Didn't your father teach you not to speak out of turn, Hayley?"

Hayley's lower lip trembled slightly. She shrank back in

her father's reassuring arms.

"What has this to do with us?" Brianna asked, taking the heat from Hayley and Michael, as she realised Blaze was using father and daughter as hostages to each other.

Blaze turned to Brianna, recognition in his eyes. "Colonel Brianna Cogan from Fifth Division, correct?" He stepped closer to watch her. "One of the best shots we had in Afghanistan after your partner Tom Richter, I believe." Brianna nodded. "A fine officer. Such a waste, even for a woman." He turned on his heel and motioned towards the soldiers. "Strap them in."

The perspex egg-shaped containers opened with a hiss, a faint wisp of vapour escaping from within them, and the soldiers grabbed Ramsey, Michael Mach and Hayley, then ushered them inside a capsule each. With their hands, feet, and bodies secured by metal clasps and straps, the containers closed over them. Hayley's piercing screams rocked from inside. Brianna wanted to move forward to free her, but the odds were too great against her not surviving the guards' bullets from such close range.

Blaze said to Brianna, but loud enough for the captives to hear from inside their prisons, "These three are our most powerful psychics. Michael Mach was the first we discovered to possess this brain energy. By genetic design, so does Hayley."

"What of the children you kidnapped?" Brianna snapped. "What do they have that you want?"

Blaze stopped, puzzlement on his face, then a grin grew to life. "You're an intelligent girl, aren't you? Or did you already know we can track some children and attract them with our Subliminal Psionics?" Brianna gave a noncommittal shrug, but Blaze didn't buy it. "Yes, you know. But there's one other thing." He pointed to Ramsey's cell. "Our mutual friend here has changed since he returned from the dead. Interestingly enough, he returned on the same night that we first tested the Neurolyser. I'd like to see if we can resurrect other psychics from the grave too."

"To increase your numbers?"

Blaze smirked. "Maybe, but that's not all. Power, Colonel Cogan, power! Power for this machine. Mister Ramsey has the same energy in his brain now, and it's more powerful than before he died! We need it to power this machine!"

At Colonel Blaze's signal, a laboratory attendant pulled down a lever in the machine's main cabinet. The maroon LEDs brightened and changed to a green colour. Internal fans hummed to life as a set of flat-screens on the walls came to life.

An instant later, a high-pitched note, short but sweet like a single strike on an empty bottle, filled the air. The machine disconnected. The humming stopped.

Brianna raised an eyebrow for a second and struggled to keep a straight face. "Perhaps you put the batteries in the wrong way?"

Blaze said nothing. A lab technician hurried towards the switches on the side of the Neurolyser's main cabinet and checked the state of things. He flicked a couple of switches, pressed another button, and shook his head in disbelief as another "lab rat" approached to examine the machine, too. They discussed the situation, scratched their heads again.

Brianna couldn't hear everything they said but caught the words "fuses" and "connection". Then something came to mind as she looked towards the perspex eggs in which her friends waited. Just like the lab geeks, Michael's facial expression was a picture of befuddlement and mild relief. But Craig Ramsey's face shone in a smile. An idea formed in her mind as recent events rushed through her head. Ramsey's smile as he approached them in the chamber reminded her of seeing Craig in Michael's living room the other morning. There had been something different about his brief smile then. What was it?

By this time, the lab technicians approached the perspex eggs with a glowing device that resembled a wand with a cord waving from the end. As one technician waved it around Hayley's container, it buzzed like a Geiger counter. The same buzz came when waved on Michael's cell. Then came Craig Ramsey's turn. No sound. The first technician turned towards Blaze, whose face had reddened upon looking at one of the caged prisoners.

"Take Mister Ramsey from the cell!" he fumed.

They unlocked the cell, unfastened Ramsey's restraints, and allowed the psychic to exit the perspex egg with a broad cheeky smile.

"That didn't go quite to plan, did it, Nigel?" His straight teeth shone in a grin.

The blast from the pistol happened before Brianna realised Blaze had drawn it. Craig Ramsey almost spun on one foot as the bullet's impact knocked him backwards. Without a cry, he fell facedown to the ground, one arm at a strange angle. Brianna was running to him before she realised it. A scream stuck in her throat. She slid across the floor to his side and held him close, one finger feeling for a pulse that had stopped. Tears burned the edges of her eyes before wetting her face as she rocked him back and forth, trying to hold his life inside. But it was too late, and she had realised the truth: this was her Craig Ramsey, the one she had known before his doppelgänger appeared from elsewhere. They must have switched places, or was the other man still stuck in his cell block? This was not the plan she intended!

Broken, Brianna kept holding Ramsey's inert body, aware yet unable to respond to either Hayley's screams or Michael's shocked and angry retorts. Neither did she hear Blaze call for the next subject to enter the vacated egg. She kept rocking back and forth, her sanity torn to the edge with grief for the man she loved without having taken the chance to admit it to him. The sound of the perspex chamber slamming shut and sealing made her glance upward in surprise at whom she saw there. "James?"

Blaze appeared distorted by the tears that obscured her vision. "Yes, James." A thinly disguised expression of smugness appeared on his face. "James is my Ace in the hole." He turned towards Michael, who appeared even more confused, his face white from shock. "You may have shielded your brain energy from me with your dampeners, Mister Mach, but James is what you might call a psychic capacitor or leech. He's been absorbing your energy ever since you took him away." He paused, his eyes keen like a rat's as he took in Michael's dumbfounded look. "You made it so easy for me when you took him. He's my battery, charged as much as you and Hayley, and I used him to track you and sit waiting."

Blaze nodded towards the lab technicians. The taller of the two reached for the controls and activated the Neurolyser. "And with the flick of a switch, I can find every psychic in the world. Some will perish when we find them. Just like Craig Ramsey…" He pulled a disgusted expression as he looked at Ramsey's body still cradled in Brianna's arms. "The others will serve our purposes."

The Neurolyser came back to life like a creature from the grave, its circuits powered by the extra energy from James' brain cells. Flat screen monitors activated and displayed satellite images of first Statton and then the rest of Australia. Data scrolled upwards upon. Geographical latitude and longitudes flashed on the screen, then came facial images with the names and addresses of each person, scrounged and scraped from other government databases. They flicked and changed so fast, but not so quickly that she missed seeing a face she'd known and grown up with since she was a child: her own!

Her eyes darted towards Blaze but noticed nothing in his expression to show if he had seen her face there too. It didn't matter. He was collecting data now. Later, he would learn when his analysts finished scouring and examining the results.

"More!" Blaze demanded. "Stretch the range. Turn on all the satellites. Let's see if we can find targets in the Middle East or Russia." On his command, more data appeared on the screen as the Neurolyser's fans whined at a higher pitch.

Brianna looked towards Michael and the others in the cells, her ideas crashing on the rocks of futility as she considered ways to stop the inevitable. Then she noticed her adoptive brother's struggle to free a hand, his fingers pressed together to attempt slipping from the clamp. A crimson creek of blood crept down his arm, dripping from the elbow to splash on the cell's floor.

A sudden explosion rocked the room. People's shouts from outside made the room's occupants glance towards the door as more blood-curdling screams approached. Amongst them mingled the angry voices of children. Machine guns fired. A child's voice roared, angry and terse. A man screamed a bloodcurdling yowl of fear, then stopped as though clipped.

Silence fell, broken only by the sound of the Neurolyser's internal fans.

A hush had fallen over the colonel and his minions as he listened, eyes darting back and forth, his fingers tensing on his holstered pistol. When he finally moved, Blaze motioned towards the six soldiers in the chamber and drew his pistol as they assembled into battle positions, their weapons trained on the door.

They waited. Fifteen tense seconds. No one dared breathe as their ears strained.

Brianna slowly released a breath, eyes darting round the room to assess the situation inside, searching for anything she could use as a weapon to help the odds from inside. She didn't know what had happened out there, but it had to be better than what they faced here. A glance revealed the soldiers were too far from her. If she dashed towards one of them, they would shoot her in a heartbeat. Blaze stepped away from her, closer to Hayley's cell, a bead of sweat trickling from his forehead. She couldn't reach his gun in time, either.

With a dying groan, the Neurolyser powered down, its screens turning black.

The soldiers' eyes focused on the doorway, fingers poised on their weapons' triggers. Their stances reflecting the same thought and purpose. Kill whoever entered.

Chapter 40

"Steady." Blaze felt anything but calm as he watched the entrance. He fought back the chills that rattled down his spine from the cries that reminded him of losing men in battle. The cold steel of the pistol he held provided small comfort as he wondered what had happened on the other side of the door—and what still lurked there. He glanced towards the egg-shaped container in which Hayley Mach sat.

Hayley returned a forbidding stare, uncharacteristic for little girls her age, that pierced the front of his skull, unwavering, and with the hint of a smile curling her lips. Something about the girl's manner gave Blaze the impression of an older, tougher mind and reminded him of his controlling mother. What did she know?

A shiver slid through Blaze's nerves and paralysed his thinking, bringing back memories of an ambush he'd experienced early in his career. A whisper from a nearby soldier snapped his attention to the present in time to witness a white mist seeping through the cracks between the door and its jamb and casing. Liquid nitrogen? Cool air wafted by him from the peculiar fog, reminding him of the strange frostbite some of his staff had received. The door's steel panel warped, curling like a sheet of paper and groaning from the strain, until hairline fissures appeared and spread across its surface. Blaze opened his mouth too slow to scream his order—too late.

The door burst inwards, slicing through the air to Blaze's left and at three guards. The projectile separated the head from its shoulders, creating a crimson fountain that spurted and splashed on Blaze's otherwise neat uniform. Screams filled his ears as the flying panel lashed two more victims with a crackling of snap frozen flesh and heavy solidified limbs. Their cries faded too fast for comfort for Blaze.

Three bursts of staccato thundered from the surviving troops' rifles, the bullets flying from the flashing barrels into the white, billowing clouds of mist that washed through the doorway. Ammunition spent. A momentary silence before fresh magazines clicked into place. The troopers stood ready, weapons aimed, with their shaky fingers resting on the trigger. The cloud advanced without a sound, as if guided by unseen intelligence towards Blaze, who inched away, his fixed stare unwavering.

The girl. It had to be her doing it. But what had she done to all the guards in the outside corridor? Where were they? What about Major Oates? Why wasn't he taking control? With his pistol still aimed at the door, Blaze side-stepped towards Hayley's perspex cell, his free hand reaching for the lock on its hatch. His finger fumbled at the latch, but he dared not take his eyes off the mist that inched closer to him. He tightened his finger on the trigger, poised….

Something smashed the pistol from his hand. It skittered across the room and stopped on the floor against the Neurolyser cabinet's base. A perfect icicle poked from its barrel, which had whitened with frost.

Thack! Thack! Thack!

The soldiers' weapons flew from their surprised hands to clatter to the floor and skittered across the surface, each impaled by an icicle through its barrel. They stepped back, surprise plastered on their faces as they sought cover from the unknown assailant.

The mist boiled further inside and a thin beam resembling sunlight shone into the room from outside the door, a man's shape silhouetted as he strolled inside. Blaze glanced at the dead man on the floor, then back at the shadowy figure that approached, aware of its similarity to…

"Craig Ramsey?" Blaze stammered the name, glancing from the dead man nearby on the ground, then to the new arrival.

"That's my name." The second Craig Ramsey grinned, showing a slight disorder to his front teeth. The smile disappeared a moment later, replaced by a dark, thundering countenance as he took in the scene. His eyes narrowed as he saw Brianna cradling the dead Ramsey and Michael and the children in the cells. He glared back at Blaze. "Hello, *Nigel No-friends*."

The soldiers rushed the new arrival at once, but three projectiles flew from the thick mist like missiles and knocked them to the concrete floor before they could reach him. Craig turned to assess the damage, shrugged, and glared at the colonel, who had regained his composure.

Blaze sucked in a breath, realising that this was an elaborate illusion on Ramsey's part. Anger and confidence filled him, tempered by decades of army discipline and training. "Your magic tricks and illusions won't work on me, Mister Ramsey," he said through gritted teeth, removing and dropping his jacket to the floor. He rolled up the sleeves of his otherwise crisp, pressed blood-stained shirt and advanced upon Craig. Now he realised what had happened. His Neurolyser had brought one Craig Ramsey to life on the night he first tested it. Tonight, it had delivered yet another, and maybe this resurrected psychic had high brain energy to power the device too. He could keep killing them one after the other and still bring them back from the dead. "I killed you over a year ago, Ramsey. Watched as my car ploughed through your worthless body and even drove my car over you twice more, to be certain. Now I'll kill you again."

"By talking me to death?" Craig Ramsey raised an amused eyebrow. "Should I have an old woman take my place?"

Angered, Blaze rushed him. "I'm a master of wushu, karate, kempo, and kickboxing." He strode closer to Craig Ramsey, ready to attack. "I'll pull you apart and—"

Blaze dropped to the ground, gasping for breath. He hadn't even seen Craig move, but he had felt the psychic's fingers strike his throat. He coughed and rasped, struggling to breathe, and rolled on his back. His face reddened more when his opponent stood over him, placed a foot on his chest, pinning him to the ground.

"Remind me to be impressed, will you, Nigel?"

Chattering voices filled the air as a mob of children entered the chamber, some of them standing next to Craig Ramsey to shower the colonel with their vindictive expressions. More passed him, and he heard the egg-shaped chambers open with a release of gas as they freed the prisoners, who staggered out. Something made him turn to watch one child, a young teenager. His face fell upon recognising her. His niece, Amy. He had forgotten his men had taken her to the base for safekeeping! For a moment, his chin shook, remembering how he had betrayed her, realising the untold damage to their relationship. She glared hard at him, then ran past his beseeching arms to meet James with a hug of her own.

Michael entered Blaze's field of vision and shook Craig Ramsey's hand. "Which one are you?"

Craig, the newcomer, gave a wink and drawled, "Well, you don't know me as well as…" He pointed towards the other Ramsey laying on the floor. "He's your Craig."

"What?" Blaze's voice croaked. He cleared his dry throat. "What do you mean by that?"

"Don't you worry about a thing, Colonel Castrati," Craig responded and delivered another kick to his side that winded him before kneeling beside his namesake. "Wake up, Ramsey. You're missing the show."

The dead man miraculously groaned and blinked his eyes. Blaze's eyes opened wide with surprise. So did Brianna's, and she gasped. "How the hell did—?"

The newly revived Ramsey pushed himself up with shaky arms into a sitting position and looked round at everyone. Blaze rolled to see him, his heart stammering and missing beats at this sight of his resurrected enemy. "But you're dead! I shot you through the heart."

The resurrected Ramsey glanced at the other Craig, and they both laughed before answering Blaze in unison. "That's our secret."

Shocked, the colonel considered how close to the truth he was. Such regenerative power would prove useful in a troop of soldiers. Excited shouts from a nearby child caught his attention, and he looked where she pointed.

"Hey, we're on TV!"

Michael, who was hugging Hayley, noticed and looked in the direction in which the little girl pointed. On the large flat-screen monitors above them, images showed of the children storming the chamber through the mist. "Check this out, guys."

Everyone else went quiet to listen as Sally Green's voice spoke through the television speakers, commenting on the recent breaking news of the children, Michael and Hayley. Blaze's eyes darted to the security cameras above him, his heart slamming when he realised what was happening. Someone had hacked them and allowed the public media to see inside his base! His mood dropped more when Michael Mach shouted to the others, "Smile, we're live."

Blaze's face fell as he watched the display. A red ribbon along the bottom of the screen displayed a scrolling text: Exclusive footage reveals mystery colonel kidnapped children for psychic experiments. More shots showed the children undergoing ESP tests. Then his face further contorted when another few seconds of video revealed the atrocities he inflicted on Craig, and how he blackmailed Hayley through Michael's torture.

Michael grinned at the two Craig Ramseys and Brianna. "It looks like our special friend really helped a bit more."

A special friend? Bile rose in Blaze's mouth as he watched in the new camera footage in slack-jawed disbelief. Older stock, it dated 18 months earlier and featured an argument he remembered having with Ramsey. He felt his career disappear in tatters upon hearing his recorded voice blurt through the speakers, "And what are you doing for the country with your psychic powers, Mister Ramsey? Your little parlour shows for the public?

Nothing!" Spittle shot from his video-self's lips as it shouted. "I am testing and studying these abilities, and I intend to turn them into something to defend Australia. Nothing can stop me from doing what's right, even if it means I have to step on your corpse to do it."

The scene transitioned to show further torturous testing as a child subject received electric shocks at every incorrect guess of a Zener card's shape. Blaze resisted the urge to shrink back as several children in the room shifted to scowl at him in response. Sally Green's voice narrated as the scenes further unfolded. "Colonel Nigel Blaze's threat turned to reality soon after as he hunted down Craig Ramsey. City cameras caught this scene that had been excised from public record, allegedly by the assailant's agencies." Everyone's attention returned to the new footage, which showed a car hurtling into Craig Ramsey with such force it threw the psychic's body hard against the car's windshield before the body slid off the front hood. A moment later, the wheels ran over him twice more before speeding away. During part of the replay, an inset video track revealed Colonel Blaze in an extreme close-up as the driver.

Blaze took advantage of their distraction and slipped out the door.

Chapter 41

Brianna gave a tired smile to the two Craig Ramseys. "I'd say we have achieved more than expected here." She searched the faces in the chamber, realising something was amiss. "Blaze!" Her eyes darted back and forth, scouring the room until her gaze fell upon the open door, and she slumped. "He's gone!"

A groan of disappointment escaped Craig's mouth. "I'm on it." He dashed out to the corridor in hot pursuit with Brianna close on his heels, leaving Michael and the resurrected Ramsey to organise the room's occupants to restrain the still unconscious soldiers.

"Watch out for the bodies," Craig shouted over his shoulder as he leapt over three corpses, his long legs carrying him along the corridor. "One kid had anger management issues towards the soldier boys here."

Brianna glimpsed and recognised the same tattoo on a dead man's arm. "You reckon? What about the strong fatherly advice to soothe him the hell down?"

"To calm *her* down," Craig huffed. "It was a girl. Her name's Beaulah Maclean."

"Then they deserved it," Brianna quipped, eliciting a raised eyebrow of amusement from the other as she retrieved a pistol from the dead man's hand. She checked the magazine and grabbed more ammunition from the pockets before following him.

They stopped at the corridor's end, where a closed lift waited. Craig rested his fingers on the adjacent panel. "We just missed him." A moment later, he nodded. "Blaze is heading up now."

"Shit!" Brianna shouted and slapped the lift's metallic doors. "How could we let him get away?"

The ding of a nearby bell drew their attention to another lift door, which slid open for them. Craig pointed to the lights above the closed one, which showed its occupant was still heading for the ground floor. "Not yet." He hurried towards the other lift, carefully poked his head around for traps, realised it was safe, and stepped inside. "Come on. He's going to the garage."

* * *

Michael had found some zip ties, formerly empty bullet casings from the floor that he had changed on the sly, which he and the recovered Ramsey used to restrain the surviving enemy troopers. No sooner had they finished when a clanging thud from the chamber's entrance surprised them. An annoying low-pitched siren played around them. "What's that?" asked Michael.

He had left the soldiers to investigate the door when Sparks' voice spoke through a television speaker. "The testing chamber has locked down, Michael."

Ramsey raised an eyebrow. "Why the siren?"

A hush fell over the children as they listened. Their eyes turned towards the racket, which now came from different points within the large testing room. Some had heard sirens at school fire drills, but even the youngest child who had never attended knew from television shows that sirens meant things like fires, ambulances, and other emergencies. They gathered together, some frowning, others shrinking into their nearest companion, and sought the only capable adults in sight: Ramsey and Michael.

Michael cast his eye on the cameras. "Sparks," he said, "is

it possible to turn them off?"

Ramsey faced him. A questioning eyebrow raised, and his expression lit up in recognition. He stepped towards the machine's flashing lights and touched it with a hesitant finger. "Sparks, this place will blow up soon, won't it?"

When the cyber-consciousness didn't answer at first, Michael frowned. His head still swam from the Neurolyser's drain on his brain earlier, yet he recognised Ramsey's concern. Blaze had set the self-destruct function to destroy everything to prevent others from gaining its technological secrets. He must have activated it remotely, a loyal soldier to the end, even if the world now knew of his project.

"Don't answer that, Sparks." Michael drew a troubled breath and exhaled in a whistling rush and spotted Ramsey. "Just try to stop the cameras from showing *everything* to the world, if you know what I mean."

"Gotcha," Sparks replied. A moment later, the siren ceased. "Blocked.".

"Sparks," Michael said, lowering his voice now that the noise had finished. "Is there a chance you can shut down the self-destruct function?" A few seconds passed. Did he hear a sigh from the speakers then? Unnerved, he asked again. "Well?"

His old friend's synthesised voice echoed through the room. "Negative, Skids. I suspect it's hard-wired in the Neurolyser."

"Then why was the siren in the other parts of the base?"

"Wi-Fi," Sparks answered. "I blocked the signals sent from the Neurolyser to the rest of the base. That will stop the entire complex exploding, but the machine itself still has a detonator inside it."

Ramsey touched the locked door, and his shoulders slumped. "The other levels will survive, but the machine's explosion…" He cast a cursory look across the other occupants in the room.

Michael shut his eyes, took another deep breath to calm his mind, and wished things had been different. If only he had stopped Blaze from taking Hayley. Memory of promising to kill the mad colonel resurfaced. He should have kept it. No! He shook his head. Time was ticking, and they didn't know how much remained. He had to act. "Die fighting, not wishing," he muttered.

Michael approached the Neurolyser; memories of the first machine that the Russians had employed in siphoning his brain's energy returned, and he shuddered. Back then, he had nicknamed it the Doomsday Machine, and its creators had hooked him up to it via electrodes, just like this time. But then he had disabled it at the connection point with his powers. Now with so many witnesses, including the captive soldiers, who were just stirring back to consciousness, he could do it again — but the cost to him and Hayley would prove too high. So could the alternative. Death or a life on the run from government organisations?

An idea came to him then.

* * *

Brianna watched the numbers on the lift's panel shrink as they approached the ground level. "Do you know if someone's waiting for us at the top?"

Craig brushed a finger across the car's doors and allowed the visions to flash and sort in his head. "To the left." Then the dreamlike prophecy further revealed itself. Shock at the bloody revelation overcame him. He patted the hand across his clothes to stop it shaking as he struggled to find objectivity in what he had witnessed.

"What is it?" Brianna asked, studying him, but Craig said nothing. "Did you see me die?"

Craig realised this Brianna was familiar with her own Ramsey, and nodded. "But we can change it." He pointed at the lift's door. "Stand here. He's to the left. Keep low and shoot in that direction through the doorway." He angled his arm to show where he meant. "It's our best chance."

"If he shoots me," Brianna said, "won't the ectoplasm bring me back?"

Craig shook his head. "I wish. We can die, so don't go gung ho." He jabbed a finger towards the floor indicator. "Ready?" They scrambled into position: Brianna behind the left front of the entrance, and Craig beside her. "Shoot at him, or whatever, to give me cover. I'm going to run out and across the space, try to get round him."

The lift's electronic bell dinged as Brianna gave a nod. Its doors slid open, and she waved a hand out. A gunshot thundered. A bullet thudded into the other interior wall. Craig tensed, shrinking from a ricochet that never happened. Brianna reached round the corner from knee height, aimed at the general heading Craig had given, and pumped two rounds in Blaze's direction. Craig bolted outside and across the concrete floor, his eyes glimpsing for the cover he sought. Behind him, Brianna fired. The gunfire distracted their target enough to prevent him firing, but Craig still expected to feel bullets knock him off his feet. His vision hadn't told him everything he wanted.

Too late, he realised what he had missed. A large soldier blocked Craig's passage beside the jeep that he had intended to use as cover. Craig stopped upon finding himself staring straight into the barrel of a rifle. Its muzzle flashed and burped, bullets zinged past Craig, one of them stinging above his ear as it whistled past. He dived. The soldier grunted something and adjusted his aim.

Craig huddled on the opposite side of the vehicle. More bullets rang through the air. This time, the shots came from Blaze's direction, but he was still shooting at Brianna. Then Blaze's gun went silent. A curse floated to his ear. Good. Blaze had spent his ammunition. At least the colonel couldn't shoot at him or Brianna. He just had to deal with Dwayne Johnson's armed loping clone on the jeep's other side.

Then Craig's jaw dropped as he realised another soldier was approaching Brianna with a long-bladed knife ready in hand. He shouted a warning, ducking as a bullet punched through the jeep at him.

* * *

Sparks' voice blasted from the television speakers. "Michael! I found the Neurolyser's self-destruct timer."

"Great!" Michael gasped in relief, looking up from his search for the manual override. "Did you stop it?"

A slight pause. "No."

"Why not?" Michael swore and kept searching.

"It's hard-coded into the machine," Sparks replied. "I can't change it."

"Next time, tell me something I should know."

"Thirty seconds remain."

"Not that useful, Sparks!" Michael sighed, wiped his arm across his forehead and eyes, finding sweat. He had no choice. The lives of children, especially Hayley and James, were too high a price to pay to keep his secret.

He placed his hand on the control panel, took a deep breath, and cleared his mind, save for one thought. The image solidified in his imagination until he felt certain of what he would do to the machine…. and he concentrated on making it happen.

"Eight seconds." Sparks' voice reflected surprise. "Skids, what did you do?"

Michael's eyebrow lifted. "Nothing yet. Why?"

"Look," replied his cyber-friend.

Something odd permeated the air surrounding Michael, and he felt his hair standing on his arms. Static electricity? The others in the room had noticed the change too and murmured things to each other. Then he saw it.

Blue and white light illuminated the surroundings. A crackle of energy jumped from a corner, drawing the queer glowing colours towards it until they formed a ball that rippled like water in its centre. More fingers of thin lightning stabbed from it.

"Oh, schick."

* * *

Caught by surprise, Brianna had tripped and fallen on her back. Her attacker lunged forward to plunge his bayonet deep into her chest. She deflected the blade and clawed with her other hand at the attacker's face, digging into his eyes. The soldier recoiled from her tiger-claw-grip, but her hand hooked his knife arm and yanked downward to the side. She twisted, rolled on top, and drove her right palm hard into his hands, pushing all her weight into him. He grunted, struggled to slash, but couldn't budge. Again and again, she rammed her knuckles into her assailant's prone throat until his windpipe snapped. She grabbed his leg, which had wrapped around her, and flung it aside before grabbing the dropped weapon.

Her eyes flicked to his bare arm, narrowing when she saw the familiar kangaroo tattoo again. Was it the same man who kidnapped Hayley? Must have been a clone. She slammed her steel-capped boot into his face, splashing more blood in the lift's car, before stepping out.

There, across the car park, she spotted Craig facing off against a larger bald-headed adversary who looked more muscle than human. She watched as the wiry man dodged a pile-driver blow that could have shattered bricks. He found an opening, swung an enormous fist, and missed the psychic by a hair's breadth. With each thrown punch, the soldier's breath whooshed with impatience. Craig's feet arced like a pendulum, carrying him away with a dancer's grace, his eyes never leaving his opponent.

Somewhere, a door slammed. An engine started.

Brianna spun about-faced and peered through the gloom, searching for the source. Headlights flicked on. A clutch popped and tyres screamed as they spun on the cement, the clamour echoing in the car park.

Something thudded. Did the ground shake? Brianna's snapped towards it in time to see Dwayne Johnson's lookalike drop to the concrete. Craig stood over him and delivered a triple punch combination to his head. He stepped away and looked towards Brianna just as the large jeep's headlights swept across the walls and caught him dead centre in their beams.

The car moved too fast. Déjà vu pinged her memory of Ramsey's murder by Blaze. The similarity of attack stunned her. Craig's name stuck in Brianna's throat. Not even a croak escaped. Her heavy feet dragged like lead.

Craig broke his stare at the headlights and bolted straight

for the oncoming juggernaut, his arms pumping hard, breath puffing his cheeks outward and exploding from his mouth. He jumped at the jeep, angled high. He rolled in midair, palms planted on the Jeep's bonnet, then flipped in a somersault over the speeding vehicle.

A glowing sphere suddenly ballooned into existence in front of the Jeep, lightning cracking from its centre. Then Blaze and his jeep hit the ball.

An unearthly wind gusted from the glowing orb, hurled Brianna to the ground. She covered her ears against the sound of the implosive rush of air washing back towards the luminous sphere.

As suddenly as it had appeared, it vanished.

Craig landed on his feet, stumbled from the momentum, and tripped.

Blaze and the Jeep had disappeared, too.

* * *

The rippling plasma and lightning faded instantly from the Neurolyser's chamber without a sound.

Michael leaned against the machine and slid to the floor. He looked up in time to catch Hayley, who jumped into his arms and clung tight. "Hey, Hayles," he said, kissing the top of his head and holding her close. "It's all over."

His daughter raised her face to look at him with large eyes that reminded him of her mother. "I knew you'd come."

"Yeah," he answered, wrapping an arm around Jason's shoulder. "We're together forever, kiddo."

The other kids were chattering amongst themselves about the ball of energy. They sounded as surprised by the events as Michael and Sparks had been. A tutting noise caught his attention. He turned to find Ramsey waving something in a tight circle, his eyebrow cocked in an ironic expression above his awkward grin.

A power cord and plug.

"You know what?" Ramsey said, shaking his head side-to-side. Then he gave a wink. "We could have just pulled the plug, saved us some trouble."

Chapter 42

Sparks had done a good job of distributing the torture scenes and ESP testing to the networks: television, bloggers, and social media.

Conspiracy theorists around the world lapped up the video footage that showed the experiments on children and the torture of Michael Mach and Craig Ramsey. Although the original Metube video disappeared from the platform—because of government intervention—it did nothing to stop those who had already downloaded it and resubmitted it on other subscriber channels. The same clips gained massive followings on other social media too. Soon it doubled and tripled across the world, thanks to more submissions through the torrent networks.

By Christmas Eve, a week later, the news still spread. Government officials tap-danced around questions the media fired at them. Parliament, which takes a break so close to the December holiday, still had no chance to rest as opposing parties pointed fingers at each other for the project. The people knew. Both conservative and left-wing parties held interests in the research and military projects, even if they were at a deeper level of secrecy.

Of course, Michael Mach held up his end of the bargain with Sally Green. Craig let this world's Ramsey fulfil his side of things.

With a glass of juice cradled in his hand, Craig watched it on the comfortable sofa in the apartment that this world's Ramsey had rented with his carefully stashed funds. This world's Sally Green was a mirror image of the one he knew on his world, and she had the same chops when interviewing the Australian minister of defence by a video hookup.

"Are we at war with other nations?" Sally asked, reminding Craig of another journalist he used to watch on Sixty Minutes in the 1980s.

"We are not at war with anyone." The official's Adam's apple bobbed above his collar and receded.

"That's not what Colonel Nigel Blaze said on the footage."

The minister chortled. "The *fake* footage. We have no alignment with any," he drew air-quotes, "clandestine operations."

"Yet, we have witnesses and the footage of children abducted in the streets by vehicles we traced to the Australian government, presumably the military." A shot appeared on the television screen of children, recognised as being in the filmed testing files, entering a van with its registration plates visible. Another image flashed that displayed its match on the government database. "How can you explain that?"

The minister's face darkened. "We have received no reports of such things."

"The Queensland police in Statton have been investigating the children's disappearances," Sally said, leaning forward. "We have footage taken on the city's security camera network. Eyewitnesses are here in the studio with us now, including two of the now recovered children."

The government member's eyes looked upward and to the side, glazed as though listening to something, then returned to the camera. "There is no further information to the ongoing investigation." With that, the connection to the government member ended.

Sally held a hand to her ear, concentrated and said, "It seems we have lost connection to the minister, which is a shame." She raised her gaze towards two of her guests. "Craig Ramsey, many people have asked, how did you survive being hit by Nigel Blaze's vehicle?"

The on-screen Ramsey offered a smile, his gaze diverted elsewhere as though he had noticed something that surprised him. "Turner? How did-" He stopped, shook his head, and said, "Sorry, Sally, I thought for a moment… never mind. It's a lot to go into about how I survived, but let's say that I relied on a lot of help from my friends to not only survive that blow from the vehicle but to, well…." Something not obvious to the cameras distracted him again. "It's a trade secret."

Footage of the two Craig Ramseys appeared on the screen. It only lasted three seconds before stopping, but there was enough to show two identical men. "Is this your twin?"

Michael Mach chuckled and pulled the on-screen Ramsey out of his discomfort. "No, Mr Ramsey won't admit this, but from his days as a stage magician, he employed a body double. That's the same man now who came when we called and helped us a lot. We owe him our lives."

A knowing smile crossed Sally Green's face. To the viewers, it would have appeared that she was appreciating the secret and choosing not to pursue it further. To Craig Ramsey, who was watching from home, the twinkle in Sally's eye was clear. The reporter was about to help avoid creating further trouble for Ramsey and Michael. "I wondered if perhaps the Neurolyser had created this double of Craig Ramsey. The man appeared on the same night of the initial test that coincided with the lightning storm. I was curious to know if he had disappeared at the same time the Neurolyser malfunctioned again in this footage."

Michael and Ramsey faced each other at the words, then turned back to Sally. "Nah," said Michael. "It sounds like a sexy story, but our friend has left for now."

Sally chuckled and faced the television camera, her face appearing to look at Craig Ramsey and Brianna Cogan as they watched the interview. "Mysterious, indeed, but this story will continue. Colonel Blaze is still missing. We presume he's dead since another witness claimed he disappeared into a ball of lightning. Meanwhile, the authorities are reuniting the other young survivors with their families. But we haven't located every parent, meaning some children will be alone for Christmas and--"

Brianna aimed the remote at the television and clicked the button to mute. She looked at Craig, studying his features. "Is that what happened?"

"What?" Craig drained his glass and rested it on the nearby coffee table.

"Did the Neurolyser create you?"

Craig paused. "No. I came from another universe, very much like this one, but different." He pulled the picture of him and his family from his wallet, and for a moment he remained silent.

"What is she like?" Brianna asked, and Craig gave her a quizzical look. "Your wife. Your Brianna."

Craig smiled. "She's brilliant. Beautiful, cunning, sexy and independent. She served in the military, just like you, and worked as a detective too."

"She doesn't work now?"

"Not as a police detective," Craig replied. "She became a mum and took time off. I supported her, married her, but we work together with special missions."

"Doing what?"

"Troubleshooting." He gave Brianna a wink. "You might find out soon enough."

Brianna looked past him at something beside him. "Does she see dead people?"

"Why, yes, she can." Craig turned in surprise to notice a little red-headed girl dressed in an old-fashioned white dress, her hair hanging down her back. "Hello!"

The youngster appeared surprised and regarded him with a searching expression. "Can you really see me?"

"We can," Craig affirmed, his gaze taking in the girl's features. Something in the way she stood reminded him of someone else, and her accent matched. "Emily, I presume?"

The little girl nodded. "Emily Fraser," she replied, her Scottish brogue recognisable to him. The Emily Craig knew from his own world was a spirit too, a cheeky Highlander lady who had been Craig's familiar guide since he was a little boy. A beam crossed his face as he watched the urchin version of Emily. "I'm here to say it's nearly time for you to go home."

Craig's expression melted with shock. Disbelief filled him. Home? Could it be true? The mellifluous tones of Bing Crosby's voice floated on a breeze through the open window, carrying the familiar seasonal lyrics of I'll Be Home For Christmas. The song's ending verse came to mind as he remembered how he had dreamed of this moment ever since his arrival. "Are you sure? How?"

"You'll learn soon enough." The little girl tapped her nose, winked, and vanished, leaving Craig with a face sodden with happy tears.

* * *

Michael and Ramsey arrived home an hour after their appearance on television, Christmas gifts filling their arms, and hid the presents in an empty room while Hayley absorbed her attention in a cartoon show. "Where's James?" Michael asked.

"Craig's talking to him about something." Brianna nodded toward the other room. "Girl trouble, I think."

Michael raised his eyebrows. "A girl?" So much had happened that he hadn't considered everything going on for his adopted son. "You're serious?"

Brianna finished pouring chilled egg nog into glasses beside a plate of pfeffernüsse for everyone to share and grinned at her adoptive brother. "I guess some boys can't always speak to their fathers about those things." She pointed to the other room. "Let them know the snacks are ready."

Michael headed down the hall and was about to knock on the ajar door when he overheard the conversation. He paused to listen.

He heard Craig's voice coming through the crack. "You can't blame Amy for being related to Blaze, mate. He didn't even tell his family about his project, so it's all on him. Anyway," Craig took a breath and continued. "There's something else. Tamsin's not the right one for you."

"How do you know?" James asked.

Craig's words carried a smile. "Because I do. Didn't you notice the way Amy cried that afternoon when Blaze had tied us up at her place? When you blamed her for being a spy, those were actual tears. She has a thing for you."

"Amy? Really?" James' voice held a tone of something more than surprise.

"Her heart's warmer than Tamsin's too."

"Yeah, she is a bit of a bitch, come to think of it."

Michael knocked on the door and poked his head through the door's crack. "We've got egg nog and biscuits out here, guys. Grab them before Hayley does." He noticed the fatherly way that Craig was sitting and facing James at the study's desk. "Is everything okay?"

James nodded, a wistful look on his face. Craig replied, "Yeah, it's all fine here. We were just having a man-to-man." The lad left the room, his fingers already reaching for the mobile phone in his pocket as he passed.

"Thanks, Craig," Michael said. He clapped a hand on the shoulder of his friend's lookalike from another world. "I have something you might like to see." When Craig gave a curious look, he added. "An early Christmas gift." He reached into his pocket and took out something that looked familiar to them both, but smaller.

"What is that?"

"A miniature version of the Neurolyser I made with you-know-what." Michael watched his friend's lookalike, waiting for a response. The psychic turned it over in his hands and studied what otherwise appeared to be a scale model of the machine, as heavy as a paperweight. Craig's face darkened for a moment, then resumed its characteristic bright expression, although a hint of uncertainty remained. "Sparks and I tried to reverse engineer some of its internal workings. We think it brought you here," said Michael.

A light turned on in Craig's eyes, and hope filled his words. "Do you mean…?"

"Those balls of lightning that appeared that night. We think the Neurolyser actually opened some kind of portal. So-"

"I'll be home for Christmas?" Craig held his hand over his mouth and nose, choked back an involuntary sob.

Michael confirmed Craig's realisation with a nod. "We think so. And if we do it right, we could probably return you to your original starting location."

Craig took the device and studied it in his hands. A huge smile crossed his face when he raised his eyes to thank Michael with a grateful handshake. "Thanks, Michael."

"But at least have something to eat and drink with us before you do, eh?" Michael replied, with a powerful emotion rippling in his voice. "We've all come through a lot together and will miss you."

Chapter 43

Craig's eyes opened. Shapes and colours whirled before his vision. He blinked, clearing his head, and lay on the turf for a few minutes until the world stopped spinning beneath him. If it moved any faster, he hoped he could hold a piece of grass to stop himself from falling. At last, the wooziness faded enough that he could look around without feeling he would slide off into space. His gaze fell upon the marble slabs, and he held his breath while reading the inscriptions.

His first wife's name, Celina, faced him from its stone. Beside that was his daughter's grave.

A shame, he thought to himself. He missed an opportunity to visit them again, to see how his first daughter could have grown up. No. That's a silly notion, he decided. To dwell upon what could have been is disrespectful for the good things that happened since. He was alive and back home. New opportunities abounded. He had his own little girl, a wonderful angel, in a life full of possibilities. And here, Brianna knew him as her husband.

Recent memories reformed of his farewell to his wife's double, his doppelgänger, and the headstrong Michael Mach. New friends. He raised his hand and examined what he held. The Neurolyser. Michael had powered it with his mind to activate it and send Craig home. Perhaps he might see them again. He hoped so.

"Oi!" a voice beside him said. Craig turned and spotted the phantasm of a man who had died twenty years ago. "You can't stay there. It's not your time yet."

Craig grinned, thanked the spirit, and stood on shaky feet to return home.

His Jaguar was missing from the car park. Someone must have retrieved it, but how long had he been away? Did time pass in the same way as in the other universe?

It didn't matter. He hailed a cab into the city and, after an hour, caught another that took him home bearing gifts for his family.

His house looked the same as when he had last seen it. In one piece, too. That was a good sign. He wondered if his double would rebuild.

Craig lifted his hand to the front door and knocked. Voices came to him from outside. Brianna. Asking someone to answer it. Who was there?

The door opened. Craig's heart jumped at the sight of the woman before him. He recognised her from a photo, but she was another man's. Not his, but Michael Mach's wife. "Alison?"

The brown-haired woman's forehead crinkled. "Yes?" She paused. "Have we met before?" Then she spotted the gifts in his arms and raised her eyes to study him again. "You must be Craig." Her smile brightened. "I recognise you from the photos!" She looked behind her and shouted, "Brianna! Come here. Quickly!"

Hurried footsteps sounded down the hallway and the love of his life burst out the front door, knocking the parcels from his arms as they embraced. His Brianna. And his daughter. He relished the warmth he had missed for the past three weeks. She looked him over, checking that he was in one piece. "Where were you?"

He was home for Christmas!

* * *

"Ah!" The voice sounded like that of a doctor. "You're awake."

Blaze opened his eyes., blinked against the sunshine that streamed through the window to his left. His throat felt dry, raspy. He coughed. Someone held a glass to his parched lips. "Sip," they urged when he tried to gulp the water. "You have been asleep for a fortnight."

His eyes shot open. Two weeks?

Then he took in his surroundings. A pained expression on his face, Jesus Christ stared down at him from the cross hanging on the opposite wall, which was painted a clinical white. A tube in his arm fed him some liquid from a bag suspended high beside him. What had happened?

Images came to mind. Memories. The strange ball of light. Forked lightning. The cascading colours that enveloped him before he lost consciousness as the jeep ploughed into a surreal place.

Then he saw her. A woman he thought he had met before, but where?

He tried to get up, but an orderly pushed him back with a gentle but firm hand.

"You aren't going anywhere," she said. Then he noticed her uniform. Military. The patch showed her rank, higher than his. A major-general! "What's your name?"

He replied, giving his serial number, too. She nodded, a slight tip of a curious eyebrow, mild surprise.

"Interesting." An assistant appeared, and the major-general read the screen of the tablet proffered. "Your DNA matches with a Colonel Nigel Blaze, but the thing is…." She paused. "You died a few years ago. We buried you."

He coughed up water that had dripped down the wrong

way. When he recovered, he said, "Years? Dead?" He raised a hand to study it in awe but noticed nothing out of the ordinary.

"You appeared from nowhere in one of our old bases," the major-general confirmed. "Obviously, we can't let you go. We have much to learn about how you came back to life."

ABOUT THE AUTHOR

Chris Johnson's stories blend science fiction, light urban fantasy, and a dash of quirky humour. He loves to include wise-cracking heroes (and heroines) who are stuck in strange situations from which they have to escape.

Chris grew up in the 1980s on a diet of Atari computers, comics, books, and lots of cool music in a small Australian town. He graduated with a Bachelors degree in Computer Science from CQU. In his varied career, he has hustled at three-card monte, read celebrities palms, publicly predicted the 1992 Los Angeles Riots a week beforehand, and hunted ghosts. But his most unusual gig is performing as a professional mentalist and psychic entertainer on stage, television, radio, and at private events.

Chris loves to hear from his readers, so be sure to:

Befriend him on Facebook
https://www.facebook.com/ChrisJohnsonAuthor

Check him out on BookBub
https://www.bookbub.com/profile/chris-johnson-71367652-f1e4-40b4-9030-a6cf37f9eaf2

Keep up with Chris Johnson behind the scenes HERE and receive a free gift!
https://www.subscribepage.com/chrisjohnsonwrites

Other Books
by
CHRIS JOHNSON

Twelve Strokes of Midnight
Deja Two (Craig Ramsey #0.5)
Dead Cell (Craig Ramsey #1)
Demon Blade (Craig Ramsey #2)
Lamia's Three Wishes (Craig Ramsey #2.5)
The Universe Crack'd (Craig Ramsey #3)
Bootstrap's Journey
While He Was Sleeping